A Manual of Russian Conversation

SALZWASSER
VERLAG

A. Paucker

A Manual of Russian Conversation

Reprint of the original, first published in 1863.

1st Edition 2022 | ISBN: 978-3-37500-744-7

Verlag (Publisher): Salzwasser Verlag GmbH, Zeilweg 44, 60439 Frankfurt, Deutschland
Vertretungsberechtigt (Authorized to represent): E. Roepke, Zeilweg 44, 60439 Frankfurt, Deutschland
Druck (Print): Books on Demand GmbH, In de Tarpen 42, 22848 Norderstedt, Deutschland

A MANUAL

OF

RUSSIAN CONVERSATION.

A MANUAL

OF

RUSSIAN CONVERSATION

CONTAINING:

1. The Russian Alphabet, 2. A Selection of Words frequently used in Conversation, 3. Examples of the Use of Verbs in Connection with Other Parts of Speech, 4. Phrases frequently used in Conversation, 5. Dialogues, 6. Outlines of Russian Grammar, 7. A Comparative Table of Russian and English Coins, Weights and Measures, 8. A List of the Principal Technical Terms for the Use of Civil Engineers, Mechanics, etc.

BY

A. PAUCKER,

English Teacher in the IMPERIAL ALEXANDER Lyceum, Author of
« *Англійская Хрестоматія для Начинающихъ.* »

ST. PETERSBURG.

1863.

CONTENTS.

V. PART IV. DIALOGUES.

VI. PART V. OUTLINES OF RUSSIAN GRAMMAR.

RUSSIAN ALPHABET.

Characters.	Pronunciation.
А, а	å; * but at the beginning and in the middle of words after *ж, ч, ш, щ* like ȧ, and in the termination *аго* of adjectives like ŏ.
Б, б	*b*; but at the end of all words, and before the hard consonants *к, п, с, т, ф, х, ц, ч, ш, щ* like *p*.
В, в	*v*; but at the end of all words, and before the hard consonants like *ff*.
Г, г	like *g* before *a, o, u*; but at the end of words, and before the hard consonants like *k*, and sometimes like *k* guttural in *lock*; in the syllable *го* at the end of words like *v*.
Д, д	*d*; but at the end of words, and before the hard consonants like *t*.
Е, е	at the beginning and at the end of words like *yè*; having the accent on *e* like *yŏ*; after *ж, ч, ш, щ* very often like *o*. Both *yè* and *yŏ* must, in the middle of words, and at the end of words when not forming a separate syllable, be contracted in the pronunciation so as to form *one* sound of èå or èŏ.
Ж, ж	*zh*; but at the end of words, and before the hard consonants like *sh*.
З, з	*z*; but at the end of words, and before the hard consonants, like *ss*.
И, и	è; at the beginning of words like *yè*.
I, i	è, used almost exclusively before vowels and й.
Й, й	ĭ, used after vowels to form a diphthong.
К, к	*k*; but before к and т, like *kh*.
Л, л	according to its position either soft like *l* in *Luke*, or harder than the sound of the English *ll* in the end of words.

Characters.	Pronunciation.	Characters.	Pronunciation.
М, м	*m.*		sonant to give it a stronger sound.
Н, н	*n.*		
О, о	ŏ; but if unaccented, like å.	Ы, ы	ůĭ, giving the ĭ the longer sound.
П, п	*p.*		
Р, р	like *r* at the beginning of syllables.	Ь, ь	placed after consonants to give them a softer pronunciation.
С, с	*ss.*		
Т, т	*t*; the soft т at the end of words, followed by ь, has a slight hissing sound resembling the combined sound of *t* and *y* in *beat-ye.*	Ѣ, ѣ	In most cases like the Russian E.
		Э, э	å, ĕ.
		Ю, ю	ů.
У, у	ů.	Я, я	*y*å; but at the beginning, and in the middle of a word, when unaccented, almost like yå.
Ф, ф	*ff, ph.*		
Х, х	like *kh* (or the German ch).		
Ц, ц	*ts.*	Ѳ, ѳ	*f, ph*; used only in words derived from the Greek, to represent the Greek letter φ.
Ч, ч	*tsh.*		
Ш, ш	*sh.*		
Щ, щ	*shtsh.*	Ѵ, ѵ	ĕ; used only in a few Greek words transferred into the Russian through the Selavonian.
Ъ, ъ	is placed at the end of words (and sometimes of syllables in compounds) after a con-		

* In the first part of the present work the pronunciation of the Russian words is marked after the method of Walker. To those who are unacquainted with that method the following directions will be useful:

å sounds like *a* in face, able, date, salvation
å » *a* » rather, father.
å » *a* » fall, scald, walk, halt.

ȧ sounds like *a* in fat, hat, lad, ham, man.
ė » *e* » me, we, he.
ĕ » *e* » met, let, get, set.
e not marked is mute.
ı sounds like *i* in pine, title, bible, kind, mild.
ĭ » *i* » pin, tittle, little.
ȯ » *o* » no, note, globe.
ŏ » *o* » move, prove, lose.
ô » *o* » nor, for, 'or.
ŏ » *o* » got, hot, not, knock.
u̇ » *u* » tube, cupid, use, confusion.
ŭ » *u* » cup, but, us.
û » *u* » full, pull.
ôĭ » *oi* » oil, toil.
ôû » *ou* » round, thou, pound.

In applying the above to the present work, instead of ôĭ sometimes ŏĭ has been used to mark a similar but shorter sound, and ȧû instead of ôû to mark a more proportionate articulation of both the sounds ȧ and û as required by the Russian tongue. The diphthong ŭĭ, when marked ‿, as ŭĭ in bŭĭk (бык), denotes not a combination of ŭ and ĭ, but something between them, a sound which can easily be caught by hearing the Russian ы pronounced by a native. In the same manner yȧ without ‿ pronounces like *ya* in *yard*, but when written yȧ the *y* becomes very soft, and much shorter.

With regard to the consonants, *zh* has been used to mark the sound of *si* in such words as *derision, division; kh,* to denote the sound of *ch* in *loch,* or ch in the German word Loch; *ll* — the strong sound of the Russian л, and *l* — the soft pronunciation of the same letter. As to the Russian semivowels ъ and ь, no equivalent has been given by any sign, for the former invariably gives the consonant by which it is preceded a stronger, and the latter a softer sound.

PART I.

SELECTION OF WORDS FREQUENTLY USED IN CONVERSATION,

and arranged according to the Parts of Speech.

NOUNS.

OBJECTS OF RELIGION.

Богъ	bŏkh	God.
Іисусъ Христосъ	ê-sûss khrê-stŏss	Jesus Christ.
архангелъ	årrkh-ång-ëll	archangel.
ангелъ	ång-ëll	angel.
діаволъ	dyå-vŏll	devil.
вѣра	våre-å	faith, belief.
законъ Божій	zå-kŏnn bŏ-zhê	God's law, religion.
церковь	tsĕrr-kŏff	church.
часовня	tshå-sŏv-nyå	chapel.
клиросъ	klê-rŏss	choir.
алтарь	åll-tår (the *r* is soft)	altar.
икона	ê-kŏ-nå	image.
крестъ	krĕst	cross.

каѳедра	kå-fè-drå	pulpit.
святая вода́	svå-tå-yå vô-då	holy water.
про́повѣдь	prô-pô-våt	sermon.
обѣдня	å-båd-nyå	mass.
вѣчéрня	vå-tshåre-nyå	vespers.
моли́тва	må-lît-vå	prayer.
би́блія	bè-blè-yå	bible.
моли́твенникъ	må-lît-vèn-nîk	prayer-book
катихизи́съ	kå-tè-khè-zîss	catechism.
рели́гія	rå-lè-gè-yå (*g* has the sound in *give*)	religion.
богослуже́піе	bô-gô-slô-zhå-nè-yè	divine service.
вѣроисповѣда́ніе	våre-ô-îss-pô-vå-då-nè-yè	confession.
проповѣдникъ	prô-pô-våd-nîk	preacher.
свяще́нникъ	svå-shtshén-nîk	priest.
пасто́ръ	på-stôrr	pastor, minister.
христіа́нинъ	khrè-stîå-nîn	a christian.
правосла́вный	prå-vô-slåv-nûî	an orthodox.
като́ликъ	kå-tô-lîk	a catholic.
протеста́нтъ	prô-tyè-stånt	a protestant.
лютера́нинъ	lû-tyå-rå-nîn	a lutheran.
жидъ	zhît	jew.
апо́столъ	å-pôs-tôll	apostle.
мона́хъ	mô-nåkh	monk.
мона́хиня	mô-nå-khè-nyå	nun.
пра́здникъ	pråz-nîk	holyday.
Но́вый годъ	nô-vûî gôt	New-year's day.
Креще́ніе	krè-shtshå-nè-yè	Twelfth-day.
ма́сляница	må-slyå-nè-tså	carnival.
вели́кій постъ	vå-lè-kôî pôst	Lent.
по́стный день	pôst-nûî dyåne (the *y* scarcely audible)	fast day.
Страстна́я пятница	stråst-nå-yå pyåt-nè-tså	Good-Friday.
Па́сха	pås-khå	Easter.
Свята́я недѣля	svå-tå-yå nå-dyå-lyå.	Easter week.

Ѳомина́я недѣля	fŏ-mē-nă-yă nă-dyă-lyă	the week beginning with the Sunday after Easter.
Тро́ицынъ день	trŏ-ē-tsĭin dyănc	Pentecost, Whitsunday.
Духовъ день	dŏ-khŏf dyăne	Whitmonday.
Ива́новъ день	ē-vă-nŏf dyăne	Midsummer's day.
Рождество́	rozh-dyĕst-vŏ	Christmas.

TEMPORAL DIGNITIES AND THE MILITARY PROFESSION.

Импера́торъ (Царь, Госуда́рь)	ĭm-pă-ră-tŏrr (tsăr, gŏ-sŭ-dăr)	Emperor.
Императри́ца (Госуда́рыня)	ĭm-pă-ră-trē-tsă (gŏ-sŭ-dă-rŭĭ-nyă)	Empress.
Вели́кій Князь	vă-lē-kŏĭ knyăs	Grand-Duke.
Вели́кая Княгиня	vă-lē-kă-yă knyă-gē-nyă	Grand-Duchess.
Коро́ль	kă-rŏl	King.
Короле́ва	kă-ră-lă-vă	Queen.
Принцъ	prĭnts	Prince.
Принцесса	prĭn-tsĕs-să	Princess.
князь *	knyăs	prince.
княгиня	knyă-ghē-nyă	princess.
княжна́	knyăzh-nă	princess (unmarried).
графъ	grăff	count.
графи́ня	gră-fē-nyă	countess.
баро́нъ	bă-rŏn	baron.
барone̍сса	bă-rŏ-nyĕs-să	baroness.
дворяни́нъ	dvŏ-ryă-nĭn	nobleman.
посла́нникъ	pă-slăn-nĭk	ambassador.

* Though *князь* is generally rendered into English by *prince*, for want of an equivalent, yet it denotes only a person of the higher nobility, occupying the next higher rank to *графъ, count*.

мини́стръ	mé-nistr	minister of state.
мини́стръ иностра́нныхъ дѣлъ	mé-nístr é-nŏ-strån-nåïkh dyåll	minister of state for foreign affairs.
фельдма́ршалъ	félt-mår-shåll (give the *l* and *t* in *felt* a very soft sound)	fieldmarshal.
генера́лъ	gå-nå-råll	general.
генералъ-лейтена́нтъ	gå-nå-råll låé-tyé-nånt	lieutenant-general.
генералъ-маіо́ръ	gå-nå-råll må-yŏrr	major-general.
адъюта́нтъ	åd-ŭ-tånt	aid-de-camp.
флигель-адъютантъ	flé-ghĕl åd-ŭ-tånt	aid-de-camp of the Emperor.
полко́вникъ	påll-kŏv-nĭk	colonel.
подполко́вникъ	pŏt-påll-kŏv-nĭk	lieutenant-colonel
маіо́ръ	må-yŏrr	major.
капита́нъ	kå-pé-tånn	captain of foot.
штабсъ-капитанъ	shtåps-kå-pé-tånn	second captain.
ро́тмистръ	rŏt-méstr	captain of horse.
пору́чикъ	på-rŭt-shĭk	lieutenant.
подпору́чикъ	pŏt-på-rŭt-shĭk	second lieutenant.
пра́порщикъ	prå-pŏr-shtshĭk	ensign.
адмира́лъ	åd-mé-råll	admiral.
ви́це-адмира́лъ	vé-tså åd-mé-råll	vice-admiral.
контръ-адмира́лъ	kŏntr åd-mé-råll	rear-admiral.
капита́нъ пе́рваго ра́нга	kå-pé-tånn pyérr-vå-vŏ rån-gå	(captain of the 1st rank) post-captain.
капита́нъ втора́го ра́нга	kå-pé-tånn ftå-rŏ-vå rån-gå	(captain of the 2d rank) post-captain.
капита́нъ-лейтена́нтъ	kå-pé-tånn låé-tyé-nånt	(lieutenant - captain) commander.
ста́ршій офице́ръ	stårr-shé- å-fé-tsérr	first lieutenant.

лейтенáнтъ	låĕ-tyĕ-nånt	lieutenant.
мичманъ	mĭtsh-mån	(a rank next lower to lieutenant, corresponding to the French « enseigne de vaisseau ».)
гардемаринъ	gårr-dyĕ-må-rĭn	midshipman.
офицéръ	å-fĕ-tsĕrr	officer.
унтеръ-офицéръ	ŭn-tyĕrr å-fĕ-tsĕrr	non-commissioned officer.
солдáтъ	sŏl-dåt	soldier.
пѣхóта	på-khŏ-tå	infantry.
кавалéрія	kå-vå-lå-rĕ-yå	cavalry.
артиллéрія	årr-tĭl-lå-rĕ-yå	artillery.
флотъ	flŏt.	fleet, navy.
полкъ	pŏllk	regiment.
рóта	rŏ-tå	company.
корабль, судно	kå-råbl, sŭd-nŏ	ship, vessel.
воéнное судно	vŏ-yĕn-nŏ-yĕ sŭd-nŏ	man of war.
пароходъ	på-rå-khŏt	steamer.
пáрусъ	på-rŭss	sail.
пушка	pŭsh-kå	cannon.
ружьé	rŭzh-yŏ	gun, musket.
ядрó	yå-drŏ	cannon-ball.
пуля	pŏ-lyå	bullet.
сабля	såb-lyå	sabre.
шпáга	shpå-gå	sword.
комендáнтъ	kå-mĕn-dånt	commander of the garrison.
парáдъ	på-råt	parade.
гауптвáхта	gŏŭpt-vakh-tå	guard-house.
будка	bŭt-kå	sentry-box.
часовóй	tshå-sŏ-vŏĭ	sentinel.
учéніе	ŏ-tshå-nĕ-yĕ	drill, exercise.

казáрма	kå-zårr-må	barracks.
непріятель	nå-pré-yå-tël	enemy.
войнá	vôî-nå	war.
битва, сраженіе	bit-vå, srå-zhå-në-yë	battle.
побѣда	på-bå-då	victory.
поражéніе	pô-rå-zhå-në-yë	rout.
миръ	merr	peace.
отéчество	å-tyå-tshëst-vô	native country.

PROFESSIONS AND TRADES.

судья́	sůd-yå	a judge.
дóкторъ	dôk-tôrr	doctor.
врачъ	vråtsh	physician.
зубнóй врачъ	zůb-nôî vråtsh	dentist.
повивáльная бабка	pô-vë-vål-nå-yå båp-kå	midwife.
аптéкарь	åp-tyå-kår	apothecary.
банки́ръ	bån-kère	banker.
купéцъ	kô-pyëts	merchant.
лáвочникъ	llå-vôtsh-nik	shopkeeper.
прикáщикъ	pré-kåsh-tshîk	clerk.
бухгáлтеръ	bôkh-gåll-tyerr	book-keeper.
мáклеръ	måk-lërr	broker.
перевóдчикъ	på-rå-vôt-shik	interpreter.
книгопродáвецъ	knë-gô-prô-då-vëts	bookseller.
переплётчикъ	på-rå-plyôt-shîk	bookbinder.
худóжникъ	khů-dôzh-nîk	artist.
ремéсленникъ	rå-må-slën-nîk	artizan.
мѣщани́нъ	mësh-tshå-nîn	citizen.
актéръ	åk-tyôrr	actor.
конди́теръ	kån-dë-tyërr	confectioner.
бýлочникъ	bô-llôsh-nîk	baker.
мясни́къ	myåss-nîk	butcher.
пивовáръ	pë-vô-vårr	brewer.

портной	pǒrrt-nǒǐ	tailor.
портниха	pǒrrt-nè-khǎ	dress-maker.
сапожникъ	sǎ-pǒzh-nǐk	bootmaker.
башмачникъ	bǎsh-mǎsh-nǐk	shoemaker.
парикмахеръ	pǎ-rǐk-mǎ-khěrr	hairdresser.
ювелиръ	ů-vǎ-lérr	jeweller.
золотыхъ дѣлъ мастеръ	zǒ-llǒ-tǔǐkh dvǎll mǎss-tyěrr	goldsmith.
часовой мастеръ	tshǎ-sǒ-vǒǐ mǎss-tyěrr	watchmaker.
плотникъ	pllǒt-nǐk	carpenter.
столяръ	stǒ-lyǎrr	joiner.
слесарь	slǎ-sǎr	locksmith.
обойщикъ	ǎ-bǒǐ-shtshǐk	upholsterer.
кузнецъ	kůz-nyěts	smith.
трубочистъ	trǒ-bǎ-tshǐst	chimney-sweeper.
хозяинъ гостиницы	khǎ-zyǎ-ǐn gǒs-tyin-nè-tsǔǐ	inn-keeper.
хозяинъ	khǎ-zyǎ-in	host, landlord, master.
лакей	llǎ-kǎǐ	lackey, footman.
слуга	sllǒ-gǎ	man-servant.
служанка	sllǒ-zhǎn-kǎ	maid-servant.
горничная	gǒrr-nǐtsh-nǎ-yǎ	chamber-maid.
поваръ	pǒ-vǎrr	he-cook.
кухарка	kǒ-khǎrr-kǎ	she-cook.
кормилица	kǎrr-mè-lè-tsa	wet nurse.
дворникъ	dvǒrr-nǐk	an ostler, a man who looks after the yard.
буточникъ	bǒ-tǒsh-nǐk	watchman.
городовой	gǒ-rǒ-dǒ-vǒǐ	policeman.
иностранецъ	è-nǒ-strǎ-nyets	foreigner.
пассажиръ	pǎs-sǎ-zhǐrr	passenger.
извощикъ	ǐz-vǒ-shtshǐk	hackney-coachman.

ломовóй извóщикъ	llo-mo-voi iz-vo-shtshik	a carter, a dray-man.
перевóзчикъ	pá-rá-vo-tshtshik	waterman.
крестьянинъ (мужи́къ)	krest-ya-nin (mo-zhék)	peasant.
пасту́хъ	pas-tukh	shepherd.
землеѣ́длецъ	zem-lyá-dyá-lets,	husbandman.
садóвникъ	sa-dov-nik	gardener.
молóшница	ma-llosh-né-tsa	dairymaid.
мѣ́льникъ	mel-nik	miller.
ни́щій	nish-tshé	beggar.
мастерска́я	mas-ter-ska-ya	workshop.
фáбрика	fa-bré-ka	manufacture.
кладова́я	klla-do-va-ya	warehouse.
лавка	llaf-ka	shop.

RELATIONSHIP.

Прéдки	pret-ké	forefathers.
дѣдъ	dyet	grandfather.
бáбушка	ba-bush-ka	grandmother.
отéцъ	a-tyets	father.
мать	mat	mother.
сынъ	suin.	son.
дочь	dotsh	daughter.
внукъ	vnuk	grandson.
вну́чка	vnutsh-ka	grand-daughter.
братъ	brat	brother.
сестрá	syess-tra	sister.
дядя	dya-dya	uncle.
тётка	tyot-ka	aunt.
племя́нникъ	pla-myan-nik	nephew.

племянница	plå-myån-nė-tså	niece.
двоюродный братъ	dvô-ů-rôd-nůĭ bråt	(male) cousin.
двоюродная сестра	dvô-ů-rôd-nå-yå syĕs-trå	(female) cousin.
родня́, ро́дственники	råd-nyå, rôtst-vĕn-nė-kė.	relations.
жени́хъ	zhå-nėkh	engaged to a lady.
невѣста	nyå-vĕs-tå,	engaged to a gentleman.
мужъ, супру́гъ	můsh, sô-prôk	husband.
жена́, супру́га	zhå-nå, sô-prô-gå	wife (lady).
вдове́цъ	vdå-vĕts	widower.
вдова́	vdå-vå	widow.
кре́стный отецъ	kryôst-nůĭ å-tyĕts	godfather.
кре́стная мать	kryôst-nå-yå måt	godmother.
кре́стный сынъ, кре́стникъ	kryôst-nůĭ sůĭn, kråst-nik	godson.
кре́стная дочь, кре́стница	kryôst-nå-yå dôtsh, kråst-nė-tså	god-daughter.
двойни	dvôĭ-nė	twins.
наслѣдникъ	nå-slåd-nik	heir.
другъ, пріятель	drůk, prė-yå-tĕl	friend.
подру́га	på-drô-gå	(female) friend.
бракъ	bråk	marriage.
супру́жество	sô-prô-zhĕst-vô	matrimony.
сва́дьба	svåd-bå	wedding.
опеку́нъ	å-på-kůn	guardian.
и́мя	ė-myå	Christian name.
фами́лія	få-mė-lė-yå	family name.

MAN, THE HUMAN BODY, ITS FACULTIES AND DISEASES.

Мужчи́на	můsh-tshė-nå	a man (person of the male sex).

мужъ *	mush	a man (with regard to moral greatness).
человѣкъ **	tsha-la-vak	man (mankind).
люди	lu-dye	people.
жéнщина	zhen-shtshe-na	woman.
ребéнокъ	ra-byo-nok	baby.
дитя́	de-tya	child.
мáльчикъ	mal-tshik	boy.
дѣвушка	dye-vush-ka	girl.
дѣви́ца, барышня	dye-ve-tsa, ba-ruish-nya	a young lady.
юноша	u-no-sha	youth.
молодóй человѣкъ	ma-lla-doi tsha-lla-vak	a young man.
господи́нъ	gos-po-dyin	gentleman, Mr.
дáма	da-ma	lady.
бáринъ	ba-rin	master (with regard to his servants).
бáрыня	ba-rui-nya	mistress of the house, gentlewoman.
стари́къ	sta-rek	an old man.
старýха	sta-ro-kha	an old woman.
сиротá	se-ro-ta	orphan.
полъ	poll	sex.
членъ	tshlen	limb, member.
головá	go-lo-va	head.
вóлосы	vo-llo-sui	the hair.
бакенбáрды	ba-ken-barr-dui	whiskers.
усы	o-sui	mustachios.
бородá	bo-ro-da	beard.
лицó	le-tso	face.

* means also *husband*.

** denotes likewise a *person*, especially when speaking of the *number* of persons; also a *servant-man*.

чéрепъ	tsha-rep	scull.
мозгъ	mozg	brain.
лобъ	llop	forehead.
глазъ	gllas (the a is short)	eye.
брóви	bro-ve	eyebrows.
щекá	shtshe-ka	cheek.
ýхо	o-kho	ear.
носъ	noss	nose.
ротъ	rott	mouth.
гýбы	go-bui	lips.
зубъ	zup	tooth.
языкъ	ya-zuik	tongue.
подборóдокъ	pod-ba-ro-dok	chin.
шéя	sha-ya	neck.
гóрло	gorr-lo	throat.
плечó	pla-tsho	shoulder.
рукá	ro-ka	arm, hand.
кулáкъ	ko-llakk	fist.
пальцы	pal-tsui	fingers.
большóй пáлецъ	bol-shoi pa-lyets	(the great finger) thumb.
нóготь	no-got	nail.
грудь	grut	breast.
	(give the *t* a very soft sound by pronouncing the *consonant* *y* after it)	
желýдокъ	zha-llo-dok	stomach.
брюхо	bru-kho	belly.
спина	spe-na	the back.
колѣно	ko-lya-no	knee.
ногá	no-ga	leg, foot.
пáлецъ (на ногѣ)	pa-lets (na no-ga)	toe.
сéрдце	serrd-tsa	heart.
кóжа	ko-zha	skin.
мясо	mya-so	flesh.

жиръ	zhĭrr	the fat.
кость	kŏsst	bone.
нéрвы	nyĕrr-vŭĭ	the nerves.
жи́ла	zhē-llă	vein.
сухáя жи́ла	sŭ-khă-yă zhē-lla	sinew.
кровь	krŏf	blood.
слёзы	slyŏ-zŭĭ	tears.
потъ	pŏt	sweat.
пульсъ	pŭlse	pulse.
дыхáніе	dŭĭ-khă-nē-yĕ	breath.
вздохъ	vzdŏkh	a sigh.
стонъ	stŏn	a groan.
чихáніе	tshē-khă-nē-yĕ	sneezing.
смѣхъ	smyĕkh	laughter.
гóлосъ	gŏ-lŏss	voice.
гóлодъ	gŏ-llŏt	hunger.
жáжда	zhăzh-dă	thirst.
сонъ	sŏnn	sleep.
храпѣніе	khră-pă-nē-yĕ	snoring.
сонъ, сновидѣніе	sŏnn, snŏ-vē-dyă-nē-yĕ	dream.
мина, видъ	mē-nă, vĭt	mien, air.
черты лицá	tshĕrr-tŭĭ lē-tsă	features.
цвѣтъ лицá	tsvĕt lē-tsă	complexion.
шагъ	shăk	step.
похóдка	pŏ-khŏt-kă	gait.
красотá	kră-sŏ-tă	beauty.
урóдливость	ŏ-rŏd-lē-vŏst	ugliness.
си́ла	sē-llă	force, strength.
здорóвье	zdŏ-rŏv-yĕ	health.
трупъ, мёртвое тѣло	trŭp, myŏrrt-vŏ-yĕ tyă-lŏ	a coprse, a dead body.
пять чувствъ	pyăt tshŭfstf	the five senses.
зрѣніе	zră-nē-yĕ	the sight.
взоръ, взглядъ	vzŏrr, vzglyăt.	a glance.

слухъ	slükh	the hearing.
шумъ	shüm	noise.
звукъ	zvük	a sound.
обоня́ніе	ŏ-bŏ-nyă-nĕ-yĕ	the smelling.
за́пахъ	ză-păkh	a smell.
вкусъ	fküss	the taste.
осяза́ніе	ŏ-syă-ză-nĕ-yĕ	the feeling.
болѣ́знь	bă-lăzn	disease, illness.
нарывъ	nă-rŭïf	abscess.
о́пухоль	ŏ-pŏ-khŏl	a swelling.
ра́на	ră-nă	a wound.
порѣ́зъ	pŏ-rĕss	a cut.
рубе́цъ	rŏ-byĕts	a scar.
головна́я боль	gă-llăv-nă-yă bŏl	head-ache.
зубна́я боль	züb-nă-yă bŏl	tooth-ache.
на́сморкъ	nă-smŏrrk	a cold in the head.
ка́шель	kă-shĕl	a cough.
охри́плость	ă-khrĭp-lŏst	hoarseness.
рво́та	rvŏ-tă	vomiting.
морска́я болѣзнь	mărr-skă-yă bă-lăzn	sea-sickness.
холе́ра	khă-lyă-ră	the cholera.
корь	kŏrr	the measles.
скарлати́на	skărr-llă-tyĕ-nă	the scarlet-fever.
о́спа	ŏss-pă	the small-pox.
пода́гра	pŏ-dă-gră	the gout.
мозо́ль	mă-zŏl	a corn.
горя́чка	gă-ryătsh-kă	fever.
чахо́тка	tshĕ-khŏt-kă	consumption.
лече́ніе	lyă-tshă-nĕ-yĕ	curing.
по́льзованіе	pŏl-zŏ-vă-nĕ-yĕ	(medical) treatment.
діе́та	dĕ-yĕ-tă	diet.
лека́рство	lyă-kărr-stvŏ	physic, medicine.
реце́птъ	rĕ-tsĕpt	prescription.

кровопусканіе	krŏ-vŏ-pŭss-kă-nĕ-yĕ	bleeding, blood-letting.
прививаніе	prĕ-vĕ-vă-nĕ-yĕ	inoculation.
прививаніе коровьей оспы	prĕ-vĕ-vă-nĕ-yĕ kă-rŏv-yăĭ ŏss-pŭĭ	vaccination
пластырь	pllăs-tŭĭr	plaster.
испанская муха	ĭss-păn-skă-yă mŏ-khă	blister.
выздоровленіе	vŭĭ-zdŏ-rŏv-lă-nĕ-yĕ	recovery.

THE SOUL, ITS FACULTIES, AND SENSATIONS.

Удивленіе	ŏ-dĭv-lă-nĕ-yĕ	admiration, astonishment.
дружба	drŭzh-bă	friendship.
привязанность	prĕ-vyă-zăn-nost	affection.
любовь	lŭ-bŏff	love.
самолюбіе	să-mŏ-lŭ-bĕ-yĕ	self-love.
сострадание	sŏ-stră-dă-nĕ-yĕ	compassion.
сожаленіе	sŏ-zhă-lă-nĕ-yĕ	regret.
ненависть	nyă-nă-vĭst	hatred.
презрѣніе	pră-ză-nĕ-yĕ	contempt.
страданіе	stră-dă-nĕ-yĕ	suffering.
прихоть, капризъ	prĕ-khŏt, kă-prĕss	caprice.
характеръ	khă-răk-tyerr	character, temper.
досада	dă-să-dă	spite.
отчаяніе	ŏt-tshă-yă-nĕ-yĕ	despair.
страхъ	străkh	dread.
скука	skŏ-kă	ennui, dulness.
охота	ă-khŏ-tă	desire.
желаніе	zhă-lă-nĕ-yĕ	wish.
надежда	nă-dyĕzh-dă	hope.
веселость	vă-syŏ-lŏst	gaiety.

радость	rå-dôst	joy.
удовольствіе	ô-dô-volst-vė-ye	pleasure.
способность	spå-sôb-nost	capacity.
понятіе	på-nyå-tė-yė	idea.
склонность	sklôn-nost	propensity.
безпокойство	bės-på-kôïst-vô	trouble.
честь	tshåst	honour.
стыдъ	stûït	shame.
память	på-myåt	memory.
мысль	mûïsl	thought.
разумъ	rå-sûm	reason.
истина	ïs-tyė-nå	truth.
воля	vô-lyå	the will.
забота	zå-bô-tå	care, anxiety.
подозрѣніе	pô-dô-zrå-nė-yė	suspicion.
горесть	gô-rėst	grief.

LIFE.

Дѣтство	dyėtst-vô	childhood.
молодость	mô-llô-dôst	youth.
старость	stå-rôst	old age.
рожденіе	rôzh-dyå-nė-yė	birth.
смерть	smėrrt	death.
счастіе	stshås-tė-yė	happiness, fortune, luck.
несчастіе	nå-stshås-tė-yė	misfortune.
состояніе	sô-stô-yå-nė-ye	condition, also a fortune.
ремесло	rå-mėss-llô	a trade.
работа	rå-bô-tå	work.
доходъ	då-khôt	an income.

póскошь	ro̊s-ko̊sh	luxury.
пра́здность	prа̊zd-no̊st	idleness.
бѣ́дность	båd-no̊st	poverty.
óбщество	o̊p-shtshe̊st-vo̊	society.
расхóды	rа̊s-kho̊-důĭ	the costs.
издéржки	ĭz-dye̊rrsh-ke̊	expenses.
наслѣ́дство	nа̊-slye̊tst-vo̊	inheritance.
прошéдшее	prа̊-she̊t-shа̊-ye̊	the past.
бýдущее	bo̊-důsh-tshа̊-ye̊	the future.
недоста́токъ	nyа̊-do̊s-tа̊-to̊k	defect, want.
на́добность	nа̊-do̊b-no̊st	need, want.
необходи́мость	nyа̊-o̊p-khа̊-dye̊-most	necessity.
привычка	pre̊-vůĭtsh-kа̊	habit.
долгъ	do̊llk	duty.
сла́ва	sllа̊-vа̊	glory.

EATING AND DRINKING.

Столъ	sto̊ll	table.
ска́терть	skа̊-tye̊rrt	table-cloth.
салфéтка	sа̊l-fe̊t-kа̊	napkin.
ножъ	no̊sh	knife.
ви́лка	vĭll-kа̊	fork.
лóжка	llo̊sh-kа̊	spoon.
блюдо	blů-do̊	dish.
тарéлка	tа̊-rye̊ll-kа̊	plate.
стака́нъ	stа̊-kа̊n	a glass, a tumbler.
рюмка	rům-kа̊	wine-glass.
графи́нъ	grа̊-fĭn	decanter.
прибóръ	pre̊-bo̊rr	a cover.
поднóсъ	pа̊d-no̊ss	tea-tray.
кофéйникъ	kа̊-fа̊ĭ-nĭk	coffee-pot.
ча́йникъ	tshа̊ĭ-nĭk	tea-pot.

самóвáръ	sa-mo-varr	tea-urn.
малóчникъ	ma-llosh-nik	milk-pot.
сáхарница	sa-kharr-ne-tsa	sugar-basin.
чáшка	tshash-ka	cup.
блюдечко	blu-detsh-ko	saucer.
прóбочникъ	pro-bosh-nik	cork-screw.
хлѣбъ	khlyep	bread.
бѣлый хлѣбъ	bya-lui khlyep	white bread.
чéрный хлѣбъ	tshorr-nui khlyep	black bread.
свѣжій хлѣбъ	svya-zhe khlyep	new bread.
хлѣбъ съ масломъ	khlyep s ma-slom	bread and butter.
кусóкъ, кусóчикъ	ko-sok, ko-so-tshik	a piece, a small piece.
бýлка	bull-ka	a roll.
щи	shtshe	cabbage-soup.
супъ	sup	soup.
ухá	o-kha.	fish-soup.
рисъ	res	rice.
говя́дина	ga-vya-de-na	beef.
жиръ	zhirr	fat.
варéное мясо	va-ryo-no-ye mya-so	boiled meat.
жаркóе	zharr-ko-ye	rost meat.
бифштéксъ	bef-shteks	beefsteaks.
телятина	tya-lya-te-na	veal.
теля́чьи котлéты	tya-lyatsh-yo kot-lya-tui	veal cutlets.
барáнина	ba-ra-nye-na	mutton.
свинина	sve-nye-na	pork.
ветчинá.	vet-she-na	ham.
дичь	dyetsh	venison.
кýрица	ko-re-tsa	fowl.
крылó	krui-llo	wing.
печéнка	pa-tshon-ka	liver.
зéлень	za-lyane	vegetables.

я́йца	yai-tsa	eggs.
я́йца въ смятку	yai-tsa f smyat-ko	poached eggs.
салатъ	sa-llat	salad.
соль	sol	salt.
пе́рецъ	pa-ryets	pepper.
горчи́ца	garr-tshe-tsa	mustard.
ма́сло	mass-llo	butter (oil).
у́ксусъ	uk-suss	vinegar.
пиро́жное	pe-rozh-no-ye	pastry.
сухари́	su-kha-re	biscuits.
пиро́гъ	pe-rok	a peculiar sort of pie.
сыръ	suirr	cheese.
блины	ble-nui	pancakes.
ва́фли	vaf-le	wafers.
са́харъ	sa-kharr	sugar.
карто́фель	karr-to-fel	potatoes.
рѣ́па	rya-pa	turnips.
морко́вь	marr-koff	carrots.
капу́ста	ka-pus-ta	cabbage.
цвѣ́тная капу́ста	tsvet-na-ya ka-pus-ta	cauliflower.
горо́хъ	ga-rokh	pease.
шпина́тъ	shpe-nat	spinage.
спа́ржа	sparr-zha	asparagus
огурцы	a-gur-tsui	cucumbers.
грибы	gre-bui	mushrooms.
вино́	ve-no	wine.
бѣ́лое вино́	bya-lo-ye ve-no	white wine.
кра́сное вино́	krass-no-ye ve-no	red wine.
шампа́нское	sham-pan-sko-ye	Champaign wine.
маде́ра	ma-dya-ra	Madeira wine.
хересъ	kha-ress	sherry.
портве́йнъ	porrt-vain	port.
пиво	pe-vo	beer.

мёдъ	myot	mead.
квасъ	kvass	a liquor made of rye flour and rye malt.
во́дка	vot-ka	brandy, gin.
чай	tshaï	tea.
ко́фе	ko-fa	coffee.
шоколадъ	she-ko-llat	chocolate.
рыба	rui-ba	fish.
треска́	tres-ka	codfish, stockfish.
се́мга	syom-ga	salmon.
форе́ль	fa-rel	trout.
щу́ка	shtsho-ka	pike.
о́кунь	o-kun	perch.
сельдъ, селе́дка	seld, sa-lyot-ka	herring.
у́горь	o-gorr	eel.
у́стрица	us-tre-tsa	oyster.
ракъ	rak	crab.
дессе́ртъ	dyes-serrt	the dessert.
плоды	pla-daï	fruit.
я́блоко	ya-blo-ko	apple.
гру́ша	gro-sha	pear.
апельси́нъ	a-pel-sin	orange.
лимо́нъ	le-mon	lemon.
вишни	ve-shne	cherries.
земляни́ка	zem-lya-ne-ka	strawberries.
клубни́ка	klub-nye-ka	garden strawberries.
мали́на	ma-lye-na	raspberries.
сморо́дина	sma-ro-dye-na	currants.
орѣхи	a-ra-khe	nuts.
виногра́дъ	ve-no-grat	grapes.

DRESS.

Бѣлье́	bel-yo	linen, linen-clothes.
руба́шка	ro-bash-ka	shirt, shift.
чулки́	tshul-ke	stockings.
носки́	nas-ke	socks.
ту́фли	tuf-le	slippers.
башмаки́	bash-ma-ke	shoes.
сапоги́	sa-pa-ghe	boots.
подшта́нники	pot-shtan-ne-ke	drawers.
ю́бка	up-ka	petticoat.
штаны, пантало́ны	shta-nui, pan-ta-lo-nui	breeches, pantaloons.
подтя́жки	pat-tyash-ke	braces.
жиле́тъ	zhe-lyett	waistcoat.
га́лстукъ	gall-stuk,	cravat.
серту́къ	syerr-tuk	surtout.
фракъ	frak	dress-coat.
рукава́	ro-ka-va	sleeves.
карма́ны	karr-ma-nui	pockets.
пу́говицы	po-go-ve-tsui	buttons.
пе́тли	pat-le	button-holes.
подкла́дка	pot-klat-ka	lining.
шине́ль	she-nyel	cloak.
шля́па	shlya-pa	hat.
ша́пка	shap-ka	cap.
пари́къ	pa-rek	wig.
бритва	brit-va	razor.
реме́нь	ra-men	strap.
корсе́тъ	korr-syet	stays.
сало́пъ	sa-lop	a (lady's) cloak.
шля́пка	shlyap-ka	a bonnet.

чéпчикъ	tshĕp-tshĭk	a (lady's) cap, a mob.
вуáль	vŭ-ăl	veil.
сéрьги	syĕrr-ghĕ	ear-rings.
браслéты	bră-slă-tŭĭ	bracelets.
лéнта	lyĕn-tă	ribbon.
туалéтъ	tŭ-ă-lyĕt	toilet, dressing-table.
передникъ	pă-răd-nĭk	apron.
носовóй платóкъ	nŏ-sŏ-vŏĭ pllă-tŏk	handkerchief.
перчáтки	pĕrr-tshăt-kĕ	gloves.
мýфта	mŭf-tă	muff.
грéбень, гребёнка	gră-bĕn, gră-byŏn-kă	comb.
щётка	shtshŏt-kă	brush.
зубнáя щётка	zŭb-nă-yă shtshŏt-kă	tooth-brush.
головнáя щётка	gă-lăv-nă-yă shtshŏt-kă	comb-brush.
платянáя щётка	pllă-tyă-nă-yă shtshŏt-kă	clothes-brush.
часы́	tshă-sŭĭ	watch.
кольцó	kăl-tsŏ	ring.
очкú	ătsh-kĕ	spectacles.
помáда	pŏ-mă-dă	pometum.
духú	dŏ-khĕ	odours, perfumes.
мы́ло	mŭĭ-llŏ	soap.
гýбка	gŭp-kă	sponge.
полотéнцо	pŏ-llŏ-tyĕn-tsŏ	towel.
трость	trŏst	cane.
зóнтикъ	zŏn-tyĭk	parasol, umbrella.
полотнó	pă-llăt-nŏ	linen, linen-cloth.
коленкóръ	kă-lyĕn-kŏrr	calico.
кисея́	kĕ-să-yă	muslin.
батúстъ	ba-tyĭst	cambric.
фланéль	fllă-nĕl	flannel.
сукнó	sŭk-nŏ	cloth.

бáрхатъ	bårr-khåt	velvet.
шерстянáя матéрія	sherr-styå-nå-yå må-tyå-rè-yå	woollen stuff.
шéлковая матéрія	shöl-kö-vå-yå må-tyå-rè-yå	silk stuff,
атлáсъ	åt-llåss	satin.
мѣхъ	myèkh	fur.
кóжа	kö-zhå	leather.
шелкъ	shölllk	silk.
нитки	nyìt-kè	thread.
бумáга	bö-må-gå	cotton.
игóлка	è-göll-kå	needle.
булáвка	bö-llåf-kå	pin.
нóжницы	nözh-nè-tsüì	scissors.
напéрстокъ	nå-pyörr-stöck	thimble.
дéньги	dyån-ghè	money.
мéлкія дéньги	myèll-kè-yå dyån-ghè	change, small coin.

THE HOUSE AND HOUSEHOLD GOODS.

Домъ	döm	house.
дáча	då-tshå	country-house.
крыльцó	krüìl-tsö	the steps.
матъ	måt	mat.
звонóкъ	zvå-nök	bell.
дверь	dvåre	door.
порóгъ	på-rök	threshold.
задвижка	zå-dvìsh-kå	bolt.
ручка	rùtsh-kå	handle.
замóкъ	zå-mök	lock.
замóкъ висячій	zå-mök vè-syå-tshè	padlock.
ключъ	klùtsh	key.
сѣни	syå-nè	entrance, vestibule.

коррпдоръ	kórr-ĕ-dŏrr	passage.
передняя	på-råd-nyå-yå	lobly, hall.
лѣстница	låse-nĕ-tså	staircase.
ступени	stŏ-på-nĕ	steps.
этажъ	å-tåsh	story.
гостиная	gås-tyĭn-nå-yå	drawing-room.
зала	zå-llå	saloon.
столовая	stå-llŏ-vå-yå	dining-room.
кабинетъ	kå-bĕ-nyĕt	study.
комната, покой	kŏm-nå-tå, på-kŏĭ	room, chamber.
обои	å-bŏ-ĕ	hangings, tapestry.
чердакъ	tshĕr-dåk	garret.
погребъ	pŏ-grĕp	cellar.
кухня	kůkh-nyå	kitchen.
кладовая	kllå-dŏ-vå-yå	store-room, pantry.
чуланъ	tshŏ-llån	pantry, lumber-room.
шкафъ	shkåf	cupboard.
окно	åk-nŏ	window.
полъ	pŏll	floor.
потолокъ	pŏ-tå-llŏk	ceiling.
каминъ	kå-mĭn	chimney.
дворъ	dvŏrr	yard.
конюшня	kå-nŭsh-nyå	stable.
сарай	så-råĭ	coach-house.
стѣна	styå-nå	wall.
крыша	krůĭ-shå	roof.
известь	ĭz-vĕst	lime, calx.
кирпичъ	kĭrr-pĭtsh	bricks.
мусоръ	mŏ-sŏrr	rubbish.
зеркало	zyĕrr-kå-llŏ	looking-glass.
картины	kårr-tyĕ-nůĭ	pictures.
портретъ	pŏrr-tryĕt	portrait.
коверъ	kå-vyŏrr	carpet.

ширмы	shirr-mui	screen.
чемоданъ	tshe-mo-dan	portmanteau.
комодъ	ka-mot	chest of drawers.
стулъ	stull	chair.
кресла	kress-lla	elbow-chair, arm-chair.
диванъ	dye-van	sofa.
постель	pa-styal	bed.
кровать	kra-vat	bedstead.
матрацъ, тюфякъ	ma-trats, tu-fyak	mattress.
перина	pa-re-na	feather-bed.
подушка	pa-dush-ka	pillow, bolster.
наволочка	na-vo-llotsh-ka	pillow-case.
простыня	pros-tui-nya	sheet.
одѣяло	a-da-ya-llo	the bed-clothes, coverlet, counterpane.
занавѣсы	za-na-va-sui	curtains.
люлька	lul-ka	cradle.
подсвѣчникъ	pat-svatsh-nik	candlestick.
свѣча, свѣчка	sva-tsha, svatsh-ka	candle.
фонарь	fo-narr	lantern.
лампа	llam-pa	lamp.
щипцы	shtship-tsui	snuffers, tongs.
спичка	spitsh-ka	a match.
кочерга	ko-tsherr-ga	poker.
дрова	dro-va	wood.
полѣно	pa-lya-no	a piece of wood.
уголь	o-gol	coals.
печь, печька	patsh, patsh-ka	oven, stove.
стѣнные часы	styen-nui-ye tsha-sui	clock.
ведро	ve-dro	pail, bucket.
корзина, корзинка	karr-ze-na, karr-zin-ka	basket.
метло	met-llo	broom.
пыль	puil	dust.

соръ	sórr	sweepings.
коры́то	ka-rui-tó	trough, wash-tub.
кастрю́ля	kas-tru-lya	stew-pan.
котёлъ	ka-tyóll	kettle.
сковорода́	skó-vó-ro-da	gridiron.
бочка	bótsh-ka	cask.
кранъ	kran	cock.
бутылка	bo-tuil-ka	bottle.
про́бка	próp-ka	a cork.

THE SCHOOL, READING, WRITING ETC.,

Университе́тъ	o-ne-verr-se-tyet	university.
акаде́мія	a-ka-dya-me-ya	academy.
учи́лище, школа	o-tshe-lish-tshe, skho-lla	school.
ко́рпусъ	korr-puss	military school.
пансіо́нъ	pan-se-ón	boarding school.
профе́ссоръ	pro-fyess-orr	professor.
дире́кторъ	de-ryek-torr	director.
директри́са	de-ryek-tre-sa	directress.
инспе́кторъ	in-spyek-torr	inspector.
гуверне́ръ	go-verr-nyorr	governor, tutor, usher.
гувернантка	go-verr-nant-ka	governess.
учи́тель	o-tshe-tyel	(a male) teacher.
учи́тельница	o-tshe-tyel-ne-tsa	(a female) teacher.
учи́тель ру́сскаго языка́	o-tshe-tel russ-ka-vo ya-zui-ka	Russian master.
учи́тель а́нглій-скаго языка́	o-tshe-tel ang-le-ska-vo ya-zui-ka	English master.
учени́къ	o-tsha-nyik	scholar, pupil, school-boy.

классъ	kllass	class.
конто́рка	kan-torr-ka	desk.
скаме́йка	ska-mai-ka	form.
(больша́я) доска́	(bol-sha-ya) doss-ka	board.
(а́спидная) доска́	(ass-pid-na-ya) doss-ka	slate.
мѣлъ	myell	chalk.
гри́фель	gre-fel	slate-pencil.
кни́га	kne-ga	book.
страни́ца	stra-ne-tsa	page.
листъ	lyist	leaf.
а́збука	az-bo-ka	the alphabet, a primer, a spelling book.
грамма́тика	gram-ma-tye-ka	grammar.
слова́рь, лексико́нъ	sllo-varr, lyek-se-kon	dictionary.
уро́къ	o-rok	lesson.
зада́ча	za-da-tsha	task.
упражне́ніе	o-prazh-nya-ne-ye	exercise.
перево́дъ	pa-ra-vot	translation.
языкъ	ya-zuik	language.
сло́во	sllo-vo	word.
слогъ	sllok	syllable.
бу́ква	buk-va	letter.
гла́сная бу́ква	gllass-na-ya buk-va	vowel.
согла́сная бу́ква	so-gllass-na-ya buk-va	consonant.
запята́я	za-pya-ta-ya	comma.
то́чка съ запятою	totsh-ka s za-pya-to-u	semicolon.
двоето́чіе	dvo-ye-to-tshe-ye	colon.
то́чка	totsh-ka	period.
ударе́ніе	o-da-ra-ne-ye	accent.
апо́строфъ	a-po-stroff	apostrophe.
кавычки	ka-vuitsh-ke	quotation, inverted commas.
ско́бки	skop-ke	parentheses.
бума́га	bo-ma-ga	paper.

почтóвая бумáга	påt-shtô-vå-yå bô-må-gå	letter-paper.
пропускнáя бумáга	prô-pûsk-nå-yå bô-må-gå	blotting-paper.
стопá	stå-på	a ream.
десть	dyåst	a quire.
листъ	lyist	sheet.
полъ листá	pôll-lis-tå	half a sheet.
тетрáдь	tå-tråt	copy-book.
черни́льница	tsherr-nyil-ne-tså	ink-stand.
черни́ла	tsherr-ne-llå	ink.
песóчница	pye-sôsh-ne-tså	sand-box.
песóкъ	nye-sôk	sand.
перó	pye-rô	pen.
стальнóе перó	stål-nô-ye pye-rô	steel pen.
перочи́нный ножикъ	pye-rô-tshin-nûi nô-zhik	pen-knife.
карандáшъ	kå-rån-dåsh	pencil.
рези́нка	re-zin-kå	Indian rubber.
линéйка	le-nyåi-kå	ruler.
циркуля́	tsir-kô-lyå	compasses.
бумáжникъ	bô-måzh-nik	pocket-book.
письмó	pis-mô	letter.
запи́ска	zå-pis-kå	note.
пóдпись	pôt-pis	signature.
сургучъ	sûr-gûtsh	sealing wax.
облáтка	ôb-llåt-kå	wafer.
печáть	pye-tshåt	seal.
газéта, вѣдомость	gå-zye-tå, vyå-dô-môst	gazette, news-paper.
журнáлъ	zhûrr-nåll	journal, magazine.
библіóтека	be-ble-ô-tye-kå	library.
библіóтека для чтенія	be-ble-ô-tye-kå dlyå tshtyå-ne-yå.	circulating library.

THE TOWN.

столи́ца, гла́вный го́родъ	stá-lyé-tsá, gllăv-nŭĭ gŏ-rŏt	metropolis, capital.
го́родъ	gŏ-rŏt	city, town.
крѣ́пость	kryă-pŏst	fortress.
прихо́дъ	prĕ-khŏt	parish.
часть	tshăst	quarter (of a town).
кварталъ	kvărr-tăll	ward, under-division of the quarters of a town.
дворе́цъ	dvă-ryĕts	palace.
тамо́жня	ta-mózh-nyă	custom-house.
ра́туша	ră-tŏ-shă	town-hall.
би́ржа	bĭrr-zhă	exchange.
адмиралте́йство	ad-mĕ-răll-tyăĭst-vŏ	admiralty.
га́вань	gă-văn	harbour, port.
на́бережная	nă-bĕ-rĕsh-nă-yă	quay.
гости́нный дворъ	găs-tyĭn-nŭĭ dvŏrr	bazar.
полиція	pă-lĕ-tsĕ-yă	police-office.
тюрьма́, темни́ца	tŭr-mă, tyĕm-nĕ-tsă	prison, jail, dungeon.
по́чта, почта́мтъ	pŏtsh-tă, pŏtsht-ămt	post-office.
го́шпиталь	gŏsh-pĕ-tăl	hospital.
ры́нокъ	rŭĭ-nŏk	market.
гости́ница	gŏs-tyĭn-nĕ-tsă	inn, hotel.
тракти́ръ	trăk-tyĭrr	eating-house.
конди́терская	kăn-dyĕ-tĕrr-skă-yă	confectioner's shop.
кофе́йная	kă-făĭ-nă-yă	coffee-house.
каба́къ	kă-băk	pot-house.
ба́ня	bă-nyă	bath.
теа́тръ	tyă-ătr	theatre.

зданіе	zda-ne-ye	bui ding.
садъ	sat	garden.
заборъ	za-borr	a wooden wall.
желѣзная дорога	zha-lyez-na-ya da-ro-ga	railroad.
улица	o-le-tsa	street.
переулокъ	pa-re-o-llok	lanc, cross-street.
тротуаръ	tro-to-arr	foot-pavement.
мостовая	mos-to-va-ya	pavement.
площадь	pllo-shtshat	square.
мостъ	most	bridge.
арка	arr-ka	arch.
ворота	va-ro-ta	gate.
застава	za-sta-va	city-gate, turnpike-gate.
предмѣстіе	pred-ma-ste-ye	suburb.
кладбище	kllad-be-shtshe	burying-ground.
могила	ma-ghe-lla	tomb, grave.
гробъ	grop	coffin.
похороны погребеніе	po-kho-ro-nui, po-gre-ba-ne-ye	funeral, burial.

COUNTRIES, NATIONS.

Азія	a-ze-ya	Asia.
Азіятецъ	a-ze-ya-tyets	an Asiatic.
Африка	a-fre-ka	Africa.
Африканецъ	a-fre-ka-nyets	an African.
Америка	a-ma-re-ka	America.
Американецъ	a-ma-re-ka-nyets	an American.
Австралія	aff-stra-le-ya	Australia.
Индія	in-de-ya	India.
Индѣецъ	in-dya-yets	an Indian.
Китай	ke-tai	China.

Китáецъ	ke-ta-yets	a Chinese.
Япóнія	ya-po-ne-ya	Japan.
Япóнецъ	ya-po-nyets	a Japanese.
Египетъ	ye-he-pet	Egypt.
Египтянинъ	ye-hip-tya-nin	an Egyptian.
Бразилія	bra-ze-le-ya	Brazil.
Бразилецъ	bra-ze-lyets	a Brazilian.
Соединéнные Штáты	so-ye-de-nyon-nui-ye shta-tui	the United States.
Еврóпа	yev-ro-pa	Europe.
Европéецъ	yev-ro-pa-yets	a European.
Россія	rass-se-ya	Russia.
Рýсскій	russ-koi	a Russian.
Пóльша	pol-sha	Poland.
Поля́къ	pa-lyak	a Pole.
Швéція	shva-tse-ya	Sweden.
Шведъ	shvet	a Swede.
Норвéгія	norr-va-ghe-ya	Norway.
Норвéжецъ	norr-va-zhets	a Norwegian.
Дáнія	da-ne-ya	Denmark.
Датчáнинъ	dat-tsha-nin	a Dane.
Великобритáнія	va-le-ko-bre-ta-ne-ya	Great Britain.
Англія	an-gle-ya	England.
Англичáнинъ	an-gle-tsha-nin	an Englishman.
Шотлáндія	shot-llan-de-ya	Scottland.
Шотлáндецъ	shot-llan-dyets	a Scotchman.
Ирлáндія	irr-llan-de-ya	Ireland.
Ирлáндецъ	irr-llan-dyets	an Irishman.
Прýссія	pruss-se-ya	Prussia.
Прусáкъ	pru-sak	a Prussian.
Саксóнія	sak-so-ne-ya	Saxony.
Саксóнецъ	sak-so-nyets	a Saxon.
Гермáнія	gherr-ma-ne-ya	Germany.
Нѣмецъ	nya-mets	a German.

Австрія	aff-stre-ya	Austria.
Австріецъ	aff-stre-yets	an Austrian.
Венгрія	ven-gre-ya	Hungary.
Венгерецъ	ven-ga-rets	a Hungarian.
Швейцарія	shvai-tsa-re-ya	Switzerland.
Швейцарецъ	shvai-tsa-ryets	a Swiss.
Бельгія	bel-ghe-ya	Belgium,
Бельгіецъ	bel-ghe-yets	a Belgian.
Голландія	goll-llan-de-ya	Holland.
Голландецъ	goll-llan-dyets	a Dutchman.
Франція	fran-tse-ya	France.
Французъ	fran-tsuss	a Frenchman.
Испанія	iss-pa-ne-ya	Spain.
Испанецъ	iss-pa-nyets	a Spaniard.
Португалія	porr-to-ga-le-ya	Portugal.
Португалецъ	porr-to-ga-lyets	a Portuguese.
Италія	e-ta-le-ya	Italy.
Итальянецъ	e-tal-ya-nyets	an Italian.
Греція	gra-tse-ya	Greece.
Грекъ	grek	a Greek.
Турція	turr-tse-ya	Turkey.
Турокъ	to-rok	a Turk.
Альпійскія горы	al-pe-ske-ya go-rui	the Alps.
Пиренейскія горы	pe-re-nyai-ske-ya go-rui	the Pyrenees.
Британскій каналъ	bre-tan-skoi ka-nall	the British Channel.
Мысъ Доброй Надежды	muiss do-broi na-dyezh-dui	the Cape of Good Hope.
Темза	tyem-za	the Thames.
Нева	nye-va	the Neva.
государство	go-so-darr-stvo	a state.
имперія	im-pa-re-ya	an Empire.
королевство	ko-ro-lyefst-vo	a kingdom.
республика	ress-po-ble-ka	a republic.

OBJECTS OF NATURE.

Природа	pre-ro-da	nature.
вселенная	fsa-lyen-na-ya	the universe.
міръ, свѣтъ	merr, svyet	the world.
небо	nya-bo	heaven, sky.
звѣзды	zvyoz-dui	the stars.
солнце	son-tse	sun.
луна́, мѣсяцъ	llo-na, ma-syats	moon.
лунный свѣтъ	llun-nui svyet	moonlight.
сѣверъ	sya-verr	the north.
югъ	ukk	the south.
за́падъ	za-pat	the west.
востокъ	vas-tok	the east.
облако	ob-lla-ko	cloud.
туча	to-tsha	dark cloud, thunder-cloud.
грязь	gryas	mud.
камень	ka-men	stone.
долина	da-lye-na	valley.
равнина	rav-nye-na	a plain.
степь	styape	heath, stepp.
холмъ	kholm	hill.
гора́	ga-ra	mountain.
мысъ, носъ	muiss, noss	cape, point.
перешеекъ	pa-ra-sha-yek	isthmus.
островъ	oss-trof	island.
полуостровъ	po-llo-oss-trof	peninsula.
берегъ	ba-rek	bank, shore.
мель	mel	shoal, sand-bank.
лѣсъ	lyess	forest, wood.
лугъ	lluk	meadow.
поле	po-lye	field.
ровъ	roff	ditch.

доро́га, путь	da-ro-ga, put	road, way.
тропи́нка	tra-pin-ka	path.
де́рево	dya-ra-vo	tree.
цвѣто́къ	tsva-tok	flower.
трава́	tra-va	grass.
ове́съ	a-vyoss	oats.
сѣ́но	sya-no	hay.
соло́ма	sa-llo-ma	straw.
хлѣбъ	khlyep	corn.
жа́тва, ўрожа́й	zhat-va, o-ro-zhai	harvest, crop.
вода́	va-da	water.
мо́ре	mo-rya	sea.
океа́нъ	o-kya-an	ocean.
прили́въ	pre-lyif	the flow, tide.
отли́въ	ot-lyif	the ebb.
во́лны	voll-nui	the billows, waves.
зали́въ, бу́хта	za-lyif, bukh-ta	gulf, bay.
рейдъ	raid	roadstead, roads.
проли́въ	pra-lyif	strait.
рѣка́	rya-ka	river.
руче́й	ro-tshai	brook.
исто́чникъ	iss-totsh-nyik	a spring.
тече́ніе	tya-tsha-ne-e	the current.
у́стье	ust-ye	the mouth.
водопа́дъ	vo-do-pat	waterfall, cataract.
о́зеро	o-zya-ro	lake.
прудъ	prut	pond.
боло́то	ba-llo-to	marsh, moor.
лу́жа	llo-zha	pool.
наводне́ніе	na-vad-nya-ne-ye	inundation.
во́здухъ	voz-dukh	air.
вѣ́теръ	va-tyerr	wind.
сѣ́верный вѣ́теръ	sya-verr-nui, va-tyerr	the north-wind.
ю́жный вѣ́теръ	uzh-nui va-tyerr	the south-wind.

западный вѣтеръ	zà-pàd-nŭi và-tyèrr	the west-wind.
восточный вѣтеръ	vàss-tòtsh-nŭi và-tyèrr.	the east-wind.
тихій вѣтерокъ	tyè-khòi và-tyè-ròk	a gentle breeze.
свѣжій вѣтеръ	svà-zhè và-tyèrr	a fresh gale.
гроза́	grà-zà	thunder-storm.
бу́ря	bò-ryà	storm, tempest.
штиль	shtèle	a calm.
ого́нь	à-gòn	fire.
и́скра	ìss-krà	spark.
пла́мя	pllà-myà	flame, blaze.
жаръ	zhàrr	heat.
дымъ	dŭim	smoke.
паръ	pàrr	steam.
зола́	zà-llà	ashes.
теплота́	tyè-pllò-tà	warmth.
хо́лодъ	khò-llòt	the cold.
моро́зъ	mà-ròss	the frost.
сы́рость	sŭi-ròst	humidity.
испаре́ніе	ìss-pà-rà-nè-yè	exhalation, evaporation.
тума́нъ	tò-màn	fog, mist.
дождь, до́ждикъ	dòsh, dòzh-dyìk	rain.
проливно́й дождь	prò-lìv-nòi dòsh	a heavy shower of rain.
роса́	rà-sà	the dew.
и́ней	è-nyài	hoar frost.
ледъ	lyòt	ice.
о́ттепель	òt-tyà-pèl	a thaw.
снѣгъ	snyèk	snow.
градъ	gràt	hail.
мо́лнія	mòll-nè-yà	lightning.
громъ	gròm	thunder.
ра́дуга	rà-dò-gà	rainbow.
затмѣ́ніе	zà-tmà-nè-yè	eclipse.

землетрясéніе	zĕm-lyá-trå-syá--nè-yĕ	earthquake.
огнеды́шущая гора́	ŏg-nyĕ-dŭĭ-shŭ-shtshå-yå gå-rå	a volcano.
темнотá, мракъ	tyĕm-nŏ-tå, mråkk	darkness.
тѣнь	tyåne	shadow, shade.

TIME.

Столѣтіе, вѣкъ	stŏ-lyá-tè-yĕ, vyĕk	a century, an age.
годъ	gŏt	year.
пóлгода	pŏll-gŏ-då	half a year.
високóсный годъ	vè-sŏ-kŏss-nŭĭ gŏt	leap-year.
мѣсяцъ	má-syåts	month.
недѣля	nå-dyá-lyå	week.
день	dyåne	day.
часъ	tshåss	hour.
полчасá	pŏll-tshå-så	half an hour.
чéтверть часá	tshå-tvĕrt tshå-så	a quarter of an hour.
минýта	mè-nŏ-tå	a minute.
заря́	zå-ryå	dawn.
сýмерки	sŏ-mĕrr-kè	twilight.
восхождéніе сóлнца	vŏss-khŏzh-dyá-nè-yĕ sŏn-tså	sunrise.
захóдъ сóлнца	zå-khŏt sŏn-tså	sunset.
ýтро	ŏ-trŏ	morning.
пóлдень	pŏll-dyåne	noon.
вéчеръ	vá-tshĕrr	evening.
ночь	nŏtsh	night.
пóлночь	pŏll-nŏtsh	midnight.
сегóдня	syá-vŏd-nyå	to-day.
вчера́	ftshå-rå	yesterday
канýнъ	kå-nŭn	the eve.

третьяго дня	trate-yå-vô dnyå	the day before yesterday.
завтра	zåf-trå	to-morrow.
послѣ завтра	pôss-lyå zåf-trå	the day after to-morrow.
завтра вечеромъ	zåf-trå vå-tshå-rôm	to-morrow evening.
времена года	vrå-mê-nå gô-då	the seasons.
весна	vyêss-nå	spring.
лѣто	lyê-tô	summer.
осень	ô-syên	autumn.
зима	zè-må	winter.
январь	yån-vårr	January.
февраль	fêv-rål	February.
мартъ	mårrt	March.
апрѣль	å-pråle	April.
май	måî	May.
іюнь	è-ûne	June.
іюль	è-ûle	July.
августъ	åv-gûst	August.
сентябрь	sên-tyåbr	September.
октябрь	ôk-tyåbr	October.
ноябрь	nô-yåbr	November.
декабрь	dyê-kåbr	December.
воскресенье	vôss-krå-såne-yê	Sunday.
понедѣльникъ	pô-nyê-dyêl-nîk	Monday.
вторникъ	ftôrr-nîk	Tuesday.
среда	srê-då	Wednesday.
четвергъ	tshêt-vêrrk	Thursday.
пятница	pyåt-nè-tså	Friday.
суббота	sûb-bô-tå	Saturday.

ANIMALS.

Дúкіе звѣ́ри	dyē-kē-yē zvā-rē	wild beasts.
слонъ	slōn	elephant.
левъ	lyēff	lion.
тигръ	tyēgre	tiger.
леопáрдъ	lyā-ō-pārrd	leopard.
медвѣ́дь	med-vāte (the *t* is very soft)	bear.
волкъ	vōllk	wolf.
лисúца	lē-sē-tsā	fox.
олéнь	ā-lyāne	deer.
сѣ́верный олéнь	syā-vērr-nūī ā-lyāne	rein-deer.
козýля	kā-zō-lyā	roe.
зáяцъ	zā-yāts	hare.
кры́са	krūī-sā	rat.
мышь	mūīsh	mouse.
обезья́на	ā-bēz-yā-nā	monkey.
домáшнія живóтныя	dō-māsh-nē-yā zhē-vōt-nūī-yā	domestic animals.
скотъ	skōtt	cattle.
стáдо	stā-dō	herd, flock.
верблю́дъ	vērr-blūt	camel.
лóшадь	llō-shāt	horse.
кобы́ла	kā-būī-llā	mare.
осéлъ	ā-syōll	ass.
бы́къ	būīk	bull.
корóва	kā-rō-vā	cow.
телёнокъ	tyā-lyō-nōk	calf.
барáнъ	bā-rān	ram.
овцá	ōff-tsā	a ewe, a sheep.
ягнёнокъ	yā-gnyō-nōk	lamb.
козёлъ	kā-zyōll	he-goat.

коза́	ka-za	she-goat.
котъ	kott	he-cat.
ко́шка	kosh-ka	she-cat.
соба́ка	sa-ba-ka	dog.
су́ка	so-ka	bitch.
свинья́	svene-ya	a swine.
поросёнокъ	pa-ra-syo-nok	pig.
саме́цъ	sa-myets	a male.
са́мка	sam-ka	a female.
ко́гти	kokh-tye	the claws, the clutches.
ла́па	lla-pa	paw.
лай	llai	the barking.
ревъ	ryeff	roar, bray.
земново́дныя животныя	zyem-no-vod-nui-ya zhe-vot-nui-ya	amphibious animals.
крокоди́лъ	kro-ko-dyill	crocodile.
змѣй, змѣя́	zmai, zma-ya	serpent.
черепа́ха	tsha-ra-pa-kha	tortoise.
ляѓушка	lya-gush-ka	frog.
бобръ	bobr	beaver.
хи́щныя пти́цы	khishtsh-nui-ya pyte-tsui	birds of prey.
оре́лъ	a-ryoll	eagle.
соко́лъ	sa-koll	falcon.
сова́	so-va	owl.
я́стребъ	yass-trep	kite.
ко́ршунъ	korr-shun	vulture.
ди́кія пти́цы	dye-ke-ya ptye-tsui	wild birds.
воро́на	va-ro-na	a crow.
соро́ка	sa-ro-ka	magpie.
ле́бедь	lya-bet	swan.
фаза́нъ	fa-zan	pheasant.
попуга́й	po-po-gai	parrot.
воробе́й	va-ra-byai	sparrow.
ла́сточка	llass-totsh-ka	a swallow.

жа́воронокъ	zhå-vô-rô-nôk	lark.
куку́шка	kô-kûsh-kå	cuckoo.
соловéй	sô-llô-våî	nightingale.
канарéйка	kê-nå-råî-kå	canary-bird.
дома́шнія пти́цы	dô-måsh-nê-yå ptyê-tsûî	domestic birds.
пѣту́хъ	på-tûkh	cock.
ку́рица	kô-rê-tså	hen.
цыплёнокъ	tsûî-plyô-nôk	chicken.
гусь	gôse	goose.
у́тка	ût-kå	duck.
го́лубь	gô-llûb	pigeon.
павли́нъ	påv-lyîn	pea-cock.
ста́я пти́цъ	stå-yå ptyêts	flight, covey.
птенцы́	ptyên-tsûî	brood.
яйцо́	yåî-tsô	egg.
носъ, клювъ	nôss, klûfe	bill, beak.
кры́лья	krûîl-yå	wings.
пе́рья	påre-yå	feathers.
хвостъ	khvôst	tail.
ла́пы	llå-pûî	feet.
ко́гти	kôkh-tyê	talons, claws.
гнѣздо́	gnyêz-dô	nest.
клѣ́тка	klyêt-kå	cage:
пѣ́ніе	på-nê-yê	the singing.
насѣко́мыя	nå-syå-kô-mûî-yå	insects.
пау́къ	på-ûk	spider.
муравéй	mô-rå-våî	ant.
моль	môl	moth.
вошь	vôsh	louse.
блоха́	bllô-khå	flea.
клопъ	klôp	bug.
пчела́	ptshê-llå	bee.
му́ха	mô-khå	fly.
кома́ръ	kå-mårr	gnat.

ба́бочка	ba-botsh-ka	butterfly.
жа́ло	zha-llo	sting.
жужжа́ніе	zhuzh-zha-ne-ye	the buzzing.
у́лей	o-lyai	bee-hive.
воскъ	vosk	wax.
медъ	myot	honey.

METALS.

зо́лото	zo-llo-to	gold.
серебро́	sya-ra-bro	silver.
желѣ́зо	zha-lya-zo	iron.
свине́цъ	sve-nyets	lead.
жесть	zhest	tin.
сталь	stal	steel.
же́лтая мѣдь	zholl-ta-ya mate	brass.
кра́сная мѣдь	krass-na-ya mate	copper.
о́лово	o-llo-vo	pewter.
ртуть	rtut	quicksilver.

ADJECTIVES.

Прекра́сный	pra-krass-nui	fine, beautiful.
те́плый	tyo-plui	warm.
жа́ркій	zharr-koi	hot.
холо́дный	kha-llod-nui	cold.
ти́хій	tye-khoi	mild.
бу́рный	burr-nui	stormy.

ясный	yass-nui	clear.
тёмный	tyom-nui	dark.
сухой	so-khoi	dry.
сырой	sui-roi	wet.
туманный	to-man-nui	foggy.
облачный	ob-llatsh-nui	cloudy.
дождливый	dazhd-lye-vui	rainy.
болотистый	ba-llo-tyiss-tui	marshy.
гористый	ga-riss-tui	mountainous.
плодоносный	pllo-do-noss-nui	fertile.
безплодный	bes-pllod-nui	sterile, barren.
здоровый	zda-ro-vui	wholesome.
нездоровый	nya-zda-ro-vui	unwholesome.

молодой	ma-lla-doi	young.
старый	sta-rui	old.
сильный	sil-nui	strong.
слабый	slla-bui	weak.
высокій	vui-so-koi	tall.
маленькій	ma-len-koi	little.
жирный	zhirr-nui	fat.
толстый	toll-stui	stout.
худощавый	kho-do-shtsha-vui	lean.
красивый	kra-sye-vui	handsome, fine.
хорошій собой	kha-ro-she sa-boi	pretty, beautiful.
дурной собой	durr-noi sa-boi	ugly.

здоро́вый	zda-ro-vui	healthy, well, strong.
нездоро́вый	nya-zda-ro-vui	indisposed, unwell.
больно́й	bal-noi	ill.
блѣ́дный	blyed-nui	pale.
горба́тый	garr-ba-tui	hunch-backed.
хромо́й	khra-moi	lame, limping.
слѣпо́й	slya-poi	blind.
криво́й	kre-voi	blind of one eye.
глухо́й	gllo-khoi	deaf.
нѣмо́й	nya-moi	dumb.

остроу́мный	oss-tro-um-nui	sharp-witted, ingenious.
у́мный, смышлё-ный	um-nui, smuish-lyo-nui	intelligent.
глу́пый	gllo-pui	stupid, foolish.
безу́мный	bez-um-nui	idiotic, silly, senseless.
сумасше́дшій	so-mas-shet-she	mad.
бѣ́шеный	bya-she-nui	furious.
серди́тый	syerr-dye-tui	angry.
дово́льный	da-vol-nui	satisfied.
недово́льный	nya-da-vol-nui	dissatisfied.
печа́льный	pa-tshal-nui	sad.
весёлый	va-syo-lui	merry, gay.
ра́достный	ra-dost-nui	joyful.

спокóйный	spa-koi-nui	quiet.
безпокóйный	bes-pa-koi-nui	troublesome.
неспокóйный	nya-spa-koi-nui	uneasy.
забóтливый	za-bot-le-vui	anxious, solicitous.
подозри́тельный	po-do-zre-tyel-nui	suspicious.
трýдный	trud-nui	difficult.
лéгкій	lyokh-koi	easy.
успѣ́шный	o-spyesh-nui	successful.
неудáчный	nya-o-datsh-nui	unsuccessful.
занимáтельный	za-ne-ma-tyel-nui	curious, interesting.
забáвный	za-bav-nui	amusing.
скýчный	skutsh-nui	wearisome, tedious.
склóнный	sklon-nui	bent, inclined.
смѣ́лый	smya-llui	bold.
дéрзкій	dyerr-skoi	impertinent.
вáжный	vazh-nui	important.
маловáжный	ma-llo-vazh-nui	unimportant.

благочести́вый	blla-go-tshes-tre-vui	pious.
безбóжный	bez-bozh-nui	impious.
добродѣ́тельный	do-bro-dya-tyel-nui	virtuous.
порóчный	pa-rotsh-nui	vicious.
дóбрый	do-brui	kind.
злой	zloi	wicked.
любéзный	lu-bez-nui	amiable.

гру́бый	gro-bui	rude.
учти́вый	utsh-tye-vui	civil, polite.
неучти́вый	nya-utsh-tye-vui	impolite.
че́стный	tshest-nui	honest.
безче́стный	bes-tshest-nui	dishonest.
открове́нный	ot-kra-vyen-nui	frank, sincere, open.
скры́тный	skruit-nui	reserved.
приле́жный	pre-lyezh-nui	diligent.
лѣни́вый	lya-nye-vui	lazy.
бережли́вый	ba-rezh-lye-vui	frugal, saving.
расточи́тельный	ras-to-tshe-tel-nui	extravagant.
благоразу́мный	blla-go-ra-zum-nui	prudent.
необду́манный	nya-ob-do-man-nui	imprudent.
хра́брый	khra-brui	brave, valiant.
трусли́вый	trus-lye-vui	cowardly.
живо́й	zhe-voi	lively.
ме́дленный	med-lyen-nui	slow.
благода́рный	blla-go-darr-nui	thankful, grateful.
неблагода́рный	nya-blla-go-darr-nui	ungrateful.
послу́шный	pa-slush-nui	obedient.
упря́мый	o-prya-mui	obstinate.
кро́ткій	krot-koi	mild, gentle.
жесто́кій	zhes-to-koi	cruel.
учёный	o-tsho-nui	learned.
невѣ́дущій	nya-va-dush-tshe	ignorant.
и́стинный	iss-tyin-nui	true.
ло́жный	llozh-nui	false.

смиренный	sme-ryen-nui	humble.
гордый	gorr-dui	proud.

молодой	ma-lla-doi	young.
новый	no-vui	new.
старый	sta-rui	old.
дѣятельный	dya-ya-tyel-nui	active.
занятый	za-nya-tui	occupied, busy.
праздный	prazd-nui	idle.
счастливый	stshast-lye-vui	fortunate, happy.
несчастный	nya-stshast-nui	unfortunate.
несчастливый	nya-stshat-lye-vui	unhappy.
богатый	ba-ga-tui	rich.
бѣдный	byed-nui	poor.
удобный	o-dob-nui	convenient.
неудобный	nya-o-dob-nui	inconvenient.

бѣлый	bya-llui	white.
черный	tshorr-nui	black.
красный	kras-nui	red.
зеленый	za-lyo-nui	green.
синій	sye-nye	deep blue.
голубой	go-llo-boi	sky-blue, azure.

же́лтый	zhôll-tüi	yellow.
сѣ́рый	syâ-rüi	gray.
ро́зовый	rô-sô-vüi	rose-coloured.
кори́чневый	kâ-rêsh-nyê-vüi	cinnamon-coloured.

прямо́й	pryâ-môi	straight.
криво́й	krè-vôi	curve, crooked.
квадра́тный	kvâ-drât-nüi	square.
кру́глый	krüg-lüi	round.
по́лный	pôll-nüi	full.
пусто́й	pûs-tôi	hollow, empty.
дли́нный	dlyîn-nüi	long.
коро́ткій	kâ-rôt-kôi	short.
большо́й	bâl-shôi	large, great.
ма́ленькій	mâ-lèn-kôi	small, little.
высо́кій	vüi-sô-kôi	high.
ни́зкій	nyîs-kôi	low.
то́лстый	tôll-stüi	thick.
то́нкій	tôn-kôi	thin.
широ́кій	shè-rô-kôi	broad, wide.
у́зкій	ûs-kôi	narrow.

NUMBERS.

Количество	kå-lyè-tshěst-vŏ	a quantity.
единица	yě-dyě-nè-tså	a unit.
цы́фра	tsŭif-rå	a figure.
нуль	nůl	a zero.
номеръ	nŏ-myěrr	a number.

одинъ, одна́	å-dyìn, åd-nå (fem.)	one.
два, двѣ	dvå, dvyå (fem.)	two.
три	trè	three.
четы́ре	tshě-tŭi-ryě	four.
пять	pyåt	five.
шесть	shěst	six.
семь	syěm	seven.
восемъ	vŏ-syěm	eight.
де́вять	dyå-vyåt	nine.
де́сять	dyå-syåt	ten.
одиннадцать	å-dyìn-nåt-såt	eleven.
двѣнадцать	dvyå-nåt-såt	twelve.
тринадцать	trè-nåt-såt	thirteen.
четы́рнадцать	tshě-tŭirr-nåt-såt	fourteen.
пятнадцать	pyåt-nåt-såt	fifteen.
шестнадцать	shěst-nåt-såt	sixteen.
семнадцать	syěm-nåt-såt	seventeen.
восемнадцать	vŏ-syěm-nåt-såt	eighteen.
девятнадцать	dyå-våt-nåt-såt	nineteen.
два́дцать	dvåt-såt	twenty.
два́дцать одинъ	dvåt-såt å-dyìn	twenty one, etc.
и т. д.		

три́дцать	trit-sat	thirty.
со́рокъ	so-rok	forty.
пятьдеся́тъ	pyat-dya-syat	fifty.
шестьдеся́тъ	shest-dya-syat	sixty.
се́мдесять	syem-dye-syat	seventy.
во́семьдесять	vo-syem-dya-syat	eighty.
девяно́сто	dya-vya-nos-to	ninety.
сто	sto	a hundred.
сто оди́нъ и т. д.	sto a-dyin	one hundred and one, etc.
двѣ́сти	dvya-ste	two hundred.
три́ста	tre-sta	three hundred.
пятьсо́тъ	pyat-sot	five hundred.
шестьсо́тъ	shest-sot	six hundred.
ты́сяча	tui-sya-tsha	a thousand.
двѣ ты́сячи	dvya tui-sya-tshe	two thousand.
пять ты́сячъ	pyat tui-syatsh	five thousand.
миллio̕нъ	mil-le-on	a million.

пе́рвый	pyerr-vui	the first.
второ́й	fta-roi	the second.
тре́тій	tra-tye	the third.
четве́ртый	tshet-vyorr-tui	the fourth.
пя́тый	pya-tui	the fifth.
шесто́й	shes-toi	the sixth.
седьмо́й	syed-moi	the seventh.
восьмо́й	vas-moi	the eighth.
девя́тый	dye-vya-tui	the ninth.

десятый	dye-sya-tui	the tenth.
одиннадцатый	a-dyin-nat-sa-tui	the eleventh.
двѣнадцатый	dvye-nat-sa-tui	the twelfth.
двадцатый	dvat-tsa-tui	the twentieth.
двадцать первый	dvat-tsat pyerr-vui	the twenty first.
тридцатый	trit-tsa-tui	the thirtieth.
сороковой	so-ro-ko-voi	the fortieth.
пятидесятый	pa-tye-dye-sya-tui	the fiftieth.
шестидесятый	shes-tye-dye-sya-tui	the sixtieth.
семидесятый	se-me-dye-sya-tui	the seventieth.
осьмидесятый	os-me-dye-sya-tui	the eightieth.
девяностый	dye-vya-nos-tui	the ninetieth.
сотый	so-tui	the hundredth.
двухъ-сотый	dvukh-so-tui	the two hundredth.
трехъ-сотый	tryokh-so-tui	the three hundredth.
четырехъ-сотый	tshe-tui-ryokh-so-tui	the four hundredth.
пятисотый	pa-tye-so-tui	the five hundredth.
шестисотый	shes-tye-so-tui	the six hundredth.
тысячный	tui-syatsh-nui	the thousandth.
двухъ-тысячный	dvukh-tui-syatsh-nui	the two thousandth.
пяти-тысячный	pa-tye-tui-syatsh-nui	the five thousandth.
милліонный	mil-le-on-nui	the millionth.

óба	o-ba	both.
двóе	dvo-ye	two together.
трóе	tro-ye	three together.
пáра	pa-ra	a pair, a couple, a brace.
трóйка	troi-ka	three pieces.
пятóкъ	pya-tok	five pieces.
полъ-дю́жины	poll-du-zhe-nui	half a dozen.
дю́жина	du-zhe-na	a dozen.
деся́токъ	dye-sya-tok	ten pieces.
два деся́тка	dva dye-syat-ka	a score.
сóтня	sot-nya	a hundred.
сóтни	sot-nye	hundreds.
ты́сячи	tui-sya-tshe	thousands.

полторá	poll-to-ra	one and a half.
половúна	po-lla-ve-na	the half.
треть	trate	the third ($^1/_3$).
чéтверть	tshate-vert	the fourth, the quarter.
пя́тая часть	pya-ta-ya tshast	a fifth.
двѣ трéти	dva tra-tye	two thirds.
три чéтверти	tre tshate-verr-tye	three fourths, three quarters.
четы́ре пя́тыхъ	tshe-tui-rye pya-tuikh	four fifths.

двойнóй	dvai-noi	double.
тройнóй	trai-noi	treble.

четверной	tshet-verr-noi	fourfold.
стокра́тный	sto-krat-nui'	hundredfold.

оди́нъ разъ	a-dyin ras	once.
два ра́за	dva ra-za	twice.
три ра́за	tre ra-za	thrice, three times.
четы́ре ра́за	tshe-tui-rye ra-za	four times.

PRONOUNS.

я	ya	I.
ты	tui	thou.
онъ	on	he.
она́	a-na	she.
оно́	a-no	it.
мы	mui	we.
вы	vui	you.
они́ (masc. a. neuter)	a-nye	they.
онѣ́ (fem.)	a-nye	they.
себя́	sye-bya	myself, thyself, himself, herself, itself, one's self, ourselves, yourselves, themselves; (refers to the subject of the sentence).
мой	moi	my, mine.

твой	tvŏĭ	thy, thine.
его́	yĕ-vŏ	his, its.
ея́	yĕ-yŏ	her, hers.
нашъ	nåsh	our, ours.
вашъ	våsh	your, yours.
ихъ	yĭkh	their, theirs.
свой	svŏĭ	my, thy, his, her, its, our, your, their, own; (refers to the subject of the sentence).
э́тотъ, (сей)	å-tŏt (syåĭ)	this.
тотъ (о́ный)	tŏt (ŏ-nŭĭ)	that.
тако́й	tå-kŏĭ	such.
таково́й	tå-kŏ-vŏĭ	such a one.
кто	khtŏ	who.
что	shtŏ	what.
кото́рый	kå-tŏ-rŭĭ	who, which.
како́й	kå-kŏĭ	what.
каково́й	kå-kŏ-vŏĭ	what kind of.
чей	tshåĭ	whose.
самъ	såm	self (myself, thyself, himself etc.)
весь	vĕs	all.
оди́нъ	å-dyĭn	alone, by himself.
са́мый	så-mŭĭ	same.
ка́ждый	kåzh-dŭĭ	each.
кто́-то (не́кто, ко́е-кто)	khtŏ-tŏ (nyå-ktŏ, kŏ-yĕ-khtŏ)	somebody, some one.
что́-то (не́что, ко́е-что)	shtŏ-tŏ (nyå-shtŏ, kŏ-yĕ-shtŏ)	something.
никто́	nyĕ-khtŏ	nobody, no one.
ничто́, ничего́	nyĕ-shtŏ, nyĕ-tshĕ-vŏ	nothing.

кто́-нибудь (кто́-либо)	khtŏ-nyè-bŭt (ktŏ-lè-bŏ)	anybody, any one.
что́-нибудь (что́-либо)	shtŏ-nyè-bŭt (shtŏ-lè-bŏ)	anything.
како́й-то	kă-kŏĭ-tŏ	a certain.
како́й-нибудь	kă-kŏĭ-nyè-bŭt	any.
ниче́й	nyè-tshăĭ	nobody's, no one's.
нѣкоторый	nyă-kŏ-tŏ-rŭĭ	a certain, some.
всякій	fsyă-kŏĭ	everybody, every.
иной	è-nŏĭ	many a, other, another.
другъ-дру́га	drŭk-drŏ-gă	each-other, one another.
другой	drŏ-gŏĭ	other, another.

VERBS.

Сотворя́ть	sŏ-tvŏ-ryăt	to create.
течь	tyătsh	to flow.
полива́ть	pŏ-lè-văt	to water.
мочи́ть	mă-tshète	to wet, to moisten.
купа́ть, купа́ться (v. n.)	kŏ-păt, kŏ-păt-syă	to bathe.
мéрзнуть	myŏrrz-nŭt	to freeze.
та́ять	tă-yăt	to thaw.
дождь идéтъ	dŏsh è-dyŏt	it rains.
снѣгъ идéтъ	snyĕk è-dyŏt	it snows.
градъ идéтъ	grăt è-dyŏt	it hails.
громъ греми́тъ	grŏm gră-mĭt	it thunders.
мо́лнія блиста́етъ	mŏll-nè-yă blĭs-tă-yĕt	it lightens.
блиста́ть	blĭs-tăt	to shine, to flash.

сверкáть	svyérr-kåt	to sparkle.
освѣщáть	å-svyå-shtshåt	to light up, to illumine.
горѣть	gå-råte	to burn.
нагрѣвáть	nå-grå-våt	to warm, to heat.
дымúться	dûî-mît-syå	to smoke, to fume.
дуть	dût	to blow.

раждáться	råzh-dåt-syå	to be born.
умирáть	å-mè-råt	to die.
жить	zhète	to live.
ѣсть	yåste	to eat.
пить	pète	to drink.
я гóлоденъ	yå gå-llå-dyèn	I am hungry.
мнѣ хóчется пить	mnyå khå-tshèt-syå pète	I am thirsty.
глотáть	gllå-tåt	to swallow.
кáшлять	kå-shlyåt	to cough.
чихáть	tshè-khåt	to sneeze.
плевáть	plyè-våt	to spit.
сморкáться	smårr-kåt-syå	to blow one's nose
кричáть	krè-tshåt	to cry.
смѣяться	små-yåt-syå	to laugh.
улыбáться	å-lûî-båt-syå	to smile.
дышáть	dûî-shåt	to breathe.
вúдѣть	vè-dyåte	to see.
слы́шать	slûî-shåt	to hear.
ходúть	khå-dyète	to go, to walk.
приходúть	prè-khå-dyète	to come.
выходúть	vûî-khå-dyète	to go out.
пáдать	på-dåt	to fall.

вставáть	fstå-våt	to rise, to get up.
одѣвáться	å-dyå-våt-syå	to dress one's self.
умывáться	ŏ-mŭĭ-våt-syå	to wash one's self.
застéгиваться	zå-styŏ-ghĕ-våt-syå	to button one's self up.
причéсываться	prĕ-tshŏ-sŭĭ-våt-syå	to comb one's self.
ложи́ться спать	llŏ-zhĭt-syå spåt	to go to bed.
раздѣвáться	råz-dyĕ-våt-syå	to undress.
спать	spåt	to sleep.
ви́дѣть во снѣ, сни́ться	vĕ-dyåte vŏ snyå, snyĭt-syå	to dream.
храпѣ́ть	khrå-påte	to snore.
просыпáться	prŏ-sŭĭ-påt-syå	to awake.
разбуждáть	råz-bŭzh-dåt	to wake.
потѣ́ть	på-tyåte	to sweat.
вздыхáть	vzdŭĭ-khåt	to sigh.
стонáть	stŏ-nåt	to groan.
дѣ́йствовать	dyåĭst-vŏ-våt	to act.
рабóтать	rå-bŏ-tåt	to work.
уставáть	ŏ-stå-våt	to grow tired.
отдыхáть	ŏt-dŭĭ-khåt	to rest.
говори́ть	gå-vå-rĕte	to speak, to tell.
скáзывать	skå-zŭĭ-våt	to say, to tell.
болтáть	bŏll-tåt	to prate.
чу́вствовать	tshŭfst-vŏ-våt	to feel.

люби́ть	lŭ-bĕte	to love, to like.
ненави́дѣть	nyĕ-nå-vĕ-dyåte	to hate.
нрáвиться	nrå-vĭt-syå	to please.
не нрáвиться	nyå nrå-vit-syå	to displease.

уважáть	o-va-zhat	to esteem.
презирáть	pre-ze-rat	to despise.
вѣ́рить	va-rete	to believe.
сомнѣвáться	so-mnya-vat-sya	to doubt.
подозрѣвáть	po-do-zrye-vat	to suspect.
пóмнить	pom-nete	to remember.
забывáть	za-bui-vat	to forget.
надѣ́яться	na-dya-yat-sya	to hope.
опасáться	o-pa-sat-sya	to apprehend.
боя́ться	ba-yat-sya	to fear.
пугáть	po-gat	to frighten.
рáдоваться	ra-do-vat-sya	to rejoice.
сожалѣ́ть	so-zha-lyate	to regret, to be sorry.
спѣши́ть	spa-shete	to hasten.
торопи́ться	to-ro-pit-sya	to make haste, to be in a hurry.
мéдлить	made-lete	to delay, to tarry.
выбирáть	vui-be-rat	to choose.
примѣчáть	pre-mya-tshat	to perceive.
замѣчáть	za-mya-tshat	to remark.
понимáть	po-nye-mat	to understand.
знать	znat	to know.
учи́ться	o-tshit-sya	to learn.
дýмать	do-mat	to think.
размышля́ть	raz-mui-shlyat	to reflect, to meditate.
ошибáться	a-she-bat-sya	to make a mistake, to err.
угáдывать	o-ga-dui-vat	to guess.
предви́дѣть	pred-ve-dyate	to foresee.

удивля́ть	ŏ-dĭv-lyăt	to astonish, to surprise.
удивля́ться	ŏ-dĭv-lyăt-syă	to be astonished, to be surprised.
склоня́ться	skllŏ-nyăt-syă	to incline.
хоте́ть	khă-tyăte	to will, to want.
жела́ть	zhă-lăt	to wish, to desire.
ожида́ть	ă-zhĕ-dăt	to expect.
забо́титься	ză-bŏ-tĭt-syă	to trouble one's self, to be concerned.
красне́ть	krăs-nyăte	to blush.
стыди́ться	stăĭ-dĭt-syă	to be ashamed.
тоскова́ть	tŏs-kŏ-văt	to grieve.
серди́ться	syĕrr-dyĭt-syă	to be angry.
жа́ловаться	zhă-llŏ-văt-syă	to complain.
повинова́ться	pŏ-vĕ-nŏ-văt-syă	to obey.
ослу́шиваться	ă-slŏ-shĕ-văt-syă	to disobey.
притворя́ться	prĕ-tvŏ-ryăt-syă	to feign.
лгать	llgăt	to lie.
клевета́ть	klă-vă-tăt	to slander.
обма́нывать	ŏb-mă-nŭĭ-văt	to deceive.
подкупа́ть	pŏt-kŏ-păt	to bribe, to corrupt.
соверша́ть преступле́ніе	sŏ-vyĕrr-shăt pră-stŏ-plă-nĕ-yĕ	to commit a crime.
ворова́ть, красть	vŏ-rŏ-văt, krăst	to steal.
убива́ть	ŏ-bĕ-văt	to kill, to murder.

стря́пать	strya-pat	to cook.
вари́ть	va-rete	to boil, to concoct, to brew.
кипяти́ть	ke-pya-tete	to boil.
кипѣ́ть	ke-pate	to seethe.
жа́рить	zha-rete	to roast.
жа́рить на ра́шпрѣ	zha-rete na rash-prya	to broil.
жа́рить на сковородѣ́	zha-rete na skó-vó-ró-dya	to fry.
жа́рить пе́редъ огне́мъ	zha-rete pa-rad ag-nyóm	to toast.
печь	patsh	to bake.
соли́ть	sa-lete	to salt.
обтира́ть	óp-te-rat	to wipe.
чи́стить	tshis-tyete	to clean.
про́бовать	pro-bó-vat	to taste.
накрыва́ть на столъ	na-krui-vat na stoll	to lay the cloth.
сади́ться за столъ	sa-dyit-sya za stoll	to sit down at table.
за́втракать	zaf-tra-kat	to breakfast, to lunch.
подава́ть обѣ́дать	pó-da-vat a-brya-dat	to serve up the dinner.
обѣ́дать	a-brya-dat	to dine.
у́жинать	o-zhe-nat	to sup.
пить за чье́ здоро́вье	pete za tshyo zda-rov-ye	to drink any one's health.
ко́фе пить, ко́фе ку́шать	ko-fya pete, ko-fya ko-shat	to drink or take coffee.
чай пить, чай ку́шать	tshai pete, tshai ko-shat	to drink or take tea.
налива́ть	na-le-vat	to pour out.

покупа́ть	po̊-ko̊-påt	to buy, to purchase.
продава́ть	pro̊-då-våt	to sell.
продава́ть по мелоча́мъ	pro̊-då-våt po̊ mye̊-llo̊-tshåm	to sell by retail.
продава́ть о́птомъ	pro̊-då-våt óp-tóm	to sell by wholesale.
торгова́ть	tórr-go̊-våt	to trade.
торгова́ться	tórr-go̊-våt-syå	to cheapen, to bargain.
поста́вить на счётъ	po̊-stå-vit nå shtshót	to carry to account.
поко́нчить счетъ	på-kón-tshe̊te, shtshót	to settle an account.
плати́ть	pllå-tye̊te	to pay.
уплати́ть по счёту	ů-pllå-tye̊te po̊ shtsho̊-to̊	to close an account.
вы́дать квита́нцію	vůi-dåt kve̊-tån-tse̊-ů	to give a receipt.
занима́ть	zå-ne̊-måt	to borrow.
быть до́лженъ	bůit dóll-zhe̊n	to owe, to be in debt.
дава́ть въ долгъ	då-våt v dóllk	to lend.
дѣлать креди́тъ	dye̊-låt krye̊-dyit	to give credit.
вступа́ть въ компа́нію	fsto̊-påt f kåm-på-ne̊-ů	to enter into partnership.
страхова́ть	strå-kho̊-våt	to insure.
обанкру́титься	o̊-bån-kro̊-tit-syå	to fail.

заключа́ть контра́ктъ	zå-klů-tshåt kón-tråkt	to make a deed.
завѣща́ть	zå-vyå-shtshåt	to bequeath,

дѣлать духóвное завѣщáніе	dyá-lât dô-khôv-nô-yè zâ-vyâ-shtshâ-nè-yè	to make a will.
имѣть тяжбу	è-myâte tyâzh-bô	to plead, to sue a law.
свидѣтельствовать	svè-dyâ-tyèlst-vô-vât	to bear wittness, to give evidence.
издáть указъ	îz-dât ô-kâs	to decree.
запретить	zâ-prâ-tyète	to prohibit.
арестовáть	â-rès-tô-vât	to arrest.
взять на поруки	vzyât nâ pâ-rô-kè	to bail.
звать въ судъ	zvât f sût	to summon.
произнести приговóръ	prô-îz-nyès-tyè prè-gô-vôrr	to pass a sentence.
подвéргнуть штрáфу	pôd-verrg-nût shtrâ-fô	to fine.
осудить на заключéніе въ темницу	â-sô-dyète nâ zâ klû-tshâ-nè-yè f tyèm-nè-tsô	to condem to confinement.
осудить на ссы́лку	â-sô-dyète nâ ssûîll-kô	to condemn to banishment.

склáдывать	skllâ-dûî-vât	to spell.
читáть	tshè-tât	to read.
линевáть	lyè-nyè-vât	to rule.
чинить перó	tshè-nète pâ-rô	to mend a pen.
писáть	pè-sât	to write.
списывать	spè-sûî-vât	to copy.
поправлять	pô-prâv-lyât	to correct.
зачéркивать	zâ-tshôrr-kè-vât	to erase.
вы́скоблить	vûî-skâ-blète	to scratch out.
подписывать	pôt-pè-sûî-vât	to sign.
стáвить числó	stâ-vète tshîs-llô	to date.

запеча́тать	za-pa-tsha-tat	to seal.
учи́ть	o-tshete	to teach.
учи́ться	o-tshit-sya	to learn.
учи́ть наизу́сть	o-tshete na-e-zust	to learn by heart.
вычисля́ть	vui-tshis-lyat	to calculate.
счита́ть	shtshe-tat	to count.
скла́дывать	sklla-dui-vat	to add up, to sum.
вычита́ть	vui-tshe-tat	to substract.
умножа́ть	o-mno-zhat	to multiply.
дѣли́ть	dye-lete	to divide.
переводи́ть	pa-ra-va-dyete	to translate.
опи́сывать	a-pe-sui-vat	to describe.
разсужда́ть	ras-suzh-dat	to reason.
дока́зывать	do-ka-zui-vat	to prove.
рисова́ть	re-so-vat	to draw.
писа́ть кра́сками	pe-sat kras-ka-me	to paint.
печа́тать	pa-tsha-tat	to print.

предпринима́ть	pret-pre-ne-mat	to undertake.
вести́ кни́ги	ves-tye kne-ghe	to keep books.
переплета́ть	pa-ra-pla-tat	to bind.
брить	brete	to shave.
мыть	muit	to wash.
чи́стить	tshis-tete	to clean.
чини́ть	tshe-nete	to mend.
шить	shete	to sew.
обруба́ть	ob-ro-bat	to hem.
золоти́ть	zo-llo-tete	to guild.
точи́ть	ta-tshete	to sharpen.
стро́ить	stro-ete	to build.

гуля́ть	gô-lyât	to walk.
бѣ́гать	byâ-gât	to run.
пры́гать	prûî-gât	to leap.
танцова́ть	tân-tsô-vât	to dance.
ката́ться на конька́хъ	kâ-tât-syâ nâ kân-kâkh	to skate.
ѣ́хать верхо́мъ	yâ-khât vèrr-khôm	to ride (on horseback).
охо́титься	â-khô-tyît-syâ	to hunt.
фехтова́ть	fèkh-tô-vât	to fence.
пла́вать	pllâ-vât	to swim.
ныря́ть	nûî-ryât	to dive.
уди́ть ры́бу	ô-dyète rûî-bô	to angle.
лови́ть ры́бу сѣтя́ми	llâ-vète rûî-bô syâ-tyâ-mè	to fish with a net.
игра́ть въ мя́чикъ	è-grât v myâ-tshîk	to play at ball.
игра́ть въ ка́рты	è-grât f kârr-tûî	to play at cards.
игра́ть въ ша́хматы	è-grât f shâkh-mâtûî	to play at chess.
игра́ть въ ша́шки	è-grât f shash-kè	to play at draughts.

копа́ть	kâ-pât	to dig.
паха́ть	pâ-khât	to plough
сѣ́ять	sâ-yât	to sow.
полива́ть	pô-lè-vât	to water.
коси́ть	kâ-sète	to mow.
жать	zhât	to reap.
пасти́	pâs-tyè	to pasture.

нестй яйца	nye̊s-tyė yåĭ-tså	to lay eggs.
пóлзать	pȯll-zåt	to creep.
летáть	lye̊-tåt	to fly.
порхáть	pȯrr-khåt	to flatter.
бѣгать рысью	byå-gåt rŭĭs-ů	to trot.
скакáть	skå-kåt	to gallop.
прыгать	prŭĭ-gåt	to jump, to skip.
колóть	kå-llȯt	to sting.
царáпать	tså-rå-påt	to scratch,
кусáть	kő-såt	to bite.
жужжáть	zhůzh-zhåt	to buzz.
пѣть	påte	to sing.
посвистывать	på-svĭs-tŭĭ-våt	to warble.
пѣть пѣтухóмъ	påte på-tő-khȯm	to crow.
визжáть	vĭz-zhåt	to squeak.
пищáть	pė-shtshåt	to yelp.
квáкать	kvå-kåt	to croak.
хрюкать	khrů-kåt	to grunt.
мяукать	myå-ő-kåt	to mew.
лáять	llå-yåt	to bark.
выть	vŭĭt	to howl.
ржать	rzhåt	to neigh.
ревѣть	rå-våte	to roar, to bray.
блéять	blå-yåt	to bleat.
мычáть	mŭĭ-tshåt	to low.
пастйсь	pås-tėse	to graze.

простудиться	prå-stő-dyĭt-syå	to catch a cold.
кáшлять	kå-shlyåt	to cough.
рáнить	rå-nėte	to wound.

па́дать въ о́бморокъ	pá-dát v ób-mó-rók	to swoon.
отрави́ть	ót-rá-véte	to poison.
распу́хнуть	rás-púkh-nút	to swell.
щу́пать пульсъ	shtshó-pát púls	to feel the pulse.
пропи́сывать	prá-pé-súi-vát	to prescribe.
принима́ть лека́рство	pré-né-mát lyé-kárst-vó	to take physic.
пуска́ть кровь	pús-kát króf	to bleed (any one).
перевя́зывать	pá-rá-vyá-zúi-vát	to dress (a wound).

рости́	rás-tyé	to grow.
увели́чивать	ó-vé-lé-tshé-vát	to enlarge (any thing).
увели́чиваться	ó-vé-lé-tshé-vát-syá	to enlarge (grow larger).
умножа́ться	ó-mnó-zhát-syá	to increase (in number).
уменьша́ть	ó-myén-shát	to lessen, to make less.
уменьша́ться	ó-myén-shát-syá	to decrease (to grow less).
расширя́ть	rás-shé-ryát	to widen.
простира́ться	pró-sté-rát-syá	to extend.
укора́чивать	ó-ká-rá-tshé-vát	to shorten.
возвыша́ть	vóz-vúi-shát	to raise.
понижа́ть	pó-né-zhát	to lower.
наполня́ть	ná-póll-nyát	to fill.
опоро́жнить	ó-pó-rózh-néte	to empty.
сгуща́ться	sgó-shtshát-syá	to thicken, to grow thick.

ADVERBS.

Хорошó	khă-ră-shŏ	well.
хýдо	khŏ-dŏ	badly.
дóрого	dŏ-rŏ-gŏ	dearly.
дéшево	dyŏ-shĕ-vŏ	cheaply, cheap.
прія́тно	prĕ-yăt-nŏ	agreeably.
печáльно	pyă-tshăl-nŏ	sadly, mournfully.
вéсело	vă-syĕ-llŏ	cheerfully, gaily.
ти́хо, потихóньку	tyĕ-khŏ, pŏ-tyĕ-khŏn-kŏ	softly, slowly.
ти́ше	tyĕ-shĕ	more softly.
по малéньку	pŏ mă-lĕn-kŏ	by little and little, by degrees.
скóро	skŏ-rŏ	fast, quickly.
поскорѣ́е	pă-skă-ră-yĕ	a little faster.
умнó	ŭm-nŏ	wisely, sensibly.
бѣ́гло	byĕg-llŏ	fluently.
нарóчно	nă-rŏsh-nŏ	on purpose.
напрáсно	nă-prăs-nŏ	in vain, wrongfully.
на-угáдъ	nă-ŏ-găt	by guess, by chance.
какъ-нибýдь	kăk-nĕ-bŭt	somehow.
по-своему	pă-svŏ-yĕ-mŏ	in one's own way.
пѣшкóмъ	pyĕsh-kŏm	on foot.
верхóмъ	vĕrr-khŏm	on horseback.
шáгомъ	shă-gŏm	at a footpace.
по-рýсски	pă-rŭss-kĕ	in Russian.
по-англíйски	pă-ăn-glĕ-skĕ	in English.
дрýжески	drŏ-zhĕs-kĕ	in a friendly manner.

мно́го	mnŏ-gŏ	much.
ма́ло	må-llŏ	little.
нѣ́сколько	nyå-skŏl-kŏ	a little, somewhat.
однажды	ŏd-nåzh-dŭi	once.
вдвое	vdvŏ-yĕ	doubly.
втрое	ftrŏ-yĕ	in three, trebly.
впятеро	fpyå-tyĕ-rŏ	five times.
стокра́тъ	stŏ-kråt	a hundred times.
вдвоёмъ	vdvå-yŏm	two together.
втроёмъ	ftrå-yŏm	three together.
сперва́	spyĕrr-vå	at first.
снача́ла	snå-tshå-llå	from the beginning.
сно́ва	snŏ-vå	anew, again.
опя́ть	å-pyåt	again.
во-пе́рвыхъ	vå-pyĕrr-vŭikh	first, in the first place.
во-вторы́хъ	vå-ftå-rŭikh	secondly, in the second place.
весьма́, о́чень	vĕs-må, ŏ-tshĕn	very, greatly.
гора́здо	gå-råz-dŏ	much, far.
сли́шкомъ	slĭsh-kŏm	too, too much.
кра́йне	kråĭ-nyĕ	extremely.
едва́	yĕd-vå	hardly, scarcely.
наси́лу	nå-sĕ-llŏ	with difficulty, hardly.
чуть	tshŭt	very nearly, just.
почти́	påtsh-tyĕ	almost.
дово́льно	då-vŏl-nŏ	enough.
по́лно	pŏll-nŏ	it is enough; cease.
бу́детъ	bŏ-dyĕt	it will do.

здѣсь, тутъ	zdyåse, tŏte	here.
тамъ	tåm	there.
вездѣ́	vĕz-dyå	everywhere.
нигдѣ́	nĕ-gdyå	nowhere.
гдѣ-нибу́дь	gdyå-nĕ-bŭt	somewhere.
до́ма	dŏ-må	at home.
домо́й	då-mŏi	home, homewards.
туда́	tŏ-då	thither, there.
сюда́	sŭ-då	hither, here.
никуда́	nyĕ-kŏ-då	no-whither, nowhere.
отту́да	åt-tŏ-då	thence.
отсю́да	åt-sŭ-då	hence.
отвсю́ду	åt-fsŭ-dŏ	from all parts.
и́здали	ĭz-då-lyĕ	from afar.
снару́жи	snå-rŏ-zhĕ	outwardly, externally.
водо́ю	vå-dŏ-ŭ	by water.
мо́ремъ	mŏ-ryĕm	by sea.
сухи́мъ путёмъ	sŏ-khĭm pŏ-tyŏm	by land.
доро́гою	då-rŏ-gŏ-ŭ	on the road.

вчера́	ftshĕ-rå	yesterday.
сего́дня	syĕ-vŏd-nyå	to-day.
за́втра	zåf-trå	to-morrow.
у́тромъ	ŏ-trŏm	in the morning.
днемъ	dnyŏm	by day.
ве́черомъ	vå-tshĕ-rŏm	in the evening.
но́чью	nŏtsh-ŭ	by night, at night.
лѣ́томъ	lyå-tŏm	in summer.
зимо́ю	zĕ-mŏ-ŭ	in winter.
весно́ю	vyĕs-nŏ-ŭ	in spring.

óсенью	ŏ-sĕn-ŭ	in autumn.
давнó	dăv-nŏ	long ago.
прéжде	prăzh-dyĕ	before, formerly.
тепéрь	tyă-pare	at present.
ны́нѣ	nŭī-myĕ	now, at present, now-a-days.
сейчáсъ, тотчáсъ	syăī-tshăs, tŏt-tshăs	directly, immediately.
пóслѣ	pŏs-lyĕ	afterwards.
ужó	ŏ-zhŏ	hereafter, by-and-by.
впредь	fprăte	henceforth.
тогдá	tăgh-dă	then.
иногдá	ē-nŏgh-dă	sometimes, occasionally.
чáсто	tshăs-tŏ	often, frequently.
всегдá	fsyĕgh-dă	always.
рѣдко	ryĕt-kŏ	seldom.
никогдá	nyĕ-kŏkh-dă	never.
рáно	ră-nŏ	early.
пóздно	pŏzd-nŏ	late.
ужé	ŏ-zhĕ	already.
ещó	yĕ-shtshŏ	more, yet, still.
нѣтъ ещé	nyĕt yĕ-shtshŏ	not yet.
всё	fsyŏ	always.

когдá?	kăgh-dă	when?
скóлько?	skŏl-kŏ	how much, how many?
зачѣмъ?	ză-tshĕm	why?
почему́?	pŏ-tshĕ-mŏ	why?
для чегó?	dlyă tshĕ-yŏ	why?

почему́ нѣтъ?	pó-tshě-mŏ nyět	why not?
гдѣ?	gdyá	where?
куда́?	kŏ-dá	whither, where?
отку́да?	ót-kŏ-dá	whence?
неуже́ли?	nyá-ŏ-zhá-lé	is it possible? really?

и́стинно	iss-tyin-nŏ.	truly.
въ са́момъ дѣлѣ	f sá-móm dyá-lyĕ	indeed.
дѣйстви́тельно	dyáist-vé-tyěl-nŏ	really.
пра́во	prá-vŏ	in truth, faith.
такъ	ták	so, thus, then, yes.
коне́чно	ká-nyěsh-nŏ	certainly.
не	nyá	not.
нѣтъ	nyět	no, not.
ника́къ	nyé-kák	in no wise.
нима́ло, ниско́лько	nyé-má-llŏ, nyé-skŏl-kŏ	not in the least.
отню́дь	át-nute	by no means.
совсѣ́мъ не	sá-fsyěm nyá	not at all.
во́все не	vŏ-fsyě nyá	not at all.

по кра́йней мѣрѣ	pá krái-nyái má-ryě	at least.
аво́сь	á-vós	it is to be hoped, perhaps.
врядъ ли	vryát lyé	hardly, scarcely.
мо́жетъ быть	mŏ-zhět búit	perhaps.
то́лько	tŏl-kŏ	only, merely.
лишь бы	lyish búi	provided that.
лишь то́лько	lyish tŏl-kŏ	no sooner, as soon as.

едѝнственно	ye-dyinst-ven-no	solely.
наравнѣ́	na-rav-nya	on an equality, on a level.
такѝмъ о́бразомъ	ta-kyim o-bra-zom	thus, by this means.
сто́лько	stol-ko	so much, so many.
ина́че	e-na-tshe	otherwise.
напро́тивъ	na-pro-tyif	on the contrary.
на оборо́тъ	na a-ba-rot	reversedly, vice versa.
вмѣ́стѣ	vmya-stya	together.
вообще́	va-ap-shtshe	in general, generally.
заодно́	za-ad-no	at the same time, together, unitedly.
вмѣ́сто	vmyes-to	instead.
и́менно	e-myen-no	namely, expressly.
то-есть	to yaste	that is.
напримѣ́ръ	na-pre-myerr	for exemple, for instance.
внеза́пно	vnya-zap-no	suddenly, unexpectedly.
вдругъ	vdruk	all at once, suddenly.
мгнове́нно	mgno-ven-no	in the twinkling of an eye, in a moment.
неча́янно	nye-tsha-yan-no	unawares, unexpectedly.

PREPOSITIONS.

Безъ	byĕz	without.
для	dlyă	for.
до	dŏ	as far as, till, to.
изъ	ĭz	out of, from.
отъ	ŏt	from.
ра́ди	ră-dyĕ	for the sake of.
у	ŏ	at, near, by, with.
изъ-за	ĭz-ză	from behind, from beyond.
изъ-подъ	ĭs-pŏt	from under, from below.
близъ	blyĭs	near.
вдоль	vdŏl	along.
вмѣсто	vmyĕs-tŏ	instead of.
внутри́	vnŏ-trĕ	within.
внутрь	vnŏtr	inwards.
внѣ	vnyă	outside.
во́злѣ	vŏz-lyă	beside, by.
по́длѣ	pŏd-lyă	beside, near.
кро́мѣ	krŏ-myĕ	besides, except.
мі́мо	mĕ-mŏ	past, by.
о́коло	ŏ-kŏ-llŏ	round, about.
позади́	pŏ-ză-dyĕ	behind.
по́слѣ	pŏs-lyĕ	after.
посре́дствомъ	pă-sryĕtst-vŏm	by means of.
пре́жде	prăzh-dyĕ	before.
про́тивъ	prŏ-tyĭf	opposite, against.
насупроти́въ	nă-sŏ-prŏ-tyĭf	opposite, on the opposite side.
сверхъ	svyĕrrkh	besides, over and above.

среди́	sr$\overset{2}{e}$-dr$\overset{1}{e}$	amidst.
къ, ко	k (kh), k$\overset{8}{o}$	to, towards.
чрезъ	tshr$\overset{2}{e}$z	over, through, after.
сквозь	skv$\overset{4}{o}$s	through.
про	pr$\overset{3}{o}$	of, about.
надъ	n$\overset{2}{a}$d	above.
мéжду	my$\overset{2}{e}$zh-d$\overset{8}{o}$	between, among.
при	pr$\overset{1}{e}$	at, on, in the presence of, in the time of.
за	z$\overset{2}{a}$	behind, beyond, for.
подъ	p$\overset{4}{o}$d	under, beneath, below.
предъ, пéредъ	pr$\overset{2}{e}$d, pá-r$\overset{2}{e}$d	before.
въ, во	v, v$\overset{3}{o}$	in, at, into, to.
на	n$\overset{2}{a}$	on, upon.
о, объ	$\overset{3}{o}$, $\overset{4}{o}$b	about, concerning.
съ	s	from, about, with.
по	p$\overset{8}{o}$	about, on account of, until, after.

CONJUNCTIONS.

и	$\overset{1}{e}$	and.
да́же	d$\overset{2}{a}$-zh$\overset{2}{e}$	even.
притóмъ	pr$\overset{1}{e}$-t$\overset{4}{o}$m	at the same time.
сверхъ-тогó	svy$\overset{1}{e}$rrkh t$\overset{2}{a}$-v$\overset{8}{o}$	besides, moreover.
та́кже	t$\overset{2}{a}$g-zh$\overset{2}{e}$	likewise, also, too.
же	zh$\overset{2}{e}$	but, then.
и́ли	$\overset{5}{e}$-l$\overset{1}{e}$	or.

и́ли—и́ли, ли́бо—ли́бо	ĕ-lĕ—ĕ-lĕ, lyĕ-bŏ—lyĕ-bŏ	either—or.
что	tshtŏ	that.
бу́дто, бу́дто бы	bŭt-tŏ, bŭt-tŏ bŭĭ	as if.
тогда́ какъ	tăgh-dă kăk	whilst, whereas.
такъ какъ	tăk kăk	as.
ни—ни	nyĕ—nyĕ	neither—nor.
ча́стію, отча́сти	tshăs-tĕ-ŭ, ŏt-tshăs-tyĕ	partly, in part.
то—то	tŏ—tŏ	now—now.
какъ—такъ и	kăk—tăk ĕ	both—and.
не́жели	nyă-zhĕ-lĕ	than.
чѣмъ—тѣмъ	tshĕm—tyĕm	the—the.
такъ же—какъ	tăg zhĕ—kăk	as well as.
е́жели, е́сли	yĕ-zhĕ-lĕ, yăse-lĕ	if, in case.
что́бы, чтобъ, дабы́	tshtŏ-bŭĭ, tshtŏp, dă-bŭĭ	in order that.
то	tŏ	then.
хотя́	khă-tyă	though, although.
пусть, пуска́й	pŭst, pŭs-kăĭ	let, granting.
пожа́луй	pă-zhă-lŭĭ	if you will, I don't care.
и́бо	ĕ-bŏ	for.
для того́ что, потому́ что	dlyă tă-vŏ tshtŏ, pŏ-tă-mŏ tshtŏ	because.
но	nŏ	but.
одна́ко	ăd-nă-kŏ	however, yet.
впро́чемъ	fprŏ-tshĕm	as for the rest, otherwise.
а	ă	and, but.
ита́къ	ĕ-tăk	and so, then, thus.
посему́	pŏ-syĕ-mŏ	on this account.
слѣ́довательно	slyă-dŏ-vă-tyĕl-nŏ	consequently.

стáло быть	stå-llȍ bůĭt	then, it seems.
наконéцъ	nå-kå-nyĕts	at last, lastly, finally.

INTERJECTIONS.

óй-ли?	ȍĭ-lyė	oh?
брáво!	brå-vȍ	bravo!
урá!	ȍ-rå	hurrah! huzza!
ей-ей!	yåĭ—yåĭ	verily!
эй!	åĭ	hey!
а? ась? что?	å, ås, tshtȍ	eh? what? Sir? Madam?
тьфу! фуй!	tfȍ, fůĭ	fy!
ну! нý-те!	nȍ, nȍ-tyĕ	now! well! come!
на! нá-те!	nå, nå-tyĕ	there!
тсъ! цыцъ!	tss, tsůĭts	hist!
ахъ!	åkh	ah! oh!
увы́!	ȍ-vůĭ	alas! oh! woe!
вотъ!	vȍt	lo! see! there! here!
вонъ!	vȍn	away! hence!

PART II.

EXEMPLIFICATIONS OF THE USE OF VERBS IN CONNECTION WITH OTHER PARTS OF SPEECH.

У меня́ есть хлѣбъ.	(With me is bread.) I have some bread.
У тебя́ есть мя́со.	Thou hast some meat.
У него́ (у нея́) есть вино́.	He (she) has some wine.
У насъ есть пи́во.	We have some beer.
У нихъ есть плоды́.	You have some fruit.
У нихъ есть я́блоки.	They have some apples.
У меня́ была́ гру́ша.	I had a pear.
У тебя́ былъ пе́рсикъ.	Thou hadst a peach.
У него́ бы́ли ви́шни.	He had some cherries.
У насъ бы́ли сли́вы.	We had some plums.
У васъ былъ виногра́дъ.	You had some grapes.
У нихъ былъ минда́ль.	They had some almonds.
У меня́ бу́детъ апельси́нъ.	I shall have an orange.
У тебя́ бу́детъ лимо́нъ.	Thou wilt have a lemon.
У него́ бу́детъ абрико́съ.	He will have an apricot.
У насъ бу́дутъ ви́нныя я́годы.	We shall have some figs.
У васъ бу́дутъ орѣ́хи.	You will have some nuts.

У нихъ бу́дутъ кашта́ны.	They will have some chestnuts.
У меня́ была́ бы говя́дина.	I should have some beef.
У тебя́ была́ бы бара́нина.	Thou wouldst have some mutton.
У него́ была́ бы теля́тина.	He would have some veal.
У насъ была́ бы ветчина́.	We should have some ham.
У васъ бы́ло бы жарко́е.	You would have some roast.
У нихъ бы́ли бы куропа́тки.	They would have some partridges.
Есть ли у меня́ но́жикъ?	Have I a knife?
Бы́ло ли у тебя́ блю́до?	Hadst thou a dish?
Бу́детъ ли у него́ кни́га?	Will he have a book?
Бу́дутъ ли у насъ пе́рья?	Shall we have any pens?
Была́ ли бы у меня́ ко́мната?	Should I have a room?
Бы́ли ли бы у нихъ цвѣты́?	Would they have any flowers?
У меня́ нѣтъ чулко́въ.	I have no stockings.
У насъ нѣтъ башмако́въ.	We have no shoes.
У тебя́ не́ было полотна́.	Thou hadst no linen.
У васъ не́ было перча́токъ.	You had no gloves.
У него́ не бу́детъ посте́ли.	He will have no bed.
У нихъ не бу́детъ сукна́.	They will have no cloth.
У меня́ не́ было бы була́вки.	I should have no pin.
У насъ не́ было бы очко́въ.	We should have no spectacles.
Нѣтъ ли у тебя́ соба́ки?	Hast thou not a dog?
Не́ было ли у него́ ковра́?	Had he not a carpet?
Не бу́детъ ли у насъ дождя́?	Shall we have no rain?
Не́ было ли бы у васъ дру́га?	Would you not have a friend.

Я о́чень радъ (ра́да).	I am very glad.
Ты лѣни́въ (лѣни́ва).	Thou art lazy.
Онъ великоду́шенъ.	He is generous.
Она́ любопы́тна.	She is curious.
Оно́ хорошо́.	It is good.
Мы счастли́вы.	We are happy.
Вы несча́стны.	You are unhappy.
Они́, онѣ́ за́няты.	They are busy.
Я былъ утомлёнъ.	I was tired.
Ты былъ серди́тъ.	Thou wast angry.
Онъ былъ дово́ленъ.	He was satisfied.
Мы бы́ли бѣдны.	We were poor.
Вы бы́ли послу́шны.	You were obedient.
Они́ бы́ли приле́жны.	They were diligent.
Я бу́ду гото́въ.	I shall be ready.

Ты бу́дешь учёнъ.	Thou wilt be learned.
Онъ бу́детъ бо́ленъ.	He will be ill.
Мы бу́демъ ве́селы.	We shall be merry.
Вы бу́дете бога́ты.	You will be rich.
Они́ бу́дутъ сла́бы.	They will be weak.
Я былъ бы де́рзокъ.	I should be impertinent.
Ты былъ бы безразсу́денъ.	Thou wouldst be thoughtless.
Онъ былъ бы безполе́зенъ.	He would be useless.
Мы бы́ли бы стро́ги.	We should be strict.
Вы бы́ли бы вино́вны.	You would be guilty.
Они́ бы́ли бы злы.	They would be wicked.
Будь че́стенъ.	Be honest.
Пусть онъ бу́детъ учти́въ.	Let him be polite.
Бу́демъ справедли́вы.	Let us be just.
Бу́дьте умны́.	Be wise.
Да бу́дутъ они́ вѣ́рны.	Let them be faithful.
Спосо́бенъ ли я?	Am I able?
Былъ ли ты досто́инъ?	Wast thou worthy?
Бу́детъ ли она́ внима́тельна?	Will she be attentive?
Бы́ли ли бы они́ (онѣ́) знамени́ты?	Would they be celebrated?
Я не легковѣ́ренъ.	I am not credulous.
Ты не былъ гордъ.	Thou wast not proud.
Онъ не бу́детъ грубъ	He will not be rude.
Она́ не была́ бы свобо́дна.	She would not be free.
Не прекра́сно ли оно́?	Is it not beautiful?
Не́ были ли мы разсѣ́яны.	Were we not absent (in mind)?
Не бу́дете ли вы миролюби́вы.	Shall you not be peaceable?
Не́ были ли бы онѣ́ небре́жны.	Would they not be negligent?

Я отвѣча́ю на вашъ вопро́съ.	I answer your question.
Ты оставля́ешь свои́хъ друзе́й.	Thou abandonnest thy friends.
Онъ вѣ́ритъ всему́ что́ ему́ ни ска́жутъ.	He believes everything they tell him.
Она́ утѣша́етъ вдовъ и сиро́тъ.	She consoles widows and orphans.
Мы ло́жно су́димъ о на́шихъ совреме́нникахъ.	We judge erroneously of our contemporaries.
Вы до́лго обду́мываете.	You reflect a long time.
Они́ разска́зываютъ о́чень прія́тно.	They relate very pleasantly.
Я шелъ впереди́.	I walked in front.

Ты зажёгъ свѣчу́.	Thou littest the candle.
Онъ встрѣ́тилъ его́ недалёко отсю́да.	He met him not far from here.
Когда́ мы проходи́ли ми́мо.	As we passed by.
Вы сопровожда́ли проце́ссію.	You attended the procession.
Они́ гото́вили обѣ́дъ.	They prepared dinner.
Я отпра́влю письмо́ съ пе́рвою по́чтою.	I shall forward the letter by the next post.
Ты избѣ́гнешь большо́й опа́сности.	Thou wilt avoid a great danger.
Моё поведе́ніе меня́ оправда́етъ.	My conduct will justify me.
Мы лиши́мся э́того удово́льствія.	We shall be deprived of that pleasure.
Вы тогда́ раска́ятесь въ своей лѣ́ности.	You will then repent of your laziness.
Они́ постара́ются заслужи́ть ва́ше одобре́ніе.	They will endeavour to deserve your approbation.
Я бы хотѣ́лъ имѣ́ть хоро́шую ло́шадь.	I should like to have a good horse.
Ты бы почи́стилъ моё пла́тье.	Thou wouldst clean my dress.
Онъ бы посовѣ́товалъ вамъ быть внима́тельнымъ.	He would advise you to be attentive.
Мы бы спря́тали свои́ де́ньги..	We should conceal our money.
Вы бы перемѣни́ли кварти́ру.	You would change your lodging.
Они́ бы жела́ли чтобъ э́то бы́ло пра́вда.	They would wish this to be true.
Дай мнѣ кни́гу.	Give me a book.
Пусть онъ говори́тъ что хо́четъ.	Let him say what he likes.
Бу́демъ поступа́ть по дру́жески и безъ церемо́ніи.	Let us act like friends and without ceremony.
Ко́нчите свою́ рабо́ту.	Finish your work.
Пусть они́ и́щутъ моего́ слугу́.	Let them look for my servant.

PART III.

PHRASES FREQUENTLY USED IN CONVERSATION.

1. PHRASES EXPRESSING AFFIRMATION, NEGATION, AND DOUBT.

Это пра́вда.	That is true.
Я ду́маю такъ.	I think so.
Ва́ша пра́вда	You are right.
Я въ э́томъ увѣ́ренъ.	I am sure of it.
Увѣря́ю васъ, что э́то такъ.	I assure you it is so.
Могу́ васъ въ томъ увѣ́рить.	I can assure you of it.
Это вѣ́рно.	That is certain.
Я полага́ю такъ.	I suppose so.
Это соверше́нно справедли́во.	It is perfectly true.
Это фактъ.	It is a fact.
Я вѣ́рю э́тому.	I believe it.
Въ э́томъ я не сомнѣва́юсь.	I do not doubt it.
Вѣ́рю вамъ.	I believe you.
Че́стное сло́во.	Upon my word of honour.
Нѣтъ сомнѣ́нія.	There is no doubt.
Безспо́рно.	It is indisputable.

Вся́кій вамъ э́то ска́жетъ.	Any one will tell you so.
Бу́дьте увѣ́рены.	Be sure (of it).
Вы ошиба́етесь.	You are mistaken.
Это не пра́вда.	That is not true.
Я не вѣ́рю э́тому	I do not believe it.
Э́то невозмо́жно.	That is impossible.
Это не мо́жетъ быть.	It cannot be.
Это невѣроя́тно.	It is improbable.
Это о́чень сомни́тельно.	It is very doubtful.
Вы шу́тите.	You are joking.
Пра́вда ли э́то?	Is it true?
Возмо́жно ли э́то?	Is it possible?
Вы хоти́те меня́ провести́.	You want to deceive me.

2. PHRASES EXPRESSING COMMAND, EXHORTATION, OR ENTREATY.

Поди́те сюда́.	Come here.
Войди́те.	Step in.
Отвори́те дверь.	Open the door.
Закро́йте окно́.	Shut the window.
Подожди́те меня́.	Wait for me.
Подожди́те мину́ту.	Wait a moment.
Отдохни́те немно́го.	Rest yourself a little.
Ся́дьте.	Sit down.
Начина́йте.	Begin.
Продолжа́йте.	Go on.
Ко́нчимъ э́то.	Let us finish it.
Говори́те гро́мко.	Speak out loud.
Говори́те ти́хо.	Speak softly.
Говори́те основа́тельно (съ то́лкомъ).	Speak resonably.
Молчи́те.	Hold your tongue.
Послу́шайте меня́.	Listen to me.
Вста́немъ.	Let us get up.
Поговори́те съ нимъ.	Speak to him.
Скажи́те э́то ему́.	Tell him so.
Не вѣ́рьте ему́.	Do not believe him.
Не говори́те э́того.	Do not say so.

Не дѣлайте этого.	Do not do so.
Будьте спокойны.	Be at ease.
Не шевелитесь.	Do not stir.
Ступайте на верхъ.	Go up stairs.
Ступайте внизъ.	Go down stairs.
Будьте осторожны.	Take care.
Остановитесь!	Stop!
Остановитесь тамъ.	Stop there.
Посторонитесь.	Move on one side
Дайте мѣсто.	Make way.
Позвольте мнѣ пройти.	Let me pass.
Не безпокойтесь.	Do not trouble yourself.
Отвѣчайте на мой вопросъ.	Answer my question.
Дѣлайте то, что я вамъ говорю.	Do what I tell you.
Надѣйтесь на Бога.	Trust in God.

3. INTERROGATIVE PHRASES.

Кто это?	Who is that?
Кто они (онѣ)?	Who are they?
Вы его родственникъ?	Are you a relation of his?
Какъ васъ зовутъ?	What is your name?
Какъ васъ зовутъ по батюшкѣ?	What is your father's christian name?
Какъ ваши имя и отчество?	What is your christian name, and your father's.
Какъ ваша фамилія?	What is your family name?
Какое вы мѣсто занимаете?	What situation have you?
Какъ идутъ ваши дѣла?	How is your business going on?
Гдѣ вы живете?	Where do you live?
Гдѣ вы будете жить?	Where are you going to reside?
Куда вы идете?	Where are you going to?
Куда мы пойдемъ?	Where shall we go?
Откуда вы идете?	Where do you come from?
Что вы дѣлаете?	What are you doing?
Что вы говорите?	What do you say? } (Sir?
Что вы сказали?	What did you say? } Madam?)
Что вы хотите сказать?	What do you wish to say?
Что скажете вы объ этомъ?	What will you say to that?
Кто сказалъ это?	Who said so?

О чемъ былъ разгово́ръ?	What was the subject of the conversation?
Понима́ете ли вы?	Do you understand?
Вы меня́ не понима́ете?	You do not understand me?
Понима́ете ли вы то, что я говорю́?	Do you understand what I say?
Почему́ вы мнѣ не отвѣча́ете?	Why do you not answer me?
О чемъ вы ду́маете?	What are you thinking of?
По́няли ли вы меня́?	Have you understood me?
Что э́то?	What is that?
Какъ э́то называ́ется?	What is that called?
Могу́ ли я васъ спроси́ть?	May I ask you?
Смѣ́ю ли проси́ть васъ объ э́томъ?	May I venture to ask you for it?
Что вамъ уго́дно?* / Чего́ вы жела́ете?	What do you wish?
Вы сомнѣва́етесь въ э́томъ?	Do you doubt it?
Что тутъ дѣ́лать?	What is to be done now?
На что рѣши́ться?	What resolution shall we take?
Что со мно́ю бу́детъ?	What will become of me?
Что я бу́ду съ э́тимъ дѣ́лать?	What shall I do with it?
Что я вамъ сдѣ́лалъ?	What have I done to you?
Какъ мнѣ вы́путаться?	How shall I get out of this difficulty.
Како́е сре́дство мнѣ употреби́ть?	What means ought I to use?
Что вы совѣ́туете мнѣ дѣ́лать?	What do you advise me to do?
Како́е ва́ше мнѣ́ніе?	What is your opinion?
Ду́маете ли вы, что э́то хорошо́?	Do you think that will do?
Что вы бы сдѣ́лали на моёмъ мѣ́стѣ?	What would you have done in my place?
На что вы жа́луетесь?	What do you complain of?
О чемъ вы пла́чете?	What are you crying about?
О чемъ вы смѣ́етесь?	What are you laughing at?
Какъ вамъ здѣсь нра́вится?	How do you like this place?
Зачѣ́мъ вы не остаётесь?	Why do you not stay?
До́лго ли вы тамъ оста́нетесь?	How long are you going to stop there?
Давно́ ли вы его́ зна́ете?	Have you known him long?
Какъ вы объ э́томъ узна́ли?	How did you know of it?
Кому́ э́то принадлежи́тъ?	To whom does this belong?
Чье э́то?	Whose is that?

* This is a politer form of address than the succeeding phrase.

4. APPROBATION.

Это о́чень хорошо́.	That is very good.
Это превосхо́дно.	That is excellent.
Это ми́ло.	That is charming.
Это удиви́тельно.	It is astonishing.
Это чуде́сно.	It is marvellous.
Это великолѣ́пно.	It is magnificent.
Я въ восхище́ніи.	I am delighted.
Онъ въ восто́ргѣ.	He is enraptured.
Это доста́вило мнѣ большо́е удово́льствіе.	It gave me much pleasure.
Это сдѣ́лаетъ вамъ честь.	It will do you credit.
Я э́тимъ чрезвыча́йно дово́ленъ.	I am exceedingly satisfied with it.
Это заслу́живаетъ внима́ніе.	This deserves to be taken notice of.
Это о́чень вы́годно.	That is very profitable.
Это о́чень удо́бно.	This is very convenient.
Это идётъ вамъ какъ нельзя́ лу́чше.	It fits you admirably.
Это у́мный человѣ́къ.	He is a sensible man.
Это замѣча́тельная осо́ба.	That is a remarkable person.
Онъ человѣ́къ съ больши́ми досто́инствами.	He is a man of great merit.
Это учёный.	That is a learned man.
Онъ литера́торъ.	He is a man of letters.
Вотъ че́стный человѣ́къ.	There is an honest man.
Это благонамѣ́ренный человѣ́къ.	That is a well-intentioned man.
Онъ человѣ́къ досто́йный довѣ́рія.	He is a trustworthy man.
Онъ бѣ́денъ, но че́стенъ.	He is poor, but honest.
Это хорошо́ воспи́танный молодо́й человѣ́къ.	He is a well-bred young man.
Это свѣ́тскій человѣ́къ.	That is a man of the world.
Это человѣ́къ степе́нный.	That is a steady man.
Онъ съ больши́ми позна́ніями.	He is possessed of great knowledge.
Я не могу́ ничего́ о нёмъ сказа́ть кро́мѣ хоро́шаго.	I can say of him nothing but what is praiseworthy.
Его́ всѣ хва́лятъ.	Everybody praises him.

Онъ отзыва́лся о васъ съ большо́ю похвало́ю.	He spoke of you in terms of great praise.
Она́ о́чень скромна́ и кротка́.	She is very modest and gentle.
Она́ съ больши́ми дарова́ніями.	She has great natural gifts.
У ней бо́льшія спосо́бности къ му́зыкѣ.	She has a great talent for music.
Она́ мнѣ о́чень нра́вится.	I like her very much.

5. DISAPPROBATION.

Это могло́ бы быть лу́чше.	This might be better.
Вы о́чень ху́до дѣ́лаете.	You do very wrong.
Како́й стыдъ!	What a shame!
Не сты́дно ли вамъ?	Are you not ashamed?
Вы мнѣ дѣ́лаете стыдъ.	You put me to shame.
Это посты́дно.	It is shameful.
Это о́чень ду́рно съ ва́шей стороны́.	It is very bad of you.
Какъ вы могли́ э́то сдѣ́лать?	How could you do it?
Это ша́лость.	It is only a boy's trick.
Я не дово́ленъ ва́ми.	I am dissatisfied with you.
Это мнѣ о́чень непрія́тно.	That is very disagreeable to me.
Это о́чень неприли́чно.	It is very indecent.
Это вамъ соверше́нно нейде́тъ.	That is not fit for you at all.
Это вамъ не приста́ло.	That does not become you.
Онъ ничего́ не зна́етъ.	He knows nothing.
Этотъ человѣ́къ не да́льнаго ума́.	That man has not much sense.
Онъ унижа́етъ себя́.	He degrades himself.
Онъ унижа́етъ свое́ досто́инство.	He derogates from his own worth.
Его посту́покъ унизи́теленъ.	His act was disgraceful.
Его́ со́вѣсть не чиста́.	His conscience is not pure.
У нея́ дурно́й нравъ.	She has a bad temper.

6. JOY AND SORROW.

Какъ я сча́стливъ!	How happy I am!
Кака́я счастли́вая мину́та!	What a fortunate moment!

Сча́стіе мнѣ благопрія́тствовало.	Fortune has favoured me.
Это его́ о́чень обра́довало.	He was overjoyed at it.
Онъ ра́дуется ва́шему сча́стію.	He rejoices at your happiness.
Это мнѣ о́чень жаль.	I am very sorry for it.
Это меня́ о́чень огорча́етъ.	It grieves me very much.
Это причиня́етъ мнѣ большо́е огорче́ніе.	That causes me a great deal of sorrow.
Я въ отча́яніи.	I am in despair.
Не должно́ отча́яваться.	You must not lose courage.
О́чень жаль!	It is a great pity!
Это ужа́сно.	It is dreadful.
Это большо́е несча́стіе.	It is a great misfortune.
Како́й непрія́тный слу́чай!	What an unpleasant accident!
Все потеря́но.	All is lost.
Онъ не въ ду́хѣ.	He is out of humour.
Мнѣ о́чень доса́дно.	I am exceedingly vexed.
Онъ се́рдится за вся́кую ма́лость.	He gets angry at the smallest trifle.
Мнѣ ску́чно.	I feel dull.

7. MEETING AND PARTING.

Жела́ю вамъ до́браго у́тра.	I wish you a good morning, Sir.
Здоро́вы ли вы?	Are you well?
Какъ вы себя́ чу́вствуете?	How do you feel?
Всѣ ли у васъ здоро́вы?	Are all well at home?
Я радъ, что ви́жу васъ въ до́бромъ здоро́вьѣ.	I am glad to see you in good health.
Все моё семе́йство вамъ кла́няется.	All my family desire their compliments.
Ми́лости про́симъ. Добро́ пожа́ловать.	You are welcome.
Мнѣ весьма́ пріятно васъ ви́дѣть.	I am very happy to see you.
О́чень радъ познако́миться съ ва́ми.	I am very glad to make your acquaintance.
Извини́те, сдѣ́лайте ми́лость, что я заста́вилъ васъ ждать.	Pray, excuse me for having made you wait.
Вы получи́ли прекра́сное мѣ́сто, — поздравля́ю васъ.	You have got a very good place, — I congratulate you.

Безъ церемо́ній.	Without ceremony.
Проща́йте.	Good-by.
До́ свида́нія.	Till I see you again.
До пріятнаго свида́нія.	Till I have the pleasure of seeing you again.
Очень благода́ренъ вамъ за вашъ раду́шный пріёмъ.	Receive my thanks for the kind reception you have given me.
Я не замѣтилъ какъ прошло́ съ ва́ми вре́мя.	I did not notice how the time passed in your company.
Это о́чень для меня́ ле́стно.	That is very flattering to me.
Прошу́ свидѣтельствовать моё почте́ніе ва́шей ма́тушкѣ.	Pray, make my respects to your mother.
Прошу́ переда́ть мой покло́нъ всѣмъ ва́шимъ.	Pray, present my compliments to all at home.

8. REQUESTING AND CONSENTING.

Съ позволе́нія ва́шего.	With your permission.
Не позво́лите ли вы мнѣ?	Will you give me leave to......?
Прошу́ васъ.	Pray.
Сдѣ́лайте ми́лость.	Do me the favour.
Сдѣ́лайте мнѣ э́то удово́льствіе.	Do me that pleasure.
У меня́ къ вамъ про́сьба.	I have to ask a favour of you.
Поко́рнѣйше прошу́ васъ.	I humbly request you.
Ещё разъ прошу́ васъ объ э́томъ.	I ask you for it once more.
Окажи́те мнѣ э́ту дру́жбу.	Do me that friendly service.
Не откажи́те мнѣ въ моей про́сьбѣ.	Do not refuse my request.
Вы бы меня́ весьма́ мно́го обяза́ли.	You would very much oblige me.
Умоля́ю васъ.	I beseech you.
Я испо́лню ва́ше жела́ніе.	I shall fulfil your wish.
Я согла́сенъ на э́то отъ всего́ се́рдца.	I consent to it with all my heart.
Я поду́маю объ э́томъ.	I shall think of it.
Я о́чень радъ, что могу́ быть вамъ поле́знымъ.	I am very glad that I can be of service to you.
Мнѣ бы пріятно было оказа́ть вамъ услу́гу.	I should be happy to render you a service.

Я сдѣ́лаю э́то едини́ственно изъ снисхожде́нія.	I shall do it merely from condescension.
Я согла́сенъ.	I consent.
Пусть бу́детъ такъ.	Let it be so.
Почему́ же нѣтъ.	And why not.
Я ни въ чемъ не могу́ вамъ отказа́ть.	I cannot refuse you anything.
Я съ удово́льствіемъ э́то сдѣ́лаю.	I shall do it with pleasure.
Э́то бу́детъ сдѣ́лано.	It shall be done.
Я постара́юсь э́то сдѣ́лать.	I will endeavour to do it.
Позво́льте мнѣ́ сказа́ть одно́ сло́во.	Give me leave to say one word.
Сдѣ́лайте ми́лость скажи́те мнѣ́.	Pray tell me.
Позво́льте мнѣ́ вамъ замѣ́тить что...	Permit me to remark to you that...
Позво́льте мнѣ́ не снима́ть шля́пы.	Allow me to keep on my hat.
Прошу́ васъ не безпоко́иться.	Pray, don't inconvenience yourself.

9. REFUSING AND BEGGING PARDON.

Я не могу́ э́того сдѣ́лать.	I cannot do it.
Э́то невозмо́жно.	That is impossible.
Не въ моéй вла́сти э́то сдѣ́лать.	It is not in my power to do it.
Э́то не зави́ситъ отъ меня́.	That does not depend on me.
Э́то до меня́ не каса́ется.	That is not my business.
Э́то не по моéй ча́сти.	It is not in my line.
Я не мѣша́юсь въ э́ти дѣла́.	I do not meddle with that matter.
Я до́лженъ отказа́ться отъ ва́шего приглаше́нія.	I am compelled to refuse your invitation.
Какъ я сожалѣ́ю что не могу́ приня́ть ва́шего дру́жескаго приглаше́нія.	How much I regret that I cannot accept your friendly invitation.
Я получи́лъ отка́зъ.	I got a refusal.
Онъ мнѣ́ на́ чисто отказа́лъ.	He gave me a downright refusal.
Онъ не подаётъ мнѣ́ никако́й надéжды.	He gives me no hopes.
Прости́те меня́.	Pardon me.
Извини́те меня́.	Excuse me.

Прошу́ у васъ проще́нія.	I beg your pardon.
Прошу́ извини́ть меня́.	Pray excuse me.
Не серди́тесь.	Don't be angry.
Прошу́ васъ прости́ть меня́ великоду́шно; я во́все не ду́малъ сдѣ́лать вамъ неудово́льствіе.	I beg you to be kind enough to pardon me; I never intended to cause you any displeasure.
Извини́те, я осмѣ́ливаюсь прерва́ть васъ.	Excuse me, if I take the liberty to interrupt you.

10. THANKING.

Да награди́тъ васъ Богъ!	May God reward you!
Да благослови́тъ васъ Госпо́дь!	May the Lord bless you!
Спаси́бо!	Thanks! (vulgar).
Благодарю́ васъ.	I thank you.
Поко́рнѣйше благодарю́ васъ.	I thank you most respectfully.
Очень обя́занъ!	Much obliged!
Я вамъ чрезвыча́йно обя́занъ.	I am very much obliged to you indeed.
Благодарю́ за ва́ше предложе́ніе.	I thank you for your proposal.
Принима́ю его́ съ благода́рностью.	I accept it with thanks.
За э́то я о́чень благода́ренъ вамъ.	I am very thankful to you for that.
Я о́чень умѣ́ю цѣни́ть э́то.	I very well know how to appreciate it.
Я вполнѣ́ чу́вствую ва́ши ми́лости.	I am perfectly sensible of your favours.
Бу́дьте увѣ́рены въ безпредѣ́льной моей́ благода́рности.	Rest assured of my extreme gratitude.

11. THE WEATHER.

Кака́я сего́дня пого́да?	What sort of weather is it to day.

Прекрáсная погóда.	It is fine weather.
Теплó.	It is warm.
Жáрко.	It is hot.
Погода я́сная.	The weather is clear.
Сóлнце свѣ́титъ.	The sun is shining.
Нестерпи́мый жаръ.	The heat is insupportable.
Тепéрь кани́кулы.	Now we are in the dog-days.
Бу́детъ грозá.	We shall have a thunderstorm.
Скóро бу́детъ дождь.	It is going to rain.
Дождь накрáпываетъ.	I feel some drops of rain.
Дождь идéтъ.	It is raining.
Идéтъ си́льный дождь.	It rains very fast.
Проливнóй дождь.	It is a pelting rain.
Мóлнія сверкáетъ.	It lightens.
Громъ греми́тъ.	It thunders.
Громъ удáрилъ.	The thunderbolt has fallen.
Какóй удáръ!	What a clap of thunder!
Грозá прошлá.	The thunderstorm has ceased.
Нéбо проясня́ется.	The sky is clearing up.
Я ви́жу рáдугу.	I see the rainbow.
Сóлнце опя́ть появля́ется.	The sun breaks out again.
Вѣ́теръ утихáетъ.	The wind is going down.
Бы́ло óчень пы́льно.	It was very dusty.
Пáдаетъ росá.	The dew is falling.
Погóда перемѣни́лась.	The weather has changed.
Дурнáя погóда.	The weather is bad.
Погóда непостоя́нна.	The weather is changeable.
Погóда пáсмурна.	The weather is gloomy.
Все нéбо покры́то облакáми.	The sky is overcast.
Нéбо óблачно.	The sky is cloudy.
Вѣ́трено.	It is windy.
Ду́етъ холóдный вѣ́теръ	There is a cold wind blowing.
Идéтъ градъ.	It hails.
Си́льная бу́ря.	We have a violent storm.
Поднимáется тумáнъ.	It is getting foggy.
Тумáнъ опускáется.	The fog is falling.
Погóда сырá.	It is damp weather.
По утрáмъ и вечерáмъ прохлáдно.	The mornings and evenings are fresh.
Хóлодно.	It is cold.
Сегóдня у́тромъ си́льно морóзило.	This morning it froze very hard.
Дни начинáютъ уменьшáться.	The days begin to shorten.

Вечера́ уже́ о́чень дли́нны.	The evenings are already very long.
Снѣгъ идётъ.	It snows.
Шелъ снѣгъ.	It has snowed.
Снѣгъ идётъ большими хло́пьями.	The snow comes down in large flakes.
Снѣгъ о́чень глубо́къ.	The snow is very deep.
Тепе́рь и́зморозь.	Sleet is falling.
Гололе́дица.	It is a hoar frost (rime-frost).
Дере́вья покры́ты и́неемъ.	The trees are covered with hoar-frost.
Си́льный моро́зъ. Си́льная сту́жа.	We have a very sharp frost.
Рѣка́ ста́ла.	The river is frozen over.
Ду́етъ пронзи́тельный вѣтеръ.	A sharp wind is blowing.
Мнѣ о́чень хо́лодно.	I am very cold.
Никогда́ ещё не́ было тако́й холо́дной зимы́.	There never was so cold a winter.
Пого́да ста́ла потеплѣ́е.	The weather has become warmer.
Начала́сь о́ттепель.	It is beginning to thaw.
Ледъ та́етъ.	The ice is thawing.
Ледъ на рѣкѣ́ тро́нулся.	The ice in the river has begun to move.
Дни прибавля́ются.	The days begin to lengthen.
Разсвѣта́етъ.	The day breaks.
Пока́зывается заря́.	The morning-twilight is appearing.
Восхо́дитъ со́лнце.	The sun is rising.
Уже́ свѣтло́.	It is day-light.
Со́лнце захо́дитъ.	The sun is setting.
Уже́ смерка́ется.	It is already growing dusky.
Стано́вится темно́.	It is growing dark.
Наступи́ла ночь.	It is night.
Луна́ восхо́дитъ.	The moon is rising.
Луна́ сія́етъ.	The moon shines.
Тепе́рь лу́нная ночь.	It is a moonlight night.
Прекра́сная ночь.	It is a beautiful night.
У насъ новолу́ніе.	We have the first quarter.
У насъ полнолу́ніе.	We have full moon.

PART IV.

DIALOGUES.

---

1. SCHOOL.

Гдѣ мнѣ сѣсть?	Where shall I sit down?
Гдѣ я дóлженъ сидѣть?	Where am I to sit.
Ся́дьте на скамью́.	Sit down upon the form.
Ся́дьте дáльше.	Sit a little lower down.
Сади́тесь на своé мѣсто.	Sit down in your place.
Не шуми́те.	Do not make a noise.
Не шевели́те столъ.	Do not shake the table.
Положи́те кни́ги на столъ.	Put your books upon the table.
Я потеря́лъ свою кни́гу.	I have lost my book.
Я не могу́ отыскáть своéй тетрáди?	I cannot find my copy-book.
Гдѣ вы ée остáвили?	Where did you leave it?
Я остáвилъ eé въ своéй контóркѣ.	I left it in my desk.
Поищи́те eé.	Look for it.
Я нашéлъ eé.	I have found it.
Вотъ онá.	Here it is.
Гдѣ онá былá?	Where was it?
Подъ скамьéй.	Under the form.

Зна́ете ли вы свой уро́къ?	Do you know your lesson?
Вы не вы́учили своего́ уро́ка.	You have not learned your lesson.
Мо́жете ли вы сказа́ть свой уро́къ?	Can you say your lesson?
Я ду́маю, что могу́.	I think I can.
Я не могу́ сказа́ть его́ безъ оши́бки.	I cannot recite it without fault.
Я вчера́ его́ зналъ.	I knew it yesterday.
Онъ о́чень тру́денъ.	It is very difficult.
Я не имѣ́лъ вре́мени его́ вы́учить.	I had no time to learn it.
Повтори́те его́.	Learn it again.
Сдѣ́лайте ми́лость, одолжи́те мнѣ́ своего́ перочи́ннаго но́жика.	Pray, lend me your penknife.
Для чего́?	What do you want it for?
Я бы хотѣ́лъ очини́ть перо́.	I want to mend my pen.
Возьми́те э́то желѣ́зное перо́.	Take this steel-pen.
Я лу́чше люблю́ гуси́ное перо́.	I prefer a quill.
Почему́ вы не употребля́ете своего́ перочи́ннаго но́жика?	Why don't you use your penknife?
Онъ не рѣ́жетъ.	It does not cut.
Онъ иступи́лся.	It is blunt.
Его на́до наточи́ть.	It wants setting.
Онъ совсѣ́мъ испо́рченъ.	It is entirely spoiled.

2. TO WRITE A LETTER.

Не мо́жете ли вы одолжи́ть мнѣ́ листа́ бума́ги?	Can you lend me a sheet of paper?
Како́й вамъ уго́дно бума́ги?	What sort of paper do you want?
Есть у васъ почтова́я бума́га?	Have you any postpaper?
У меня́ цѣ́лая десть.	I have a whole quire.
Я купи́лъ стопу́.	I have bought a ream.
Одолжи́те мнѣ́ оди́нъ листъ.	Oblige me by lending me one sheet.
Мнѣ́ на́добно писа́ть письмо́?	I have a letter to write.
Къ кому вы хоти́те писа́ть?	To whom to you want to write?
Къ мои́мъ роди́телямъ.	To my parents.
На́добно сего́дня его отпра́вить.	It (the letter) must go to-day.

Кото́рое число́?	What is the day of the month.
Сего́дня тре́тье.	To-day is the third.
Я ко́нчилъ.	I have done.
Да́йте мнѣ конве́ртъ.	Give me an envelope.
Тепе́рь остаётся мнѣ то́лько написа́ть а́дресъ.	Now I have only the address to write.
Письмо́ ещё не запеча́тано.	The letter is not sealed yet.
Запеча́тайте э́то письмо́.	Seal this letter.
Здѣсь нѣтъ сургучу́.	There is no sealing wax.
Принеси́те мнѣ обла́тку.	Bring me a wafer.
Куда́ дѣва́лась моя́ печать?	What has become of my seal?
Отнеси́те э́то письмо́ на по́чту.	Take this letter to the post-office.

3. TIME.

Кото́рый часъ?	What o'clock is it?
Сдѣ́лайте ми́лость, скажи́те мнѣ, кото́рый часъ.	Pray, tell me what o'clock it is.
Че́тверть втора́го.	It is a quarter past one.
Полови́на втора́го.	It is half past one.
Три че́тверти втора́го.	It is a quarter to two.
Два часа́ безъ десяти́ мину́тъ.	It wants ten minutes to two.
Ещё нѣтъ двухъ часо́въ.	It is not yet two.
Двѣна́дцать часо́въ.	It is twelve o'clock (noon).
По́лночь.	It is midnight.
Около трехъ часо́въ.	It is about three o'clock.
Три часа́ ро́вно.	It is exactly three o'clock.
Сію́ мину́ту бу́детъ бить три часа́.	It is going to strike three.
Тепе́рь три часа́ де́сять мину́тъ.	It is ten minutes past three.
По́здно.	It is late.
Ра́но.	It is early.
Ещё не по́здно.	It is not yet late.
Тепе́рь гора́здо по́зже, не́жели я ду́малъ.	It is much later than I thought.
Я не ду́малъ, чтобъ бы́ло такъ по́здно.	I did not think it was so late.
Стѣнны́е часы́ о́чень отстаю́тъ.	The clock loses a good deal.
Часы́ иду́тъ впере́дъ.	The clock goes to fast.

Мои карма́нные часы́ несхо́дны со стѣнны́ми.	My watch does not go by the clock.
Въ ва́шихъ часа́хъ что то сло́мано.	There is something broken in your watch.
Стрѣ́лка слома́лась.	The hand is broken.
Пружи́на ло́пнула.	The main spring is broken.
Они́ останови́лись.	It has stopped.
Они́ нейду́тъ.	It does not go.
Они́ испо́рчены.	It is out of order.
Мои часы́ поста́влены по со́лнцу.	My watch goes by the sun-dial.
Посмотри́те на со́лнечные часы́.	Look at the sun-dial.
Посмотри́те кото́рый часъ на ва́шихъ часа́хъ.	See what o'clock it is by your watch.
Они́ иногда́ остана́вливаются.	It stops now and then.
Они́ не заведены́.	It is not wound up.
На́добно завести́ мои часы́.	I must wind up my watch.

4. A VISIT.

Стуча́тъ.	There is a knock.
Кто-то стучи́тъ.	Somebody knocks.
Кто-то звони́тъ.	Some one rings.
Посмотри́те, кто э́то.	Go and see who it is.
Отвори́те дверь.	Open the door.
Это господи́нъ Н.	It is Mr. N.
Здра́вствуйте, г-нъ Н.	Good morning, Mr. N.
Жела́ю вамъ до́браго у́тра.	I wish you a good morning.
Ми́лости про́симъ; я́ о́чень ра́дъ ви́дѣть васъ.	You are welcome, Sir; I am very glad to see you.
Цѣ́лый вѣкъ я не видался съ ва́ми.	I have not seen you this age.
Какъ ва́ше здоро́вье?	How is your health?
Очень хорошо́, какъ ви́дите.	Very good, as you see.
По обыкнове́нію.	As usual.
Какъ нельзя́ лу́чше.	As well as can be.
Прошу́ сади́ться.	Pray, be seated.
Не уго́дно ли сѣсть?	Won't you sit down?
Ся́дьте на дива́нъ.	Sit down on the sofa.

Надѣюсь, что вы сдѣлаете мнѣ честь, останетесь обѣдать у меня́.	I hope you will do me the honour to stay and take some dinner with me.
Благодарю́ васъ, я не могу́ остáться.	I thank you, I cannot stay.
Я зашёлъ къ вамъ тóлько узнáть о вáшемъ здорóвьѣ.	I only came in to know how you were.
Мнѣ нáдобно идти́.	I must go.
Вы óчень спѣши́те.	You are in great haste.
У меня́ мнóго дѣ́ла.	I have many things to do.
Остáньтесь хоть на корóткое врéмя.	Surely you can stay a little longer.
Мнѣ ещё нáдобно быть въ рáзныхъ мѣстáхъ.	I have many places to call at.
Въ другóй разъ я остáнусь у васъ дóлѣе.	I will stay longer another time.
Благодарю́ васъ за посѣщéніе.	I thank you for your visit.
Надѣ́юсь скóро уви́дѣться съ вáми.	I hope I shall see you soon again.

5. DINNER.

Порá обѣ́дать.	It is dinner-time.
Ку́шанье пóдано, ся́демте за столъ.	Dinner is served, let us sit down to table.
Пойдéмте въ столóвую.	Let us walk into the dining-room.
Сдѣ́лайте ми́лость, сади́тесь.	Pray, be seated.
Какóй супъ вы бóлѣе лю́бите?	What soup do you prefer?
Говя́жій бульóнъ или супъ съ ри́сомъ и́ли вермичéлью.	Gravy soup, rice or vermicelli?
Я попóтчую васъ паштéтомъ.	I am going to send you a piece of this pie.
Благодарю́ васъ. Я попрошу́ немнóго говя́дины.	I thank you. I will trouble you for a little beef.
Какóй кусóкъ вы лу́чше лю́бите?	What part do you like best?
Съ котóрой стороны́ отрѣ́зать?	Which way shall I cut it?
Съ котóрой нибу́дь.	Any way.
Подáйте мнѣ тарéлку.	Give me a plate.

Надѣюсь, этотъ кусокъ по вашему вкусу.	I hope this piece is to your liking.
Не угодно ли картофелю?	Shall I help you to some potatoes?
Не хотите ли гороху или цвѣтной капусты?	Will you have peas or cauliflower?
Возьмите рыбы.	Take a little fish?
Эта рыба превосходна, и очень хорошо изготовлена.	This is excellent fish, and it is very well prepared.
Неугодно ли вамъ немного этого жаркаго?	Will you have a little of this roast meat?
Любите ли вы жиръ?	Do you like fat?
Пожалуйте мнѣ безъ жиру.	Give me some lean, if you please.
Немного того и другаго.	A little of both.
У васъ нѣтъ подливки.	You have no gravy.
Извините, у меня ея довольно.	I beg your pardon, I have plenty.
Не угодно ли вамъ зелени?	Shall I help you to some vegetables?
Вотъ шпинатъ и броколи.	Here is spinage and brocoli.
Какого вамъ угодно хлѣба: бѣлаго или чернаго?	Will you take white or black bread?
Мнѣ все равно.	It is quite indifferent to me.
Вы не кушали пуддинга.	You have not eaten any pudding.
Я попрошу самый маленькій кусокъ, только отвѣдать.	I will thank you for a very small piece, just to taste it.
Позвольте мнѣ только не много.	Give me only a little of it.
Вы ничего не кушаете.	You eat nothing.
Напротивъ, я ѣмъ очень много.	I beg your pardon, I eat very heartily.
У васъ отличный поваръ.	You have an excellent cook.
Да; онъ знаетъ свое дѣло.	Yes, he knows his business.
Не хотите ли бѣлаго вина?	Do you take white wine?
Я болѣе люблю красное.	I prefer red.
Отвѣдайте этого шампанскаго, оно не дурно.	Taste some of that Champaign; it is not bad.
Превосходно; я давно не пилъ такого пріятнаго вина.	Excellent; it is long since I drank such delicious wine.
Чокнемся.	Let us touch glasses.
Ваше здоровье!	Your health!
Имѣю честь пить за ваше здоровье.	I have the honour to drink your health.
Любите ли вы пирожное?	Are you fond of pastry?
Кушайте что вамъ болѣе нравится.	Take what you like best.

Подай десертъ.	Serve the dessert.
Возьмите кисть винограду или персикъ.	Will you take a bunch of grapes or a peach.
Вы кушаете очень мало.	You are a poor eater.
Я хорошо пообѣдалъ.	I have made an excellent dinner.

6. TEA.

Чай готовъ.	Tea is ready.
Васъ ожидаютъ.	They are waiting for you.
Я здѣсь.	Here I am.
Я иду за вами.	I follow you.
У насъ не достаетъ чашекъ.	We have not cups enough.
Намъ нужны ещё двѣ чашки.	We want two cups more.
Возьмите сахару.	Take some sugar.
Вы пьёте чай безъ сливокъ?	Do you take no cream?
Возьмите булку.	Take a roll.
Я возьму хлѣба съ масломъ.	I shall take a slice of bread and butter.
Какъ вамъ нравится чай?	How do you like your tea?
Можетъ быть, онъ не довольно крѣпокъ для васъ?	Perhaps you do not find it strong enough?
Я не люблю крѣпкаго.	I do not like strong tea.
Я прибавлю немного кипятку.	I will fill up your cup with water.
Намъ надобно ещё воды.	We want some more water.
Потрудитесь позвонить.	Ring the bell, if you please.
Довольно ли сладокъ у васъ чай.	Is your tea sweet enough?
Я не люблю очень сладкаго.	I do not like it quite so sweet.
У васъ очень хорошій чай.	Your tea is very good.
Гдѣ вы его покупаете?	Where do you buy it?
Я покупаю у Б.	I buy it at B....'s.
Это лучшій магазинъ кофе и чаю.	It is the best shop for coffee and tea.
Какой у васъ прекрасный чайный приборъ.	You have a very fine set of tea-things.
Чайникъ съ большимъ вкусомъ.	The tea-pot is very tasty.
Сахарница и сливочникъ очень красивы.	The sugar-basin and the milk-jug are very handsome.
Не хотите ли ещё чашки?	You will take another cup?

Я ужé вы́пилъ три чáшки, и болѣе никогдá не пью.	I have taken three cups, and I never take more.
Я налью́ вамъ полчáшки.	I will pour you out half a cup.
Покóрнѣйше благодарю́.	I thank you.
Убери́те со столá.	Take away.

7. MORNING.

Вы ужé встáли?	You are up already?
Ужé съ часъ какъ я всталъ.	I have been up this hour.
Вы встáли óчень рáно.	You got up very early.
Я обыкновéнно встаю́ рáно.	I generally get up early.
Это прекрáсная привы́чка.	It is a very good custom.
Это óчень хорошó для здорóвья.	It is very good for the health.
Чѣмъ бáльше спишь, тѣмъ больше спать хóчется.	The more one sleeps, the more one wants to sleep.
Какъ вы спáли?	How have you slept?
Какъ вы э́ту ночь спáли?	How did you sleep last night?
Хорошó ли вы спáли.	Did you sleep well?
Очень хорошó. Я крѣпко спалъ.	Very well. I slept soundly.
Я спалъ безъ прóсыпу.	I slept without waking.
А вы хорошó почивáли?	And you, how did you rest?
Не óчень хорошó.	Not very well.
Я не óчень хорошó спáлъ.	I did not sleep very well.
Я не могъ спать.	I could not sleep.
Я не могъ сомкну́ть глазъ.	I could not sleep a wink.
Я не смыкáлъ глазъ во всю ночь.	I never closed my eyes all night.
Какóе прекрáсное у́тро!	What a fine morning!
Какъ вы ду́маете, не прогуля́ться ли намъ?	What do you think of taking a walk?
Успѣ́емъ ли мы до зáвтрака?	Shall we have time before breakfast?
Зáвтракъ бу́детъ не рáнѣе какъ чрезъ часъ.	They won't breakfast this hour.
Мы мóжемъ располагáть цѣ́лымъ чáсомъ.	We have full an hour before us.
Прогу́лка придáстъ намъ аппети́та.	The walk will give us an appetite.
Одѣ́ньтесь скорѣ́е.	Dress yourself quickly.
Я недóлго бу́ду одѣвáться.	I shall not be long dressing.

8. EVENING.

День оканчивается.	The day is almost spent.
Солнце только что зашло.	The sun has just set.
Совершенно темно.	It is perfectly dark.
Подайте огня: я невижу болѣе.	Give me a light. I cannot see any longer.
Мнѣ хочется спать.	I am sleepy.
Постлана ли моя постель?	Is my bed made?
Я лягу сегодня въ десять часовъ.	I shall go to bed at ten o'clock to-night.
Ещё рано.	It is early yet.
Я вчера очень поздно легъ.	I went to bed very late last night.
Мнѣ надобно встать на разсвѣтѣ.	I must get up at break of day.
Г-нъ А. ещё не вовратился.	Mr. A. has not come home yet.
Я думаю, что онъ не опоздаетъ.	I don't think he will be long.
Я почти увѣренъ, что онъ не замедлитъ придти.	I dare say he will not be long.
Онъ обыкновенно приходитъ рано.	He generally comes home early.
Я слышу — стучатъ.	I hear a knock.
Это, вѣроятно, онъ стучитъ.	Very likely, it is he who is knocking.
Посмотрите.	Go and see.
Посвѣтите ему.	Light the way for him.
Такъ точно. Это онъ.	Just so. It is he.
Надѣюсь, что я не заставилъ васъ ждать.	I hope I have not made you wait.
Вовсе нѣтъ. Ещё только десять часовъ.	Not in the least. It is only ten o'clock.
Мы никогда не ложимся спать ранѣе половины одиннадцатаго.	We never go to bed before half past ten.
Я пришелъ во-время.	I have come just in time.
Теперь прекрасный вечеръ.	It is a charming evening.
Какова была ваша вечерняя прогулка.	How did you like your evening's walk.
Очень пріятна.	Delicious.
Не устали ли вы?	Are you not tired?
Не очень.	Not much.

Не хоти́те ли немно́го отдохну́ть?	Will you rest yourself a little.
Поко́рно благодарю́; я ля́гу спать.	I thank you; I shall go to bed.
Пора́ идти́ спать.	It is time to go to bed.
Я не люблю́ по́здно ложи́ться.	*I do not like sitting up late.*
Я люблю́ ложи́ться ра́но.	I like to go to bed early.
Жела́ю вамъ споко́йной но́чи.	I wish you a good night.
Разбуди́те меня́ пора́ньше.	Call me early to-morrow.
Смотри́те не забу́дьте.	Do not fail.
Бу́дьте споко́йны.	You need not doubt it.

9. WALKING.

Не пойти́ ли намъ прогуля́ться.	Shall we go and take a little walk?
Съ больши́мъ удово́льствіемъ.	With much pleasure.
Позво́льте мнѣ взять мою́ трость?	I must beg leave to go and take my stick.
Тепе́рь я гото́въ идти́ съ ва́ми.	Now, I am ready to follow you.
Куда́ мы пойдёмъ?	Which way shall we go?
Пойдёмъ въ дере́вню?	Let us go into the fields.
Я бою́сь, несли́шкомъ ли пы́льно на доро́гахъ.	I am afraid the roads are very dusty.
Дождь немно́го прибилъ пыль.	The rain has laid the dust a little.
Мо́жно ли перейти́ чрезъ э́то по́ле?	May we cross this field?
Пойдемъ э́той тропи́нкой.	Let us take this path.
Скро́емся въ тѣнь.	Let us walk in the shade.
Мы бу́демъ защищены́ отъ со́лнца.	We shall be sheltered from the sun.
Э́то мѣ́сто преле́стно.	This place is delightful.
Мнѣ здѣсь нра́вится.	I like this place.
Все э́то превзошло́ мои́ ожида́нія.	All this exceeds my expectation.
Посмотри́те на э́ту сто́рону.	Look that way.
Отку́да открыва́ются са́мыя живопи́сныя мѣстоположе́нія.	Where the most picturesque sites are discovered to the view.
Э́то до́лженъ быть прекра́сный паркъ.	I believe it is a fine park.

Войдёмъ туда́.	Let us go in.
Если вы уста́ли, то отдохнёмъ на траве́.	If you are tired, let us rest ourselves on the grass.
Я не уста́лъ; бу́демъ продолжа́ть на́шу прогу́лку.	I am not tired; let us continue our walk.
Я здѣсь иногда́ прогу́ливаюсь ве́черомъ, чтобъ подыша́ть свѣ́жимъ во́здухомъ.	I walk here of an evening in order to breathe the fresh air.
Мнѣ бы хотѣ́лось пора́нѣе возврати́ться домо́й.	I want to be home in good time.
Такъ отдохнёмъ пре́жде, не́жели пойдёмъ домо́й.	Well, let us take a little rest before going home.

10. MEETING A FRIEND.

Какъ! это вы?	What! is it you?
Да вы ли э́то?	Is it really you?
Я самъ.	It is I myself.
Вы меня́ о́чень удиви́ли.	You quite surprise me.
Я не ожида́лъ встрѣ́тить васъ здѣсь.	I did not expect to meet you here.
Я о́чень радъ, что встрѣ́тился съ ва́ми.	I am very glad to meet you.
Давно́ ли вы возврати́лись?	When did you return?
Я при́былъ вчера́ ве́черомъ.	I came home last night.
Какъ вы пріѣ́хали?	How did you come?
Я пріѣ́халъ въ дилижа́нсѣ.	I came by the stage-coach.
Я пріѣ́халъ по желѣ́зной доро́гѣ.	I came by the rail.
Я пріѣ́халъ на почтовы́хъ.	I came by post.
Вы при́были неожи́данно.	You are come rather unexpectedly.
Я предполага́лъ оста́ться тамъ все лѣ́то.	I thought to stay there all the summer.
Что же заста́вило васъ такъ ско́ро возврати́ться?	What made you return so soon?
Нѣ́которыя дѣла́ тре́буютъ моего́ прису́тствія здѣсь.	Some business requires my presence here.
Какъ вы соверши́ли своё путеше́ствіе?	How did you like your journey?
Какъ нельзя́ лу́чше.	As well as can be.

Я здѣлалъ са́мую прія́тную поѣздку.	I have had a very pleasant journey.
Когда́ я бу́ду имѣ́ть удово́льствіе ви́дѣть васъ у себя́.	When shall I have the pleasure of seeing you at my house?
Не зна́ю. Мнѣ на́добно ко́нчить нѣкоторыя дѣла́.	I don't know. I have a little business to do.
Бу́дете ли вы за́втра свобо́дны?	Will you be at leisure to-morrow.
Я бу́ду имѣ́ть удово́льствіе ви́дѣться съ ва́ми за́втра.	I shall wait upon you to-morrow.
Мы бу́демъ о́чень ра́ды васъ ви́дѣть.	We shall be very happy to see you.

11. IN A SHOP.

Куда́ вы хоти́те идти́?	Where do you wish to go?
Мнѣ ну́жно ко́е-что купи́ть.	I have to buy a few things.
Не уго́дно ли вамъ идти со мной?	Will you go with me?
Съ больши́мъ удово́льствіемъ.	With great pleasure?
Не на́добно ли вамъ сами́мъ чего́ нибу́дь купи́ть?	Don't you want to buy something yourself?
Ничего́ осо́бенно.	Not anything in particular.
Я хочу́ купи́ть ко́е-какія бездѣлицы.	I am going to buy a few trifles.
Отпра́вимтесь скорѣ́й, намъ ну́жно возврати́ться къ ча́ю.	Let us go directly, for we must be back to tea.
Сдѣлайте ми́лость, покажи́те мнѣ обра́щики то́нкаго сукна.	Pray, let me see some patterns of fine cloth.
Како́го цвѣта вы жела́ете? Не уго́дно ли, я покажу́ вамъ си́няго цвѣта?	What colour do you prefer? Shall I show you some blue ones?
Я лу́чше люблю́ чёрный цвѣтъ, онъ всегда́ въ мо́дѣ.	I prefer black, it is always in fashion.
Како́го со́рта сукна́ вы жела́ете?	What sort of cloth do you wish to have?
Въ каку́ю цѣну?	What price would you wish to go to?
У насъ есть су́кна ра́зныхъ цѣнъ.	We have some of different prices.
Покажи́те мнѣ са́маго лу́чшаго.	Show me the best you have.
Покажи́те мнѣ са́маго то́нкаго.	Let me see the finest you have.

Вотъ два куска́.	Here are two pieces.
Это превосхо́дное сукно́.	This is excellent cloth.
Но цвѣтъ не про́чный, я бою́сь, чтобъ оно́ не полиняло.	But the colour is rather delicate, I fear it will soon fade.
Вы ошиба́етесь, я отвѣча́ю вамъ за него́.	You are mistaken, I will answer for it.
Совѣ́тую вамъ взять э́то сукно́.	I advise you to take this cloth.
Что сто́итъ арши́нъ?	How much do you sell it an arsheen?
Шесть рубле́й серебро́мъ.	Six silver roubles.
Это о́чень до́рого.	I find it very dear.
Скажи́те кра́йнюю цѣ́ну; я не люблю́ торгова́ться.	What is the lowest price, for I do not like to bargain.
Ничего́ нельзя́ сба́вить: э́то опредѣлённая цѣна́.	I cannot sell it for less: it is a fixed price.
Не мо́жете ли вы мнѣ уступи́ть за...?	Can you let me have it for....?
Ника́къ не могу́ ме́нѣе взять.	I cannot take less.
Отрѣ́жьте мнѣ три арши́на.	Cut me three arsheens.
Не жела́ете ли ещё́ чего́ ни-бу́дь?	Do you want anything else?
Мнѣ на́добно мате́ріи на жиле́тъ.	I want some stuff for a waistcoat.
Вотъ здѣсь вся́каго цвѣ́та.	Here are some of all colours.
Любите ли вы бѣ́лый?	Do you like white?
У меня́ есть прекра́сный пике́.	I have some beautiful quilting.
Этотъ казими́ръ о́чень хоро́шъ.	This cassimer is very good.
Могу́ рекомендова́ть вамъ э́ту мате́рію.	I can recommend you this stuff.
Этотъ цвѣтъ о́чень те́менъ.	This colour is too dull.
А тотъ сли́шкомъ свѣ́телъ.	And that is too light.
Я жела́ю имѣ́ть таку́ю мате́рію, кото́рая не была́ бы марка́.	I want some stuff that does not get dirty.
Я жела́ю таку́ю, кото́рую мо́жно бы́ло бы мыть.	I want something that washes well.
Мнѣ дово́льно нра́вится э́тотъ рису́нокъ, но бою́сь чтобы не сошла́ кра́ска.	I like this pattern well enough, but I fear the colour won't stand.
Бою́сь, что э́та мате́рія не бу́детъ прочна́.	I fear this stuff will not wear.
Никогда́ не изно́сите.	You will never wear it out.
Мо́жете её́ взять и положи́ться на моё́ сло́во.	You may take it upon my word
Мнѣ нужна́ ше́лковая шля́па.	I wish to have a silk hat.

Примѣрьте э́ту.	Try this.
Поля́ слишкомъ широки́.	The brim is too broad.
Тепе́рь въ мо́дѣ широ́кія поля́.	Broad brims are in fashion.
Это очень хоро́шая и мо́дная шля́па.	This is a very good and fashionable hat.
Тулья́ сли́шкомъ узка́.	The shape is too small.
Вотъ другая той же доброты́.	Here is another of the same quality.
Она́ мнѣ пра́вится; что она́ сто́итъ.	This will do; what does it cost?
Пять рубле́й серебро́мъ.	Five silver roubles?
Тепе́рь скажи́те мнѣ, ско́лько я вамъ до́лженъ?	Now let me know what I owe you?
Что все э́то сто́итъ?	How much does it come to?
Все э́то составля́етъ два́дцать пять рубле́й.	It comes in all to twenty five roubles.
Отпра́вьте все э́то неме́дленно ко мнѣ.	Send it to my house immediately.

12. A TAILOR.

Я посла́лъ за ва́ми, что́бы вы сня́ли съ меня́ мѣ́рку для фра́ка.	I have sent for you to measure me for a coat.
Сними́те съ меня́ мѣ́рку.	Take my measure.
Какъ вамъ уго́дно его́ сдѣ́лать?	How will you have it made?
Сдѣ́лайте мнѣ такъ, какъ ны́нче но́сятъ.	Make it as they wear them now.
Не жела́ете ли та́кже заказа́ть жиле́тъ и пантало́ны?	Do you want also a waistcoat and pantaloons?
Да. Я купи́лъ сукна́ для по́лной па́ры пла́тья.	Yes, I have bought enough cloth for a complete suit of clothes.
Какъ уго́дно вамъ сдѣ́лать жиле́тъ?	How do you wish your waistcoat made?
Сдѣ́лайте по ны́нѣшней мо́дѣ?	Make it in the newest fashion.
Какі́я вамъ уго́дно пу́говицы?	What sort of buttons will you have?
Изъ той же са́мой мате́ріи.	Of the some stuff.
Очень хорошо́.	Very well.
Сдѣ́лайте мнѣ пантало́ны со штри́пками.	Make my pantaloons with straps.

Не дѣлайте штрипокъ къ моимъ панталонамъ.	Don't put any straps to my pantaloons.
Сдѣлайте ихъ пошире; я не люблю тѣсныхъ.	Make them wide, for I don't like tight ones.
Онѣ будутъ сдѣланы по вашему вкусу.	They shall be made to suit your taste.
Помните, что все это мнѣ непремѣнно нужно къ воскресенью.	Remember that I must have every thing by next Sunday without fail.
Вы получите все въ воскресенье утромъ.	You shall have it on Sunday morning.
Принесли вы моё платье?	Have you brought me my dress?
Точно такъ, вотъ оно.	Yes, Sir; here it is.
Вы сдержали своё слово. Но, признаться, я ужé начиналъ безпокоиться.	You have kept your word. But I confess I began to grow impatient.
Ещё только десять часовъ, а я обѣщалъ вамъ принести въ продолженіе утра.	It is but ten o'clock, and I promised you to bring it in the course of the morning.
Примѣрьте его на мнѣ.	Try it on me.
Посмотримъ, хорошо ли оно на мнѣ сидитъ.	Let's see whether it fits me well.
Посмотримъ, какъ оно на мнѣ сидитъ?	Let me see how it fits me.
Вы сдѣлали рукава слишкомъ длинные и широкіе.	You have made the sleeves too long and too wide.
Теперь носятъ очень большіе рукава.	They are worn very wide now.
Мой фракъ тѣсенъ.	My dress-coat is too close.
Мнѣ жметъ подъ мышками.	It pinches me under my arms.
Талія очень длинна.	It is too long-waisted.
Талія очень коротка.	It is too short-waisted.
Между плечами складки.	It sits in wrinkles between the shoulders.
Оно сидитъ на васъ какъ нельзя лучше.	It fits you as well as can be.
Вы никогда не были лучше одѣты.	You were never better dressed.

13. A SHOEMAKER.

Мнѣ нужна́ па́ра сапого́въ.	I want a pair of shoes.
Сними́те мѣ́рку.	Take my measure.
У меня́ ужé есть ва́ша мѣ́рка.	I have your measure at home, Sir.
Сдѣ́лайте мнѣ ихъ посвобо́днѣе.	Make them wide enough.
Не дѣ́лайте о́чень у́зкихъ.	Don't make them too tight.
Я постара́юсь сдѣ́лать ихъ такъ, какъ вы жела́ете.	I will take care to make them to your liking.
Сдѣ́лайте ихъ какъ мо́жно скорѣ́е.	Get them ready as soon as may be.
Сдѣ́лайте мнѣ за-одно́ и ба́льные башмаки́.	Make me also a pair of dancing pumps.
Вы полу́чите все на бу́дущей недѣ́лѣ.	You shall have everything in the course of next week.
Я принёсъ вамъ ва́ши сапоги́.	Sir, I have brought your shoes.
Посмо́тримъ.	Let me see.
Не уго́дно ли вамъ надѣ́ть ихъ?	Will you please to try them on?
Они́ совсѣ́мъ не лѣ́зутъ мнѣ на́ ногу.	I cannot get my foot in.
Зачѣ́мъ вы мнѣ сдѣ́лали такі́е остроно́сые?	Why have you made them so pointed?
Такъ ны́нче но́сятъ.	They wear them so now.
Хорошо́; да я не хочу́ му́чить себя́ для мо́ды.	Well; but I don't like to suffer pain for the sake of being in fashion.
Они́ о́чень у́зки.	They are a good deal too narrow.
Они́ жмутъ мнѣ большо́й па́лецъ.	They hurt my great toes.
Они́ бу́дутъ просто́рнѣе, когда́ разно́сятся.	They will get wide enough by wearing.
Но въ ожиданіи, поку́да они́ сдѣ́лаются просто́рнѣе, я во́все не хочу́ быть хромоно́гимъ.	But till they get wide enough, I have no mind to be lame.
Я не могу́ ходи́ть въ нихъ.	I cannot walk in them.
Я не хочу́ получи́ть мозо́лей.	I don't like to get corns.
Голени́ще э́того сапога́ сли́шкомъ высоко́.	The leg of this boot is too high.
Я говори́лъ вамъ, чтобъ вы сдѣ́лали мнѣ каблуки́ са́мые высо́кіе.	I told you to make the heels as high as possible.

Я терпѣ́ть не могу́ ни́зкихъ каблуко́въ.	I detest low heels.
Возьми́те э́ти сапоги́, ихъ на́добно передѣ́лать.	Take these boots back, they must be altered.
Принеси́те ихъ скорѣ́й.	Bring them me back as soon as possible.
Принесли́ ли вы мои́ башмаки́?	Have you brought my shoes?
Вотъ они́.	Here they are.
Ко́жа плоха́.	The leather is bad.
Передки́ никуда́ не годятся.	The upper-leathers are good for nothing.
Подо́швы сли́шкомъ тонки́.	The soles are too thin.
Я увѣ́ренъ, что э́ти башмаки́ во́все не для меня́ сдѣ́ланы.	I am sure these shoes were never made for me.
Возьми́те ихъ наза́дъ, и сдѣ́лайте мнѣ какъ мо́жно скорѣ́е другу́ю па́ру.	Take them back, and make another pair as soon as possible.

14. AT A BOOKSELLER'S.

Вы неда́вно получи́ли вы́боръ францу́зскихъ книгъ; я бы о́чень жела́лъ ихъ ви́дѣть.	You have lately received a selection of French books; I should like to see them.
Съ больши́мъ удово́льствіемъ.	With great pleasure, Sir.
Ихъ то́лько сего́дня у́тромъ распакова́ли. Вы пе́рвый ихъ уви́дите.	They were unpacked only this morning. You are the first to see them.
Все э́то но́выя кни́ги?	Are these all new books?
Нѣтъ, есть и но́выя и ста́рыя.	No. Some are new, some are old.
Надѣ́юсь, вы найдёте что вы́брать изъ нихъ по ва́шему жела́нію.	I hope you will find some that will suit you.
Покажи́те тѣ кни́ги, кото́рыя мы неда́вно получи́ли.	Show the gentleman the books we have received lately.
Что же, нашли́ ли вы что́ нибудь по ва́шему жела́нію?	Well, Sir, have you found anything to suit you?
Да. Вотъ вы́писка книгъ, кото́рыя я жела́ю имѣ́ть.	Yes. Here is a list of the books I wish to have.
Какъ вы жела́ете получи́ть ихъ, въ листа́хъ или въ переплётѣ?	How do you like to have them, in sheets or bound?

Пришлите мнѣ ихъ въ брошю́рахъ.	Let me have them stitched.
Я желаю въ переплётѣ.	I should like to have them bound.
Какой переплётъ вы желаете?	What sort of binding do you wish for?
Я желаю, чтобы э́та книга была́ переплетена́ въ сафья́нъ съ золоты́мъ обрѣзомъ.	I wish to have that book bound in morocco with gilt edges.
Какого цвѣта желаете вы сафья́нъ?	What colour would you prefer?
Одна́ ли цѣна́ за всякій цвѣтъ?	Is the price the same for all colours?
Все одна́; цвѣтъ не перемѣня́етъ цѣны́.	Exactly the same. The colour makes no difference in the price.
Въ тако́мъ слу́чаѣ я предпочита́ю зелёный сафья́нъ.	In that case I prefer green morocco.
Этотъ цвѣтъ живѣ́е и не такъ ма́рокъ.	That colour is more striking, and does not get dirty so easily.
Какъ желаете вы переплёсть другія кни́ги?	How do you wish the other books bound.
Я хочу́ переплёсть ихъ въ ко́жу съ загла́віями на корешкѣ́.	I wish to have them bound in calf with the titles on their backs.
Изво́льте; я позабо́чусь, чтобы онѣ́ переплетены́ бы́ли по ва́шему жела́нію.	Very well, Sir; I shall take care to have them bound to your liking.
Не на́добно ли вамъ ещё чего́ нибу́дь?	Do you want anything else, Sir?
Я бы о́чень хотѣ́лъ имѣ́ть экземпля́ръ словаря́ Н...а.	I should like to have a copy of N...'s dictionary.
У меня́ есть оди́нъ подёржанный экземпля́ръ, кото́рый о́чень хорошо́ сохранёнъ и не до́рогъ.	I have a second-hand copy which is in very good condition, and not dear.
Мнѣ бы хотѣ́лось имѣ́ть но́вый.	I prefer to have it new.
Это невозмо́жно; все изда́ніе разошло́сь.	That is impossible; the book is out of print.
Не ду́маютъ ли вновь напеча́тать? Эта кни́га чрезвыча́йно поле́зна.	Don't they think of reprinting it? The book is exceedingly useful.
Тепе́рь на́чали её печа́тать.	It is now in the press.
Но ещё неизвѣ́стно, когда́ она́ вы́йдетъ въ свѣтъ.	But nobody knows when it will appear.

Въ такóмъ слýчаѣ я лýчше воспóльзуюсь вáшимъ экземпля́ромъ.
In that case I had better make sure of the copy you have here.

Скóлько вы за негó хоти́те?
What do you ask for it?

Я разсчи́тывалъ продáть его за четы́рнадцать рублéй серебрóмъ.
I should have asked two guineas and a half for it.

Но такъ какъ вы берéте у меня́ мнóго други́хъ книгъ, то я уступлю́ вамъ зá десять рублéй.
But as you have bought several other books, I will let you have it for ten silver roubles.

Это дорóже, чѣмъ стóилъ нóвый экземпля́ръ.
It is more than it cost when new.

Это прáвда. Но онъ сталъ такъ рѣ́докъ, что цѣнá его увели́чивается со дня нá день.
That is true. But it is so scarce that the price advances every day.

Вы не мóжете взять мéнѣе?
You cannot let me have it for less?

Нѣтъ, по сóвѣсти, я тутъ не имѣ́ю почти́ никакóй вы́годы.
No, upon my word, I hardly get anything by it.

Отложи́те егó, и пришли́те ко мнѣ́ съ прóчими кни́гами.
Put it by, and send it me with the other books.

15. THE DOCTOR.

Извини́те, я рѣши́лся послáть за вáми.
Excuse me, Sir, I have taken the liberty to send for you.

Что съ вáми?
What is the matter with you?

Я совсѣ́мъ нездорóвъ.
I am not at all well.

Я чýвствую себя́ óчень нездорóвымъ.
I feel very unwell.

У меня́ чрезвычáйная слáбость.
I am unusually weak.

Какъ начaлáсь вáша болѣ́знь?
How were you taken ill?

Трéтьяго дня у меня́ сдѣ́лался ознóбъ.
It began the day before yesterday by a shivering.

Потóмъ я былъ въ си́льной испáринѣ.
Then I perspired profusely.

Не чýвствовали ли вы тошнотьí?
Did you feel a nausea?

Да, сначáла; но потóмъ это прошлó, и у меня́ остáлась сильная головнáя боль.	Yes, at first; but that went off. and I have had a terrible headache ever since.
Гдѣ вы тепéрь чу́вствуете боль?	Where do you feel pain now?
Я чу́вствую боль въ желу́дкѣ.	I feel a pain in my stomach.
У меня́ боли́тъ головá.	My head aches.
У меня́ боли́тъ гóрло.	I have a sore throat.
У меня́ нáсморкъ.	I have a cold in the head.
У меня́ два дня продолжáется кáшель.	I have had a cough these two days.
Всю ночь я чу́вствовалъ ознóбъ.	I have had a shivering the whole night long.
Я чу́вствую боль во вну́тренностяхъ.	I feel a pain in my bowels.
У меня́ боль въ боку́, и я съ трудóмъ могу́ дышáть.	I feel pains in my side, and I breathe with difficulty.
Есть ли у васъ аппети́тъ?	Have you any appetite?
Я почти́ ничегó не ѣлъ въ продолжéніе двухъ дней.	I have hardly eaten anything these two days.
Покажи́те вашъ язы́къ.	Let me see your tongue.
У васъ нечи́стъ желу́докъ.	Your stomach is overloaded.
Вамъ нáдобно приня́ть лекáрство.	You must take some medicine.
Позвóльте вáшу ру́ку.	Give me your hand.
Позвóльте пощу́пать вашъ пульсъ.	Let me feel your pulse.
Онъ си́льно бьетъ.	It is rather high.
У васъ лихорáдка.	You are feverish.
Не полагáете ли вы мою́ болѣ́знь опáсною?	Do you think my illness dangerous?
Нѣтъ; но нáдобно взять предосторóжности, чтóбы онá не сдѣлалась опáсною.	No; but you must be careful lest it become so.
Чтожъ я дóлженъ дѣлать?	And what must I do?
Я пропишу́ вамъ кóе-что, а зáвтра у́тромъ опя́ть приду́ къ вамъ.	I will write a prescription, and call on you again to-morrow morning.
Не нáдобно ли мнѣ ещé чегó нибу́дь?	What else must I do?
Нѣтъ. Старáйтесь тóлько держáть себя́ въ теплѣ́.	Nothing but keep yourself warm.
Остерегáйтесь просту́ды.	Be careful you do not catch cold.

За́втра увидимъ не ну́жно ли бу́детъ пусти́ть вамъ немно́го кро́ви.	To-morrow I shall see whether it will not be proper to bleed you a little.

16. TRAVELLING.

Нѣтъ ли у васъ како́го поруче́нія въ Б...?	Have you any commissions to give me for B.?
Вы отправля́етесь въ Б...?	Are you going to B.?
Такъ то́чно. Не могу́ ли я для васъ что́ нибудь сдѣлать тамъ?	Just so, Sir. Is there anything that I can do for you there?
Вы о́чень любе́зны.	You are very obliging.
Когда́ вы ду́маете ѣхать?	When do you think of going?
Я ѣду за́втра у́тромъ.	I shall set off to-morrow morning.
Вы ѣдете въ дилижа́нсѣ?	Do you go by the stage-coach?
Нѣтъ, я ѣду на почтовы́хъ.	No, I shall go by post.
Я отпра́влюсь по желѣзной доро́гѣ.	I shall go by rail.
Какъ до́лго ду́маете вы проб́ыть тамъ?	How long do you mean to stay there?
Когда́ вы возврати́тесь?	How soon will you come back?
Я ду́маю оста́ться пять въ или шесть мѣ́сяцевъ.	I think of staying four or five months.
Если я могу́ быть вамъ въ чемъ нибу́дь тамъ поле́знымъ, то скажи́те.	If I can be of any use to you there, give me your commands.
Я воспо́льзуюсь ва́шимъ обяза́тельнымъ предложе́ніемъ, и потому́ прійду къ вамъ сего́дня ве́черомъ.	I shall avail myself of your kind offer, and in order to do so, I will call on you in the evening.
Вы навѣ́рно заста́нете меня́ до́ма.	You will be sure to find me at home.

Вотъ мы и на путево́мъ дворѣ́.	Here we are at the railway-station.

Поѣздъ отправится чрезъ пять минутъ.	The train will start in five minutes.
Возьмите скорѣй билетъ.	Take a ticket directly.
Какое вы берете мѣсто?	In which class will you go?
Я возьму въ первомъ классѣ.	I shall go in the first class.
Я отправлюсь въ вагонѣ втораго класса.	I shall go in second class carriage.
Какая у васъ поклажа?	What luggage have you, Sir?
У меня два чемодана, дорожный мѣшокъ и шляпный футляръ.	I have two portmanteaus, one travelling-bag, and a hat-box.
Поберегите мой шляпный футляръ.	Take care of my hat-box.
Вотъ и паровозъ, который насъ повезетъ.	Here is the engine that is to take us.
У насъ два паровоза.	We have two engines.
Надобно большую силу, чтобъ везти поѣздъ въ двадцать пять экипажей.	Much force is required to propel a train of twenty five carriages.
Во сколько силъ эти машины?	Of how many horse-power are these engines?
Каждая во сто лошадиныхъ силъ.	Of a hundred horse-power each.
Въ которомъ часу отправляется товарный поѣздъ?	At what time does the goods-train start?
Каждый день ходятъ по два: одинъ отправляется въ десять часовъ утра, а другой въ три часа по полудни.	There are two trains every day: one starts at ten o'clock in the morning, and the other at three in the afternoon.
Вашъ пріятель ѣдетъ съ нами?	Does your friend go with us?
Нѣтъ, онъ поѣдетъ въ двѣнадцать часовъ (въ полдень) съ поспѣшнымъ поѣздомъ.	No, he will go at twelve o'clock (at noon) by the fast train.
Долго ли онъ пробудетъ въ Н.?	Does he mean to stay long at N.?
Онъ долго тамъ не останется.	He will not stay there long.
Онъ думаетъ завтра вечеромъ возвратиться съ обыкновеннымъ поѣздомъ.	He intends to return to-morrow evening by the ordinary train.
Садитесь по мѣстамъ, господа!	Take your seats, gentlemen!
Поторопитесь, поѣздъ сію минуту отправляется.	Make haste, the train is going to start directly.
Вотъ и знакъ къ отъѣзду.	That was the signal for starting.
Вотъ мы и двинулись.	Now the train is moving.
Мы ѣдемъ очень скоро.	We are going very fast.

Такáя скóрость привóдитъ меня́ въ страхъ.	Such rapidity frightens me.
Не бóйтесь ничегó.	Don't be afraid.
Вотъ идéтъ пóѣздъ.	There is a train coming.
Это обрáтный пóѣздъ.	It is a return-train.
Вотъ мы прíбыли на пéрвую стáнцію.	Now we have reached the first station.
Мы остáнемся здѣсь не бóлѣе трехъ минýтъ.	We only stop here three minutes.
Вотъ мы и опя́ть поѣ́хали.	Now we are moving again.
Гдѣ мы тепéрь?	Where are we now?
Кáжется, какъ бýдто мы висíмъ на вóздухѣ.	It looks as if we were suspended in the air.
Мы ѣ́демъ чрезъ мостъ.	We are passing over a viaduct.
Вотъ предпослѣ́дняя стáнція.	This is the last station but one.
Мы скóро бýдемъ у цѣ́ли нáшей поѣ́здки.	We shall soon have reached the end of our journey.
Это послѣ́дняя стáнція.	This is the last station.
Позвóльте взять вашъ билéтъ.	Your ticket, please.
Вотъ онъ.	Here it is.
Пойдéмъ искáть нáши вéщи.	Let us go and look for our things.

Когдá вы отправля́етесь въ Р.?	When do you start for R.?
Чéрезъ два дня.	In two days.
Въ котóромъ часý отхóдитъ парохóдъ?	At what o'clock does the steamer sail?
Въ четы́ре часá по полýдни.	At four o'clock in the afternoon.
Совѣ́тую вамъ немéдленно взять мѣ́сто.	I advise you to secure a berth at once.
Если вы бýдете мéдлить, то, можетъ быть, не найдéте для себя́ каюты.	If you wait any longer, perhaps you will not find a cabin.
Пéрвое или вторóе мѣ́сто вы возьмéте?	Which class do you wish to take, the first or the second?
Какíя цѣ́ны мѣстáмъ?	What is the fare?
Пéрвыя пятнáдцать рублéй, а вторы́я семь.	For first-cabin passengers it is fifteen roubles, and for the second class seven.
Возьмéмъ пéрвыя мѣстá.	Let us take first-cabin.

Гдѣ ва́ши ве́щи?	Where is your luggage?
Я уже́ отпра́вилъ ихъ на при́стань.	I have already sent it on to the landing place.
Вы о́чень хорошо́ сдѣ́лали.	You have done very well.
Бы́ли ли вы на пароходѣ́, что́бы взять для себя́ каю́ту?	Did you go on board to secure a berth?
У меня́ прекра́сная каю́та.	I have an excellent cabin.
Прекра́сно.	That's very good.
Во ско́лько вообще́ вре́мени вы дѣ́лаете э́тотъ путь?	What is the average time for the passage?
Мы обыкнове́нно употребля́емъ о́коло восемна́дцати часо́въ на весь путь.	The whole passage is generally about eighteen hours.
Не теря́йте вре́мени, парохо́дъ чрезъ по́лчаса отхо́дитъ.	Don't lose any more time; the steamer is going to start in half an hour.
Я слы́шу ко́локолъ.	I hear the bell.
Пойде́мте скорѣ́й.	Let us make haste.
Парохо́дъ мо́жетъ уйти́ безъ насъ.	The steamer might go without us.
Намъ на́добно разста́ться.	We must part.
Жела́ю вамъ счастли́ваго пути́.	I wish you a prosperous voyage.
Да благослови́тъ васъ Богъ!	May God bless you!
Пиши́те мнѣ скорѣ́й.	Let me hear from you soon.
Гдѣ моя́ каю́та?	Where is my berth?
Вотъ здѣ́сь; тутъ напи́сано ва́ше и́мя.	Here it is; your name is written on it.
Потруди́тесь отнести́ мой доро́жный мѣшо́къ въ каю́ту.	Please to take my travelling bag into my cabin.
Пойде́мте на па́лубу.	Let us go on deck.
Кто э́тотъ человѣ́къ, кото́рый стои́тъ на кожухѣ́?	What man is that on the paddle-box there?
Это капита́нъ.	It is the captain.
Мы идёмъ ско́ро.	We are going at a quick rate.
Мы такъ ско́ро не пойдёмъ, когду́ бу́демъ въ откры́томъ мо́рѣ.	We shall not go so fast, when we get into the open sea.
Здѣ́сь вода́ тиха́.	Here the water is calm.
Мо́ре о́чень бу́рно.	The sea is very rough.
Кака́я ужа́сная бу́ря!	What a terrible storm!
Не бо́йтесь, нѣтъ никако́й опа́сности.	Don't fear, there is no danger.
Не поста́вите ли вы па́русъ?	Are you going to hoist sail?
Нѣтъ, вѣтеръ проти́вный.	No, the wind is contrary.

Тѣмъ ху́же, переѣздъ бу́детъ продолжи́теленъ.	So much the worse; the passage will be long.
Я пойду́ въ каю́ту; я чу́вствую себя́ не о́чень хорошо́.	I shall go into my cabin; I do not feel well.
Мнѣ о́чень ду́рно.	I feel qualmish.
Это дѣйствіе морско́й болѣ́зни.	It is the effect of sea-sickness.
Поню́хайте ке́льнской воды́.	Try some eau-de-Cologne.
Вы́пейте немно́го джи́ну, э́то укрѣпи́тъ желу́докъ и вы почу́вствуете облегче́ніе.	Take a little gin; that will strengthen your stomach, and you will feel some relief.
Я о́чень слабъ.	I feel very weak.
Ля́гте, и вамъ бу́детъ лу́чше.	Lie down, and you will feel better.
Какъ вы провели́ ночь?	How have you passed the night?
Дово́льно ху́до; ма́шина не дава́ла мнѣ спать.	Rather badly; the engine would not let me sleep.
Гдѣ мы тепе́рь?	Where are we at present?
Мы ско́ро уви́димъ бе́регъ.	We shall soon see the shore.
Мо́ре ста́ло споко́йнѣе.	The sea is calmer.
Вѣ́теръ ужé не такъ силе́нъ, какъ пре́жде.	The wind does not blow so hard as it did before.
Ско́лько мы дѣ́лаемъ узло́въ въ часъ?	How many knots do we make an hour?
Спро́симъ объ э́томъ у рулева́го?	Let us ask the steersman.
Мы дѣ́лаемъ по десяти́ узло́въ въ часъ.	We are making ten knots an hour.
Мнѣ ка́жется, я ви́жу бе́регъ.	I think I can see the shore.
Мы ско́ро прибу́демъ.	We shall soon arrive.

17. ARRIVAL AT AN HOTEL.

Скажи́те мнѣ, сдѣ́лайте ми́лость, кака́я здѣсь лу́чшая гости́ница?	Pray tell me which is the best hotel here?
Вы мо́жете съ по́лною увѣ́ренностью идти́ въ гости́ницу...	You may go to the ......hotel with safety.
Въ како́й э́то у́лицѣ?	In what street is it?
Если хоти́те, я провожу́ васъ туда́.	If you like, I will go with you.
Эта гости́ница имѣ́етъ дово́льно хоро́шую нару́жность.	This inn has a very good appearance.

Войдёмъ.	Let us go in.
Можно ли у васъ поужинать?	Have you anything to give us for supper?
Есть у васъ свободныя комнаты?	Have you any spare rooms?
Можемъ мы здѣсь ночевать?	Can we sleep here?
Да, господа; вы найдёте здѣсь прекрасныя комнаты и хорошія постели.	Yes, gentlemen; you will find here excellent rooms, and good beds.
Я не забочусь о комнатѣ, лишь бы постель была хороша.	I don't care for the room provided the bed is good.
Вы нигдѣ не найдёте лучшихъ постелей.	You will nowhere find better beds.
Господа, чего вы желаете для вашего ужина?	Gentlemen, what do you wish for supper?
Подайте намъ бифстексъ, пирогъ съ уткой и сыру.	Let us have beefsteaks, a duck-pie, and some cheese.
Сверхъ того, дайте намъ лучшаго вашего вина.	And also, give us some of your best wine.
Больше ничего не желаете?	Do you want nothing else?
Нѣтъ. Только велите поскорѣй подавать намъ ужинать, мы хотимъ спать.	No. Only let us have our supper quickly, we want to go to sleep.
Сію минуту вамъ все подадутъ.	You will be served in a moment.
Чемоданы наши у насъ въ комнатахъ?	Are our trunks in our rooms?
Точно такъ, господа; я при себѣ велѣлъ перенести ихъ туда.	Certainly, gentlemen; I had them carried there in my presence.
Готовы ли наши комнаты?	Are our rooms ready?
Постланы ли постели?	Are the beds made?
Не забудьте, что завтра ровно въ шесть часовъ мы хотимъ ѣхать.	Don't forget that we want to set off to-morrow morning at six precisely.
Я непремѣнно разбужу васъ.	I shall not fail to call you.
Приготовили ли вы намъ счетъ?	Have you made out our bill?
Сколько мы вамъ должны?	How much do we owe you?
За все слѣдуетъ четыре рубля.	Four roubles in all.
Вотъ вамъ деньги.	Here is the money.
Покорнѣйше благодарю.	I thank you, Sir.
Прощайте.	Good-by.
Счастливый путь!	A prosperous journey to you!

18. TO HIRE A LODGING.

Мнѣ сказáли, что у васъ отдаю́тся кóмнаты въ наёмъ.	I have been told that you have apartments to let.
Позвóльте мнѣ ихъ вúдѣть.	Let me see them.
У меня́ ихъ мнóго и въ рáзныя цѣ́ны. Какъ вамъ угóдно нанять, на̀ день, на недѣ́лю или на мѣ́сяцъ?	I have several, and at different prices. How do you wish to hire them, by the day, the week or the month?
Покажи́те мнѣ ихъ, и потóмъ я скажу́ рѣши́тельно.	Show me them, and then I will tell you my decision.
Вотъ прекрáсная кóмната; онá въ пéрвомъ этажѣ́, и при ней есть осóбый кабинéтъ.	Here is a nice room; it is on the first floor, and there is a separate closet appertaining to it.
Онá не óчень великá, однáкожъ годи́тся для меня́.	It is not very large, but it will do for me.
Вы ви́дите, что тутъ есть все, что нýжно, и мéбель сáмая прили́чная.	You see that there is everything necessary, and the furniture is very neat.
Вся мéбель крáснаго дéрева.	All furniture is mahogany.
Вотъ два крéсла, шесть стýльевъ, нóвый ковéръ, прекрáсное зéркало и сáмые чи́стые зáнавѣсы.	Here are two armchairs, six chairs, a new carpet, a fine looking glass, and very neat curtains.
Сверхъ тогó два шкáпа по обѣ́имъ сторонáмъками́на.	Besides that, there are cupboards on both sides of the chimney-piece.
Что вы хоти́те за э́ту кóмнату?	How much do you ask for this apartment?
Если вы берéте её тóлько на нѣ́сколько дней, то по рублю́ за̀ день; на недѣ́лю — пять рублéй, а éжели вы нанимáете на мѣ́сяцъ, то бýдетъ стóить двáдцать рублéй.	If you take it only for a few days, a rouble a day; if by the week — five roubles; but if you hire it by the month, it will you cost twenty roubles.
Мнѣ кáжется, э́то немнóго дóрого.	I think that is rather dear.
Вы ви́дите, какъ здѣсь все прекрáсно.	You see how elegant every thing is here.

Ко́мната выхо́дитъ на у́лицу?	Does the room look into the street?
Нѣтъ, о́кна ея́ выхо́дятъ въ садъ.	No, Sir, it looks into the garden.
Тѣмъ лу́чше.	So much the better.
Посмо́тримъ, хорошо́ ли постéль, э́то гла́вное.	Let us see whether the bed is good, that is the principal thing.
Вы не мо́жете и жела́ть лу́чшей.	You cannot wish for a better one.
Ско́лько разъ вы перемѣня́ете просты́ни?	How often do you change the sheets?
Чрезъ ка́ждыя двѣ недѣли.	Every fortnight.
Не дыми́ться ли ками́нъ?	Does the chimney smoke?
Нима́ло не дыми́тся.	Not in the least.
Если все такъ, то я беру́ ко́мнату на три мѣ́сяца.	If every thing is as you say, I will take the room for three months.
Я велю́ принести́ мои́ вéщи, и заплачу́ вамъ за мѣ́сяцъ впере́дъ.	I will have my things carried here, and pay you one month in advance.

19. INQUIKING THE WAY.

Дале́ко ли отсю́да почта́мтъ?	Is the post-office far from here?
Не такъ дале́ко; въ тре́тьей у́лицѣ, на пра́во.	Not very; it is in the third street on the right hand.
На по́чтѣ должны́ быть пи́сьма къ намъ.	There must be some letters for us lying at the post-office.
Въ каку́ю сто́рону мнѣ на́добно идти́?	Which way must I go?
Иди́те все пря́мо.	Straight along.
Ступа́йте по э́тому переу́лку, онъ вы́ведетъ васъ на большу́ю у́лицу.	Go along this lane, and it will lead you into a wide street.
Сдѣ́лайте ми́лость, покажи́те мнѣ доро́гу въ...	Pray, show me the way to .....
Не мо́жете ли сказа́ть мнѣ, какъ пройти́ къ... воро́тамъ?	Can you tell me which is the way to go to .....gate?

Возьмите на лѣво и ступайте все прямо.	Turn to the left, and then go straight along.
Покорнѣйше благодарю.	I thank you, Sir.
Нé за что.	Oh don't mention it.
Не знаете ли вы здѣсь господина Н.?	Do you know Mr. N. in this place?
Я знаю его очень хорошо.	I know him very well.
Не можете ли сказать, гдѣ онъ живётъ?	Can you tell me where he lives?
Онъ живётъ близъ... моста.	He lives near the .....bridge.
Это далеко отсюда?	Is it far from here?
Очень близко.	It is but a very little way.
Не можете ли показать мнѣ его домъ?	Can you direct me to his house?
Я покажу вамъ, гдѣ онъ живётъ.	I will show you where he lives.
Я иду самъ въ ту сторону.	I am going that way myself.
Вы меня очень обяжете.	You will greatly oblige me.

20. DRIVING IN A DROSHKEY OR AN OMNIBUS.

Куда вы пойдете сегодня утромъ?	Where shall you go this morning?
Мнѣ надобно сдѣлать нѣсколько визитовъ.	I have several visits to pay.
Прежде всего мнѣ надобно сходить къ нашему пріятелю, господину Н.	First of all I must give a call to to our friend, Mr. N.
Отправимтесь къ нему вмѣстѣ.	Let us go to him together.
Пойдёмъ.	Come along.
На извощикѣ или пѣшкомъ мы отправимся?	Shall we take a droshkey or go on foot?
Возьмёмъ извощика, а то устанемъ.	Let us take a droshkey, or else we may be tired.
Какъ вамъ угодно.	Just as you like.
Вотъ извощикъ стоитъ.	There I see a cabman.
Извощикъ! въ ....улицу?	Cabman, (how much is it) to ....street?
Только туда?	Only there?

То́лько туда́.	Yes.
Туда́ и обра́тно.	No, you are to bring us back again.
А до́лго ли тамъ пробу́дете?	And how long are you going to stop there?
Мину́тъ де́сять, не бо́льше.	Not longer than about ten minutes.
Полти́нникъ, безъ ли́шняго.	Fifty copeeks — that's the least I can take.
Мно́го — со́рокъ копе́екъ.	That is too much — forty copeeks is enough. *
Поми́луйте, су́дарь, вѣдь въ два конца́.	For pity's sake, Sir; why, it is a double journey.
Ну, со́рокъ пять копе́екъ.	Well, I'll give you forty five copeeks.
Эхъ, господи́нъ, не жалѣ́йте пяти́ копе́екъ.	Ah, Sir! you needn't mind the five copeeks.
Бо́льше не дамъ.	I shall not give you any more.
Хорошо́, сади́тесь.	Well, get in.
Поѣзжа́й поскорѣ́е.	Drive on a little faster.
Поми́луйте, су́дарь, вѣдь вы са́ми зна́ете, кака́я у насъ ны́нче худа́я доро́га.	For pity's sake, Sir; you can see how bad the roads are just now.
Вотъ, наконецъ, мы пріѣ́хали.	Here we are arrived at last.
Останови́сь у тре́тьяго крыльца́ (у вторы́хъ воро́тъ) по пра́вой рукѣ́.	Stop at the third street-door (the second gate) on the right hand side.
Нѣтъ ли у тебя́ сда́чи на рубль?	Can you give me change for a rouble?
Ниче́го нѣтъ, су́дарь; я то́лько что съ почи́ну.	No, Sir, I have no money at all about me; this is my first job this day.
Ну, такъ я размѣня́ю въ ла́вкѣ.	In that case I must get some small change at the next shop.
Вотъ тебѣ́ де́ньги.	Here is your money.

* This is a literal translation of the Russian, and is constantly employed in this sense by the lower classes.

Дайте знакъ кучеру, чтобъ онъ остановился.	Make the coachman a sign to stop.
Позовите кондуктора.	Call the conductor.
Нѣтъ мѣста.	There is no room left.
Экипажъ полонъ.	The omnibus is quite full.
Есть одно только мѣсто.	There is room for only one person more.
Надобно подождать.	We must wait.
Вотъ другой омнибусъ.	There is another omnibus.
Онъ ѣдетъ въ другую сторону.	It is going in a different direction.
Кондукторъ, куда вы ѣдете?	I say, conductor, where are you going?
Мы ѣдемъ въ.... улицу.	We are going to .....street.
Вотъ омнибусъ, который намъ нуженъ.	This is the omnibus we want.
Сядемъ.	Let us get in.
Взойдите вы прежде.	You get in first.
Я не могу сѣсть.	I cannot sit down here.
Сдѣлайте милость, подвиньтесь немного.	Make a little room there, if you please.
Здѣсь довольно мѣста для двухъ.	Here is plenty of room for two.
Садитесь возлѣ меня.	Sit down beside me.
Сядьте на этомъ мѣстѣ.	Sit down in that place.
Я сяду здѣсь.	I shall take my seat here.
Подвиньтесь поближе.	Move this way.
Мнѣ здѣсь хорошо.	I am all right here.
Вы иностранецъ?	Are you a foreigner, Sir?
Да, я Англичанинъ.	Yes, Sir. I am an Englishman.
Давно ли вы въ Петербургѣ?	How long have you been at St. Petersburg?
Я здѣсь двѣ недѣли.	I have been here this fortnight.
Какъ вамъ здѣсь нравится.	How do you like this place?
Петербургъ мнѣ очень нравится.	I like St. Petersburg very well.
Долго ли вы здѣсь пробудете?	Are you going to stay here long?
Я намѣренъ провести лѣто въ Петербургѣ.	I intend passing the summer at St. Petersburg.
Видѣли ли вы все достойное примѣчанія?	Have you seen all the curiosities of the place?
Нѣтъ еще.	Not yet.
Мы ѣдемъ очень тихо.	We are driving very slowly.
Тише ѣдешь, дальше будешь.	«Fair and softly goes far.»
Когда я спѣшу, то никогда не ѣзжу въ городской каретѣ.	When I am in a hurry, I never go in an omnibus.

Гдѣ мы тепéрь?	Where are we now?
Въ.... ýлицѣ.	In .....street.
Мы ещé только на половúнѣ дорóги.	We have only made half the way.
Потéрпимъ немнóго.	We must have patience for a little while.
Посмотрúте на э́тотъ прекрáсный домъ.	Look at that fine house.
Какóй прекрáсный видъ.	What a beautiful sight.
Вотъ прекрáсное мѣ́сто для прогýлку.	Here is a very nice place for a promenade.
Вотъ домъ, гдѣ я живý.	There is the house in which I live.
Кондуктóръ, вы́садите меня́ на углý.... ýлицы.	Conductor, put me down at the corner of .....street.
Остановúте, пожáлуйста.	Stop here, if you please.
Позвóльте мнѣ прéжде вы́дти.	Let me get down first.
Дáйте рýки.	Give me your hand.
Не спѣшúте.	Do not be in too great a hurry.
Берегúтесь, чтобъ не упáсть.	Be careful lest you fall.
Я провожý васъ.	I shall accompany you.
Благодáрю за вáше предложéніе.	I thank you for your offer.
Проводúте меня́ до концá ýлицы.	Accompany me as far as the end of that street.
Благодарю́ васъ за вашъ трудъ.	I thank you for your trouble.

PART V.

OUTLINES OF RUSSIAN GRAMMAR. *

SUBSTANTIVES. **

In the Russian language there are three genders: the *masculine*, *feminine*, and *neuter*.

The *gender* of substantives may be known by their *meaning* or their *termination*.

By their *meaning:* all the names of living beings of the male sex are *masculine*, as дядя, uncle, левъ, lion, and those of the female sex are *feminine*, as дочь, daughter, львица, lioness.

By their *termination:* those ending in *ъ* and *й* are *masculine*, as орёлъ, eagle, муравей, ant; those ending in *а* and *я* are *feminine*, as шпага, sword, лилія, lily; those ending in *о*, *е*, and *мя* are *neuter*.

* In these outlines no definitions of grammatical terms have been given, the student being considered to be acquainted with general grammar.

** There are no articles in the Russian language.

as окно́, window, мо́ре, sea, вре́мя, time. To the *neuter* gender belongs also the word *дитя́*, child. As to the nouns ending in *ь*, some are *masculine*, as кора́бль, ship, and others *feminine*, as тѣнь, shadow: the gender of these nouns may be known by the termination of the genitive case.

Some substantives denoting living beings of either sex are of the *common* gender, as сирота́, orphan.

Some nouns are employed only in the singular number, others only in the plural, even when the latter denote but *one* object.

Such as have *no plural* are: 1. The greater part of *proper nouns*, as Москва́, Moscow, Во́лга, the Volga; 2. many *names of material*, as зо́лото, gold, молоко́, milk; 3. names of *virtues* and *vices*, as терпѣ́ніе, patience, лѣ́ность, laziness; many names of abstract qualities, as ста́рость, old age, мо́лодость, youth; 4. many names of plants, especially vegetables, as морко́вь, carrots, лукъ, onion.

Those that want the *singular* denote various objects, as лю́ди, men, people, са́ни, a sledge, но́жницы, scissors, дрова́, wood; also ancient towns and places, f. ex. Ѳи́вы, Thebes, Аѳи́ны, Athens.

There are seven *Cases* in the Russian language: the *Nominative, Vocative, Genitive, Dative, Accusative, Instrumental,* and *Prepositional.*

Rem. The vocative case is like the nominative. The prepositional is always employed after the prepositions о, объ (of), въ, во (in), на (on), при (by, near), по (after).

There are three *declensions* in the Russian language. The 1st declension comprises all nouns of the *masculine* gender ending in *ъ*, *й*, and *ь*; the 2d all substantives, *masculine* or *feminine*, ending in *а* and *я*, and *feminine* nouns in *ь*; the 3d includes all nouns ending in *о*, *е*, and *мя* belonging to the *neuter* gender.

Substantives are declined after the following table:

	I.			II.			III.		
	Singular.								
N. V.	ъ	й	ь	а	я	ь	о	е	я
Gen.	а	я	я	ы(и)	и	и	а	я	ени
Dat.	у	ю	ю	ѣ	ѣ	и	у	ю	ени
Acc.	like the Nom. or Gen.			у	ю	ь	о	е	я
Instr.	омъ	емъ	емъ	ою	ею	ію, ью	омъ	емъ	енемъ
Prep.	ѣ	ѣ	ѣ	ѣ	ѣ	и	ѣ	ѣ	ени
	Plural.								
N. V.	ы	и	и	ы(и)	и	и	а	я	ена
Gen.	овъ	евъ	ей	ъ	ь	ей	ъ	ей	енъ
Dat.	амъ	ямъ	ямъ	амъ	ямъ	ямъ	амъ	ямъ	енамъ
Acc.	like the			Nominative			or Genitive.		
Instr.	ами	ями	ями	ами	ями	ями	ами	ями	енами
Prep.	ахъ	яхъ	яхъ	ахъ	яхъ	яхъ	ахъ	яхъ	енахъ

EXAMPLES OF THE 1ST DECLENSION.

Singular.

N. V.	слонъ, * an elephant.	столъ, a table.	покой, a chamber.	царь, the Tsar.
G.	слона́, of an elephant.	стола́.	поко́я.	царя́.
D.	слону́, to an elephant.	столу́.	поко́ю.	царю́.
A.	слона́, an elephant.	столъ.	поко́й.	царя́.
I.	слоно́мъ, by or with an elephant.	столо́мъ.	поко́емъ.	царе́мъ.
P.	о слонѣ́,** of or about an elephant.	о столѣ́.	о поко́ѣ.	о царѣ́.

Plural.

N. V.	слоны́, elephants.	столы́.	поко́и.	цари́.
G.	слоно́въ, of elephants.	столо́въ.	поко́евъ.	царе́й.
D.	слона́мъ, to elephants.	стола́мъ.	поко́ямъ.	царя́мъ.
A.	слоно́въ, elephants.	столы́.	поко́и.	царе́й.
I.	слона́ми, by or with elephants.	стола́ми.	поко́ями.	царя́ми.
P.	о слона́хъ, of elephants.	о стола́хъ.	о поко́яхъ.	о царя́хъ.

* There being no articles in the Russian language, *слонъ* may be rendered either by *an* elephant or *the* elephant, and in the vocative by ŏ elephant! In every other respect the English translation of the cases of any other noun is like that of *elephant* as given here, and for this reason is not repeated.

** The prepositional case has no signification without a preposition; о, объ, of, is therefore prefixed as being the preposition most commonly used with it.

Singular.

N. V.	льстецъ, a flatterer.	урожа́й, a crop.	трофе́й, a trophy.	ключъ, a key.
G.	льстеца́.	урожа́я.	трофе́я.	ключа́.
D.	льстецу́.	урожа́ю.	трофе́ю.	ключу́.
A.	льстеца́.	урожа́й.	трофе́й.	ключъ.
I.	льстецо́мъ.	урожа́емъ.	трофе́емъ.	ключо́мъ.
P.	о льсте́цѣ́.	объ урожа́ѣ.	о трофе́ѣ.	о ключѣ́.

Plural.

N. V.	льстецы́.	урожа́и.	трофе́и.	ключи́.
G.	льстецо́въ.	урожа́евъ.	трофе́евъ.	ключе́й.
D.	льстеца́мъ.	урожа́ямъ.	трофе́ямъ.	ключа́мъ.
A.	льстецо́въ.	урожа́и.	трофе́и.	ключи́.
I.	льстеца́ми.	урожа́ями.	трофе́ями.	ключа́ми.
P.	о льстеца́хъ.	объ урожа́яхъ.	о трофе́яхъ.	о ключа́хъ.

EXAMPLES OF THE 2ND DECLENSION.

Singular.

N. V.	слуга́, a servant.	звѣзда́, a star.	пу́ля, a bullet.	часть, a part.
G.	слуги́.	звѣзды́.	пу́ли.	ча́сти.
D.	слугѣ́.	звѣздѣ́.	пу́лѣ.	ча́сти.
A.	слугу́.	звѣзду́.	пу́лю.	часть.
I.	слуго́ю.	звѣздо́ю.	пу́лею.	ча́стью.
P.	о слугѣ́.	о звѣздѣ́.	о пу́лѣ.	о ча́сти.

Plural.

N. V.	слу́ги.	звѣ́зды (pr. zvyŏz-dŭĭ).	пу́ли.	ча́сти.
G.	слугъ.	звѣздъ.	пу́лей.	часте́й.
D.	слуга́мъ.	звѣ́здамъ.	пу́лямъ.	частя́мъ.
A.	слу́ги.	звѣ́зды.	пу́ли.	ча́сти.
I.	слуга́ми.	звѣ́здами.	пу́лями.	частя́ми.
P.	о слуга́хъ.	о звѣ́здахъ.	о пу́ляхъ.	о частя́хъ.

Singular.

N. V.	вельмóж*а*, a grandee.	дя́дя, an uncle.	ли́лія, a lily.	рóщ*а*, a grove.
G.	вельмóж*и*.	дя́д*и*.	ли́лі*и*.	рóщ*и*.
D.	вельмóж*ѣ*.	дя́д*ѣ*.	ли́лі*и*.	рóщ*ѣ*.
A.	вельмóж*у*.	дя́дю.	ли́лію.	рóщ*у*.
I.	вельмóж*ею*.	дя́д*ею*.	ли́лі*ею*.	рóщ*ею*.
P.	о вельмóж*ѣ*.	о дя́д*ѣ*.	о ли́лі*и*.	о рóщ*ѣ*.

Plural.

N. V.	вельмóж*и*.	дя́д*и*.	ли́лі*и*.	рóщ*и*.
G.	вельмóжъ.	дя́д*ей*.	ли́лі*й*.	рощъ.
D.	вельмóж*амъ*.	дя́д*ямъ*.	ли́лі*ямъ*.	рóщ*амъ*.
A.	вумьмóжъ.	дя́д*ей*.	ли́лі*и*.	рóщ*и*.
I.	вельмóж*ами*.	дя́д*ями*.	ли́лі*ями*.	рóщ*ами*.
P.	о вельмóж*ахъ*.	о дя́д*яхъ*.	о ли́лі*яхъ*.	о рóщ*ахъ*.

EXAMPLES OF THE 3D DECLENSION.

Singular.

N. V.	дѣло, an affair.	по́ле, a field.	мнѣ́ніе, an opinion.	і́мя, a name.
G.	дѣла.	по́ля.	мнѣ́нія.	і́мени.
D.	дѣлу.	по́лю.	мнѣ́нію.	і́мени.
A.	дѣло.	по́ле.	мнѣ́ніе.	і́мя.
I.	дѣломъ.	по́лемъ.	мнѣ́ніемъ.	і́менемъ.
P.	о дѣлѣ.	о по́лѣ.	о мнѣ́ніи.	объ і́мени.

Plural.

N. V.	дѣла́.	поля́.	мнѣ́нія.	имена́.
G.	дѣлъ.	поле́й.	мнѣ́ній.	име́нъ.
D.	дѣла́мъ.	поля́мъ.	мнѣ́ніямъ.	имена́мъ.
A.	дѣла́.	поля́.	мнѣ́нія.	имена́.
I.	дѣла́ми.	поля́ми.	мнѣ́ніями.	имена́ми.
P.	о дѣла́хъ.	о поля́хъ.	о мнѣ́ніяхъ.	объ имена́хъ.

Singular.

N. V.	лицó, a face, a person.	учи́лище, a school.
G.	лиц*á*.	учи́лищ*а*.
D.	лиц*ý*.	учи́лищ*у*.
A.	лиц*ó*.	учи́лищ*е*.
I.	лиц*óмъ*.	учи́лищ*емъ*.
P.	о лиц*ѣ́*.	объ учи́лищ*ѣ*.

Plural.

N. V.	ли́ц*а*.	учи́лищ*а*.
G.	лицъ.	учи́лищъ.
D.	ли́ц*амъ*.	учи́лищ*амъ*.
A.	ли́ц*а*.	учи́лищ*а*.
I.	ли́ц*ами*.	учи́лищ*ами*.
P.	о ли́ц*ахъ*.	объ учи́лищ*ахъ*.

OBSERVATIONS.

1. Words ending in *жъ, чъ, шъ, щъ* form their genitive plural in *ей*, and not in *овъ*, as ключъ, a key, ключ*é́й*; падé*жъ*, case, падеж*éй*.

2. The letter *ы* can never be put after *г, ж, к, х, ч, ш, щ*, but must be replaced by *и*; therefore the nominative plural of nouns ending in *г*, and the genitive singular and nominative plural of those in *а*, should be: враг*и́*, enemies, нож*и́*, knives, кни́г*и*, of the book, рýк*и*, the hands, and not врагы́, ножы́, кни́гы, рýкы.

3. After the same letters, *я* is replaced by *а*, and *ю* by *у*; thus the genitive singular of сéрдце, the heart, is сéрдц*а*, not сéрдц*я*, and the dative сéрдц*у*, not сéрдц*ю*.

4. The letter *о* after *ж, ц, ч, ш, щ*, is generally changed into *е*; thus the instrumental of рóща, a grove, вельмóжа, a grandee, is

рощею, вельможею, and not рощою, вельможою. Sometimes *o* is not changed into *e*, when the last syllable has the accent, as ножъ. knife, ножо́мъ.

5. The letter *ь*, after a vowel, is changed into *й*; thus шея, the neck, лилія, a lily, have in the genitive plural шей, лилій.

6. Substantives ending in *дя* and *ря*, terminate in the genitive plural in *ей*, as дядя, uncle; дядей, буря, a storm, бурей.

7. The letter *ѣ* never follows *i*, consequently the dative and prepositional singular of nouns ending in *ія*, and the prepositional singular of those terminating in *ій* and *іе* should be written with *и*, not with *ѣ*, as Франціи, to France, о лиліи, of the lily, въ сочиненіи, in the composition.

8. Many names of material ending in *й*, *ъ* and *ь*, form their genitives by taking the termination of the dative *у* and *ю*, as фунтъ чаю, a pound of tea, кусо́къ бархату, a piece of velvet.

9. The accusative singular of masculine substantives in *ъ*, *й* and *ь*, which denote an inanimate or abstract object, is like the nominative; but of those which denote an animate being, like the genitive. The same rule applies to the accusative case of substantives of all the three genders in the plural number.

10. The vocative is always like the nominative, but in some substantives it has peculiar terminations proper to the Slavonic church dialect, for example Богъ, God, Бо́же! Госпо́дь, the Lord, Го́споди! Іису́съ, Jesus, Іисусе! Христо́съ, Christ, Христе́! Оте́цъ, Father, Отче! Влады́ка, Lord, Master, Влады́ко! Богоро́дица, the mother of God, Богоро́дице! Царь, Tsar, Царю́!

11. Of the substantives in *мя* one only, сѣмя, seed, has an irregular termination, its genitive plural being сѣмянъ, not сѣменъ.

12. The words: не́бо, heaven, and чу́до, miracle, are thus declined in the plural: небеса́, чудеса́, небе́съ, чуде́съ, and so on; but when чу́до, denotes a prodigy, a monster, its plural is inflected: чу́ды, чудъ, чу́дамъ.

13. The genitive plural of nouns ending in *іе*, is *ій*, not *іей*, f. ex. мнѣній, of the opinions, not мнѣніей.

14. The following words: человѣкъ, man, солдатъ, a soldier, драгу́нъ, a dragoon, гуса́ръ, a hussar, ула́нъ, a lancer, каде́тъ, a cadet, Ту́рокъ, a Turk, гренаде́ръ, a grenadier, ре́крутъ, a recruit, and several others undergo no change in the genitive plural. The same rule applies also to the words: арши́нъ, an arsheen (2 feet 4 inches), пудъ, a pood (36 pounds 2 ounces), чуло́къ, a stocking. Саже́нь, a Russian fathom, has са́женъ in the genitive plural, not са́жень or саженей.

15. Some substantives ending in *й* and *ъ* form their prepositional cases by taking *у* or *ю* instead of *ѣ*, when their last syllables are accented, as на бок*у́*, on one side, въ ряд*у́*, in the row, въ лѣс*у́*, in the wood, въ ра*ю́*, in paradise, на кра*ю́*, on the brink.

Examples of substantves deviating still more from the general rules:

1. Nouns ending in *анинъ* and *янинъ*. They are declined regularly in the singular, and as follows in the plural:

N. V. Англича́н*е*, Englishmen, крестья́н*е*, peasants; G. Англича́нъ, крестья́нъ; D. Англича́н*амъ*, крестья́н*амъ*; A. Англича́нъ, крестья́нъ; I. Англича́н*ами*, крестья́н*ами*; P. объ Англича́н*ахъ*, о крестья́н*ахъ*.

2. Nouns denoting animals and terminating in *ёнокъ:*

Singular.

N.V. телёнокъ, a calf.
G. телёнк*а*.
D. телёнк*у*.
A. телёнк*а*.
I. телёнк*омъ*.
P. о телёнк*ѣ*.

Plural.

N.V. тел*я́та*.
G. тел*я́тъ*.
D. тел*я́тамъ*.
A. тел*я́тъ*.
I. тел*я́тами*.
P. тел*я́тахъ*.

According to this example are declined: ребёнокъ, an infant, жеребёнокъ, a foal, поросёнокъ, a pig, цыплёнокъ, a chicken, etc.

Singular.

волчёнокъ, a young wolf.
волчёнк*а*.
волчёнк*у*.
волчёнк*а*.
волчёнк*омъ*.
о волчёнк*ѣ*.

Plural.

волч*а́та*.
волч*а́тъ*.
волч*а́тамъ*.
волч*а́тъ*.
волч*а́тами*.
о волч*а́тахъ*.

According to this example is declined: медвѣжёнокъ, a young bear; but львёнокъ, a lion's whelp, changes in the plural into львёнки, мышёнокъ, a little mouse, into мышёнки.

The declension of the following substantives is perfectly irregular:

Singular.

N. V.	дитя́, a child.	мать, a mother.	це́рковь, a church.	путь, a way.
G.	дитя́*ти*.	ма́т*ери*.	це́рк*ви*.	пут*и́*.
D.	дитя́*ти*.	ма́т*ери*.	це́рк*ви*.	пут*и́*.
A.	дитя́.	ма́ть.	це́рковь.	путь.
I.	дитя́*тею*.	ма́т*ерью*.	це́рковью.	пут*е́мъ*.
P.	о дитя́*ти*.	о ма́т*ери*.	о це́рк*ви*.	о пут*и́*.

Plural.

N. V.	д*ѣ́ти*.	ма́т*ери*.	це́рк*ви*.	пут*и́*.
G.	д*ѣте́й*.	мат*ере́й*.	церкв*е́й*.	пут*е́й*.
D.	д*ѣ́тямъ*.	мат*еря́мъ*.	церкв*а́мъ*.	пут*я́мъ*.
A.	д*ѣте́й*.	мат*ере́й*.	це́рк*ви*.	пут*и́*.
I.	д*ѣтьми́*.	мат*еря́ми*.	церкв*а́ми*.	пут*я́ми*.
P.	о д*ѣ́тяхъ*.	о мат*еря́хъ*.	о церкв*а́хъ*.	о пут*я́хъ*.

Rem. The word дочь, a daughter, is declined like мать.

N. Христо́съ, Christ, Госпо́дь, the Lord. G. Христа́, Го́спода. D. Христу́, Го́споду. A. Христа́, Го́спода. V. Христе́, Го́споди. I. Христо́мъ, Го́сподомъ. P. о Христѣ́, о Го́сподѣ.

The following substantives undergo peculiar alterations in the the genitive as well as the other oblique cases:

by changing *e* into *ь*:

левъ, a lion, льва.
ледъ, ice, льда.
ленъ, flax, льна.
ручéй, a brook, ручья́.
у́лей, a bee-hive, у́лья.
воробéй, a sparrow, воробья́.
муравéй, an ant, муравья́.
соловéй, a nightingale, соловья́.
жилéцъ, a lodger, жильца́.

by changing *e* into *й*:

наéмъ, rent, hire, найма́.
заéмъ, a loan, займа́.
перешéекъ, an isthmus, перешейка.
боéцъ, a champion, бойца́.

by changing *я* into *й*:

за́яцъ, a hare, за́йца.

by the elision of *e*:

молéбенъ, Te Deum, молéбна.
Па́велъ, Paul, Па́вла.
орéлъ, an eagle, орла́.
котéлъ, a kettle, котла́.
у́зелъ, a knot, узла́.
пéпелъ, ashes, пéпла.
козéлъ, a he-goat, козла́.
осéлъ, an ass, осла́.
купéцъ, a merchant, купца́.
отéцъ, father, отца́.
ка́мень, a stone, ка́мня.
пéнь, a stump, пня.
день, a day, дня.
ремéнь, a strap, ремня́.
ковéръ, a carpet, ковра́.
вѣ́теръ, wind, вѣ́тра.
шатéръ, a tent, шатра́,
костéръ, a pile, костра́.
хребéтъ, a ridge, хребта́.
Еги́петъ, Egypt, Еги́пта.

овёсъ, oats, овса́.
песъ, a cur, пса.
а́гнецъ, lamb, а́гнца.
самодéржецъ, an autocrat, самодéржца.
стéбель, stalk, стéбля.
ка́шель, cough, ка́шля.
сéлезень, drake, сéлезня.
кулёкъ, a mat-bag, кулька́, and others ending in *екъ*.

by the elision of *o*:

сонъ, sleep, сна.
хохо́лъ, crest, хохла́.
но́готь, a finger-nail, но́гтя.
ого́нь, fire, огня́.
псало́мъ, a psalm, псалма́.
у́голъ, a corner, угла́.
у́голь, coal, у́гля.
у́горь, an eel, угря́.
лобъ, the forehead, лба.
посо́лъ, an ambassador, посла́.
чехо́лъ, a cover, чехла́.
баго́ръ, a boathook, багра́.
буго́ръ, a hillock, бугра́.
вихо́ръ, forelock, вихра́.
свёкоръ, a husband's father, свёкра.
ротъ, mouth, рта.
за́мокъ, a castle, за́мка.
замо́къ, a lock, замка́.
дёготь, birch-tar, дёгтя.
шовъ, seam, шва.
уча́стокъ, a share, уча́стка.
ломо́ть, a slice, ломтя́.
ло́коть, the ebow, ло́ктя.
чуло́къ, a stocking, чулка́, and many nouns ending in *окъ*.

The following substantives have peculiar terminations in the nominative plural:

о́ко, the eye, о́чи.
у́хо, the ear, у́ши.
рука́въ, a sleeve, рукава́.
лѣ́карь, a physician, лѣкаря́.
глазъ, the eye, глаза́.
боя́ринъ, a lord, боя́ре.
ба́ринъ, master, ба́ре.
го́сподинъ, a gentleman, господа́.
хозя́инъ, landlord, хозя́ева.
шу́ринъ, a wife's brother, шу́рья.
братъ, brother, бра́тья.
кумъ, godfather, кумовья́.
другъ, a friend, друзья́.
князь, a prince, князья́.
со́лнце, the sun, со́лнцы.
о́блако, a cloud, облака́ (genitive облако́въ, etc.).

Домъ, a house, has домá and дóмы; учи́тель, a teacher — учителя́ and учи́тели; профéссоръ, a professor — профессорá and профéссоры. The former terminations are more frequently employed in conversation, and the latter in writing.

Стулъ, a chair, has стýлья; прутъ, a twig — прýтья; сукъ, a bough — сýчья. Like them, other nouns easily noticed in practice take the termination *ья*.

The following substantives have two meanings, and take two forms in the plural:

Хлѣбъ, a loaf, has хлѣбы.
— corn, хлѣбá.
Цвѣтъ, a flower, цвѣты́.
— colour, цвѣтá.
Зубъ, a tooth, зýбы.
— — (of instruments), зýбья.
Мѣхъ, bellows, мѣхи.
— fur, мѣхá.

Листъ, a sheet, листы́.
— a leaf, ли́стья.
Мужъ, a man, мужи́.
— a husband, мужья́.
Сынъ, son (of a father), сыновья́.
— son (of his country), сыны́.

The substantives: дéрево, a tree; кáмень, a stone; ýголь, coal; кóрень, a root; крюкъ, a hook, have also two forms in the plural: деревá and дерéвья; кáмни and камéнья; ýгли and ýголья; кóрни and корéнья, крю́ки and крю́чья. The latter terminations are given to these words, when they are employed as collective nouns.

The vowels *о* and *е* are very often inserted in the genitive plural of feminine substantives in *а* and *я*, and neuter ones in *о*, preceded by two consonants. Thus the genitive plural of пáлка, stick, is not палкъ, but пáлокъ; of ю́бка, petticoat, ю́бокъ; of оши́бка, a fault, оши́бокъ; of кóшка, a cat, кóшекъ. In the same manner is formed the genitive of the following words: буты́лка, a bottle, бóчка, a cask, овцá, a sheep, земля́, the earth, коню́шня, a stable, дерéвня, a village, веслó, an oar, числó, a number, крéсло, an arm-chair, oкнó, a window, etc., namely: бутылокъ, бочекъ, овецъ, земель, конюшенъ, деревень, весел, чисел, кресел, оконъ. — For the same reason, the genitive plural of substantives ending in йка, лька, дьба, takes the terminatitions екъ, лекъ, дебъ: thus чайка, a gull, has чаекъ, копейка, a copeck, копеекъ; Полька, a (female) Pole, Полекъ; свадьба, a wedding, свадебъ.

Кушанье, eating, has кушаньевъ; помѣстье, an estate, помѣстій.

Substantives having the *plural number only*, if masculine, are declined according to the 1st declension; if feminine, according to the 2d; and if neuter, according to the 3d.

The gender of these nouns may be known by their *nominative* and *genitive* cases:

1. Substantives ending in the nominative in *ы* or *и*, and in the genitive in *евъ* and *овъ*, are *masculine*, as щипцы, pincers, щипцовъ; тиски, a press, тисковъ; обои, hangings, обоевъ. Eccept: оковы, fetters, оковъ, which is feminine.

2. All other nouns ending in the nominative plural in *ы* or *и*, whatever be the termination of the genitive, are *feminine*, as сани, a sledge, саней; ножницы, scissors, ножницъ; сливки, cream, сливокъ. Except: люди, men, people, which is masculine.

3. All substantives whose nominative plural terminates in *а* are *neuter*, as ворота, the gate, дрова, fuel, уста, the lips.

In compound substantives only the last word is declined, as мореходецъ, seafarer, мореходца. мореходцу, etc.

If two nouns stand separately, and at the same time in different cases, only the first, which is in the nominative, is declined, as *отецъ* семейства, father of a family, *отца* семейства, *отцу* семейства; *опись* вещамъ, an inventory of the articles, *описью* вещамъ, etc.

All nouns of which *полъ* or *полу* (half) forms a component part, as пóлдень, noon, пóлночь, midnight, полумѣра, half-measure, have *полу* in all their cases: полудня, полýдню, полýднемъ, о полýднѣ.

ADJECTIVES.

Adjectives must agree with their substantives in gender, number and case.

Adjectives have *seven* terminations in the nominative singular: *ый, ой, ій* are of the masculine gender; *ая, яя* of the feminine; and *ое, ее* of the neuter gender.

Adjectives in general are varied by their declensions; but *qualificative** adjectives, may further change in form by *apocopating* their terminations, and taking the *degrees of comparison.*

Apocopation is the abbreviation of the full termination, for ex. changing стрóг*ій, ая, ое,* strict, into строгъ, стрóг*а*, стрóго. The terminations of apocopated adjectives are: in the singular number *ъ, ь* for the *masculine, а, я* for the *feminine,* and *о, е* for the *neuter;* in the plvral *ы, и* for all three genders.

Adjectives called *personal possessive* have only the last-mentioned apocopated terminations. They are formed from names of persons, professions etc. by changing the masculine terminations into *овъ* and *евъ*, and the feminine into *инъ* and *ынъ*, as ивáновъ from Ивáнъ, John, андрéевъ from Андрéй, Andrew, отцéвъ from отéцъ, father, мáрьинъ from Мáрья, Mary, сéстринъ from сестрá, sister.

There are three *degrees of comparison:* 1. the *positive,* as, *вáжный* проéктъ, an important project, *высóкая* горá, a high mountain, *чéрное* сукно, black cloth; 2. the *comparative,* as, вы оказáли мнѣ *важнѣйшую* услýгу, нéжели онъ, you have rendered me a more important service than he, это сукнó *чернѣе*, нéжели твоé, this

* i. e. expressing the quality or property of an object.

cloth is blacker than yours, братъ мой *вы́ше* тебя́, my brother is taller than you; 3. the *superlative*, as, вы избрали *са́мую ва́жную* до́лжность, you have chosen the most important duty, онъ чита́етъ *весьма́ поле́зную* книгу, he reads a very useful book, вотъ *са́мое че́рное* сукно́, here is the blackest cloth, это *наилу́чшее* сре́дство, this is the best means.

Adjectives in the comparative degree have a *full* termination and an *apocopated* one. The full termination is *ѣйшій* and *айшій*, as сильн*ѣйшій*, the strongest, глубоч*айшій*, the deepest; the apocopated one is *ѣе, ѣй, же, че, ше, ще*, as сильн*ѣе*, сильн*ѣй*, stronger, глу́б*же*, deeper, ле́г*че*, easier, ти́*ше*, calmer, сла́*ще*, sweeter.

Rem. The terminations *ѣйшій* and *айшій* may sometimes be employed to indicate the superlative degree, as, Россія есть величайшее государство въ свѣтѣ, Russia is the largest empire in the world.

The superlative degree is formed: 1. by prefixing the word *са́мый* or *пре* to the full termination of the positive or the comparative degree, for ex. *са́мый* пріятный день, the most pleasant day, *са́мая* высоча́йшая гора́, the very highest mountain, *пре*краснѣйшій цвѣто́къ, a very beautiful flower, *пре*поле́знѣйшее сре́дство, a most useful means; 2. by prefixing the adverbs *весьма́, о́чень*, to the full termination of the positive degree, for ex. *весьма́* поле́зное изобрѣтеніе, a very useful invention, *о́чень* пріятная встрѣча, a very pleasant meeting; 3. by prefixing the particle *наи* to some adjectives in the comparative degree, for ex. *наи*лу́чшій спо́собъ, the best method, *наи*бо́лѣе поле́зное дѣло, the most useful thing of all.

To increase the energy of expression *гора́здо*, much, is sometimes prefixed to the apocopated termination of the comparative, as, онъ *гора́здо* умнѣе, he is much wiser, *гора́здо* краси́вѣе, much handsomer, *гораздо* ху́же, much worse. On the other hand, to give the signification of slight superiority, the particle *по* is prefixed to the comparative, as, она *по*краси́вѣе бра́та, she is rather handsomer than her brother.

The following adjectives are compared irregularly:

	Comparative full:	Comparative apocopated:	Superlative
Вели́кій, great,	бо́льшій,	бо́лѣе and бо́льше,	велича́йшій.
Большо́й, large,	бо́льшій,	бо́лѣе and бо́льше,	велича́йшій.
Ма́лый, little,	ме́ньшій,	ме́нѣе and ме́ньше,	малѣ́йшій.
Высо́кій, high,	вы́сшій,	вы́ше,	высоча́йшій.
Ни́зкій, low,	ни́зшій,	ни́же,	нижа́йшій.
Хоро́шій, good,	лу́чшій,	лу́чше,	наилу́чшій.
Худо́й, bad,	ху́дшій,	ху́же,	наиху́дшій.
Ста́рый, old,	старѣ́йшій,	старѣ́е and ста́рше,	ста́ршій.
Молодо́й, young,		моло́же,	мла́дшій.

Qualificative adjectives may take a *diminutive* or an *augmentative* form. *Augmentative* adjectives end in *е́хонькій* and *о́хонькій*, as чёрный, black, чер*не́хонькій*, quite black. *Diminutive* adjectives are of two kinds: the first terminate in *онькій* and *енькій*, and relate to the diminutiveness of the object, as бѣ*ле́нькій* плато́чикъ, a (pretty) little white handkerchief; the second end in *еватый* and *оватый*, and may be rendered in English by an adjective terminating in *ish* or preceded by the particle *rather*, as кра́сный, red, крас*нова́тый*, reddish, сла́бый, weak, сла*бова́тый*, rather weak.

Some adjectives are used as common nouns, as вы́бор*ный*, a deputy, со́тск*ій*, a peasant-superintendent, гости́н*ая*, a parlour, столо́*вая*, a dining-room, жа́рк*о́е*, a roast. On the other hand, adjectives having become appellations, are used as proper nouns, as Толст*о́й*, Задуна́йск*ій*, Че́сменск*ій*, etc.

To some adjectives the particles *не, без* are prefixed; which imparts to them an opposite meaning, as *не*вѣ́рный, unfaithful, *без*у́мный, unwise, *без*вку́сный, tasteless, *без*вре́дный, harmless, *без*опа́сный, free from danger, etc.

TABLE FOR THE DECLENSION OF ADJECTIVES HAVING FULL TERMINATIONS.

	Mas.		Fem.		Neut.	
			Singular.			
N. V.	ый, ой	ій, ній	ая	яя	ое	ее
G.	аго	яго	ой	ей	аго	яго
D.	ому	ему	ой	ей	ому	ему
A.	like the Nom. or Gen.		ую	юю	ое	ее
I.	ымъ	имъ	ою, ой	ею, ей	ымъ	имъ
P.	омъ	емъ	ой	ей	омъ	емъ
			Plural.			
N. V.	ые	іе	ыя	ія	ыя	ія
G.	ыхъ	ихъ	ыхъ	ихъ	ыхъ	ихъ
D.	ымъ	имъ	ымъ	имъ	ымъ	имъ
A.		like the	Nominative		or Genitive.	
I.	ыми	ими	ыми	ими	ыми	ими
P.	ыхъ	ихъ	ыхъ	ихъ	ыхъ	ихъ.

EXAMPLES.

1. DECLENSION OF MASCULINE ADJECTIVES.

Singular.

N. V.	по́лный, пусто́й, си́ній стака́нъ.	стро́гій учи́тель.
	(a) full*, (an) empty, (a) blue tumbler.	(a) strict teacher.
G.	по́лнаго, пуста́го, си́няго стака́на.	стро́гаго учи́теля.
D.	по́лному, пусто́му, си́нему стака́ну.	стро́гому учи́телю.
A.	по́лный, пусто́й, си́ній стака́нъ.	стро́гаго учи́теля.
I.	по́лнымъ, пусты́мъ, си́нимъ стака́номъ.	стро́гимъ учи́телемъ.
P.	о по́лномъ, пусто́мъ, си́немъ стака́нѣ.	о стро́гомъ учи́телѣ.

Plural.

N. V.	по́лные, пусты́е, си́ніе стака́ны.	стро́гіе учи́тели.
G.	по́лныхъ, пусты́хъ, си́нихъ стака́новъ.	стро́гихъ учи́телей.
D.	по́лнымъ, пусты́мъ, си́нимъ стака́намъ.	стро́гимъ учи́телямъ.
A.	по́лные, пусты́е, си́ніе стака́ны.	стро́гихъ учи́телей.
I.	по́лными, пусты́ми, си́ними стака́нами.	стро́гими учи́телями.
P.	о по́лныхъ, пусты́хъ, си́нихъ стака́нахъ.	о стро́гихъ учи́теляхъ.

* The translation into English of the different cases of Adjectives is like that of the cases of nouns. See p. 130.

2. DECLENSION OF FEMININE ADJECTIVES.

Singular.

N. V.	по́лная, пуста́я, си́няя рю́мка.	стро́гая гуверна́нтка.
	(a) full, (an) empty, (a) blue wine-glass.	(a) strict governess.
G.	по́лной, пусто́й, си́ней рю́мки.	стро́гой гуверна́нтки.
D.	по́лной, пусто́й, си́ней рю́мкѣ.	стро́гой гуверна́нткѣ.
A.	по́лную, пусту́ю, си́нюю рю́мку.	стро́гую гуверна́нтку.
I.	по́лною (ой), пусто́ю (ой), си́нею (ой) рю́мкою.	стро́гою (ой) гуверна́нткою (ой).
P.	о по́лной, пусто́й, си́ней рю́мкѣ.	о стро́гой гуверна́нткѣ.

Plural.

N. V.	по́лныя, пусты́я, си́нія рю́мки.	стро́гія гуверна́нтки,
G.	по́лныхъ, пусты́хъ, си́нихъ рю́мокъ.	стро́гихъ гуверна́нтокъ.
D.	по́лнымъ, пусты́мъ, си́нимъ рю́мкамъ.	стро́гимъ гуверна́нткамъ.
A.	по́лныя, пусты́я, си́нія рю́мки.	стро́гихъ гуверна́нтокъ.
I.	по́лными, пусты́ми, си́ними рю́мками.	стро́гими гуверна́нтками.
P.	о по́лныхъ, пусты́хъ, си́нихъ рю́мкахъ.	о стро́гихъ гуверна́нткахъ

3. DECLENSION OF NEUTER ADJECTIVES.

Singular.

N. V.	по́лное, пусто́е, си́нее блю́до.	солда́тское ружье́.
	(a) full, (an) empty, (a) blue dish.	(a) soldier's musket.
G.	по́лнаго, пуста́го, си́няго блю́да.	солда́тскаго ружья́.
D.	по́лно́му, пусто́му, си́нему блю́ду.	солда́тскому ружью́.
A.	по́лное, пусто́е, си́нее блю́до.	солда́тское ружье́.
I.	по́лнымъ, пусты́мъ, си́нимъ блю́домъ.	солда́тскимъ ружьёмъ.
P.	о по́лномъ, пусто́мъ, си́немъ блю́дѣ.	о солда́тскомъ ружьѣ́.

Plural.

N. V.	по́лныя, пусты́я, си́нія блю́да.	солда́тскія ру́жья.
G.	по́лныхъ, пусты́хъ, си́нихъ блюдъ.	солда́тскихъ ру́жей.
D.	по́лнымъ, пусты́мъ, си́нимъ блю́дамъ.	солда́тскимъ ру́жьямъ.
A.	по́лныя, пусты́я, си́нія блю́да.	солда́тскія ру́жья.
I.	по́лными, пусты́ми, си́ними блю́дами.	солда́тскими ру́жьями.
P.	о по́лныхъ, пусты́хъ, си́нихъ блю́дахъ.	о солда́тскихъ ру́жьяхъ.

Several possessive adjectives derived from animate objects, and ending in *ій*, as вра́жій, hostile, рыба́чій, a fisherman's, во́лчій, wolf's, are declined in the following way:

Singular.

N. V.	оле́н*ій*, deer's.	ры́бь*я*, fish-.	пти́чь*е*, bird's.
G.	оле́нь*яго*.	ры́бь*ей*.	пти́чь*яго*.
D.	оле́нь*ему*.	ры́бь*ей*,	пти́чь*ему*.
A.	оле́н*ій*.	ры́бь*ю*.	пти́чь*е*.
I.	оле́нь*имъ*.	ры́бь*ею*.	пти́чь*имъ*.
P.	объ оле́нь*емъ*.	о ры́бь*ей*.	о пти́чь*емъ*.

Plural.

N. V.	оле́нь*и*.	ры́бь*и*.	пти́чь*и*.
G.	оле́нь*ихъ*.	ры́бь*ихъ*.	пти́чь*ихъ*.
D.	оче́нь*имъ*.	ры́бь*имъ*.	пти́чь*имъ*.
A.	оле́нь*и*.	ры́бь*и*.	пти́чь*и*.
I.	оле́нь*ими*.	ры́бь*ими*.	пти́чь*ими*.
P.	объ оле́нь*ихъ*.	о ры́бь*ихъ*.	о пти́чь*ихъ*.

The possessive adjective Бо́жій, God's, is declined as follows:

	Singular.			Plural.
N. V.	Бо́ж*ій*,	Бо́ж*ія*,	Бо́ж*іе*,	Бо́ж*іи*.
G.	Бо́ж*ія*,	Бо́ж*іей*,	Бо́ж*ія*,	Бо́ж*іихъ*.
D.	Бо́ж*ію*,	Бо́ж*іей*,	Бо́ж*ію*,	Бо́ж*іимъ*.
A.	Бо́ж*ій*,	Бо́ж*ію*,	Бо́ж*іе*,	Бо́ж*іи*.
I.	Бо́ж*іимъ*,	Бо́ж*іею*,	Бо́ж*іимъ*,	Бо́ж*іими*.
P.	о Бо́ж*іемъ*,	о Бо́ж*іей*,	о Бо́ж*іемъ*,	о Бо́ж*іихъ*.

TABLE FOR THE DECLENSION OF ADJECTIVES HAVING APOCOPATED TERMINATIONS.

	Mascul.	Fem.	Neut.	All Genders.
	Singular.			Plural.
N. V.	ъ	а	о	ы
G.	а	ой	а	ыхъ
D.	у	ой	у	ымъ
A.	like the Nom. or Gen.	у	о	like the Nom. or Gen.
I.	ымъ	ою	ымъ	ыми
P.	омъ	ой	омъ	ыхъ

EXAMPLES.

	Singular.	Plural.
N. V.	отцо́въ домъ.	отцо́вы до́мы.
	the father's house.	the father's houses.
G.	отцо́ва до́ма.	отцо́выхъ домо́въ.
D.	отцо́ву до́му.	отцо́вымъ дома́мъ.
A.	отцо́въ домъ.	отцо́вы до́мы.
I.	отцо́вымъ до́момъ.	отцо́выми дома́ми.
P.	объ отцо́вомъ до́мѣ.	объ отцо́выхъ дома́хъ.

	Singular.	Plural.
N. V.	сéстрин*а* шля́пка. a sister's bonnet.	сéстрин*ы* шля́пки. a sister's bonnets.
G.	сéстрин*ой* шля́пк*и*.	сéстрин*ыхъ* шля́покъ.
D.	сéстрин*ой* шля́пкѣ.	сéстрин*ымъ* шля́пкамъ.
A.	сéстрин*у* шля́пку.	сéстрин*ы* шля́пки.
I.	сéстрин*ою* шля́пкою.	сéстрин*ыми* шля́пками.
P.	о сéстрин*ой* шля́пкѣ.	о сéстрин*ыхъ* шля́пкахъ.

	Singular.	Plural.
N. V.	ивáнов*о* перó. John's pen.	ивáнов*ы* пéрья. John's pens.
G.	ивáнов*а* перá.	ивáнов*ыхъ* пéрьевъ.
D.	ивáнов*у* перý.	ивáнов*ымъ* пéрьямъ.
A.	ивáнов*о* перó.	ивáнов*ы* пéрья.
I.	ивáнов*ымъ* перóмъ.	ивáнов*ыми* пéрьями.
P.	объ ивáнов*омъ* перѣ́.	объ ивáнов*ыхъ* пéрьяхъ.

NUMERALS.*

Cardinal numbers are declined as substantives; ordinal numbers have the termination and declension of adjectives.

Rem. The ordinal number пéрвый, when denoting *the best* or *excellent,* takes the degrees of comparison: as пéрв*ый*, перв*ѣйшій*, *сáмый* пéрвый.

* For a list of numbers see p. 51.

Several numerals have a declension of their own, as will be seen by the following examples:

	Singular.			Plural.	
	masc.	fem.	neut.	masc. and neuter.	fem.
N.	одíнъ.	однá.	однó.	однí.	однѣ́.
G.	одногó.	однóй.	одногó.	однíхъ.	однѣ́хъ.
D.	одномý.	однóй.	одномý.	однíмъ.	однѣ́мъ.
A.	like the N. or G.	однý.	однó.	N. G.	N. G.
I.	однíмъ.	однóю.	однíмъ.	однíми.	однѣ́ми.
P.	объ однóмъ.	объ однóй.	объ однóмъ.	объ однíхъ.	объ однѣ́хъ.

N.	два, двѣ (fem.).	три.	четы́ре.	пять.	вóсемь.
G.	двухъ.	трехъ.	четырéхъ.	пятí.	осьмí.
D.	двумъ.	тремъ.	четырéмъ.	пятí.	осьмí.
A.	N. G.	N. G.	N. G.	пять.	вóсемь.
I.	двумя́.	тремя́.	четырьмя́.	пятью́.	вóсемью.
P.	о двухъ.	о трехъ.	о четырéхъ.	о пятí.	объ осьмí.

N.	одíннадцать.	сóрокъ.	пятьдеся́ть.	сто.	двѣ́сти.	пять сотъ.
G.	одíннадцати.	сорокá.	пятíдесяти.	ста.	двухъ сотъ.	пятí сотъ.
D.	одíннадцати.	сорокý.	пятíдесяти.	сту.	двумъ стамъ.	пятí стамъ.
A.	одíннадцать.	сóрокъ.	пятьдеся́ть.	сто.	двѣ́сти	пять сотъ.
I.	одíннадцатью.	сорокá.	пятьюдесятью.	ста.	двумя́ стáми.	пятью стáми.
P.	объ одíннадцати.	о сорокѣ́.	о пятíдесяти.	о стѣ́.	о двухъ стахъ.	о пятí стахъ.

It must be observed that сóрокъ, сто (and девянóсто, 90) are declined according to the above examples only when standing alone; but being joined to substantives the dative, instrumental, and prepositional cases are like the genitive, as сорокá рубля́мъ, to 40 roubles, ст*а* аршíнами, by or with 100 arsheens, въ девя́ност*а* трехъ рубля́хъ, in 193 roubles. After the preposition по, however, the dative retains its regular termination *у*, as по ст*у* рублей, by a 100 roubles (at a time).

---

	masc. and neut.	fem.	all genders.	all genders.
N.	óба, both.	óбѣ.	трóе, three (in all).	чéтверо, four (in all).
G.	обóихъ.	обѣ́ихъ.	троíхъ.	четверы́хъ.
D.	обóимъ.	обѣ́имъ.	троíмъ.	четверы́мъ.
A.	N. G.	N. G.	N. G.	N. G.
I.	обóими.	обѣ́ими.	троíми.	четверы́ми.
P.	объ обóихъ.	объ обѣ́ихъ.	о троíхъ.	о четверы́хъ.

Like трóе are declined: двóе, two (in all), обóе, both; and like чéтверо — пáтеро, five (in all), шéстеро, six (in all).

masc. and neut.	fem.	all genders.
N. полторá, one and a half.	полторы́.	полторáста, 150.
G. полу́тора.	полу́торы.	полу́тораста.
D. полу́тору.	полу́торѣ.	полу́торасту.
A. полторá.	полторы́.	полторáста.
I. полу́торымъ.	полу́торою.	полу́тораста.
P. о полу́торѣ.	о полу́торѣ.	о полу́торастѣ.

In compound cardinal numbers each component part is declined according to its own termination, and in accordance with its substantive and adjective, as, трехъ-сотъ солдáтъ, of 300 soldiers, семи́стамъ нóвымъ кни́гамъ, to 700 new books, ты́сячею вóсемью-стáми тридцатью́ шестью́ рубля́ми, by or with 1836 roubles, etc.

In compound ordinal numbers only the last word is declined together with its substantive and adjective, f. ex. въ ты́сяча вóсемь сотъ шестьдеся́тъ *трéтьемъ* году, in the year 1863, до двáдцать пя́той страни́цы, as far as the 25th page.

Collective and fractional numbers being joined to substantives, the former two only are declined, whilst the latter retain the genitive in all the cases, f. ex. деся́токъ огурцéвъ, half a score of cucumbers, пáры лошадéй, of a pair of horses, чéтверти листá, to a quarter of a sheet, etc.

Substantives being preceded by the nominative and accusative of the numerals два, три, четы́ре, óба and полторá, must have the genitive singular, as, три человѣ́ка, three men, полторá пу́да, a pood and a half. But if these numerals are followed by an adjective, it ought to be in the nominative or genitive plural, as, три кáменныхъ дóма or три кáменные дóма, three stone houses. After all other numerals in the nominative or accusative beginning from пять, the genitive plural must be employed, as пять лошадéй, five horses сóрокъ корóвъ, forty cows.

PRONOUNS.

Pronouns may be divided into personal, reflective, demonstrative, possessive, relative, interrogative, determinative and indefinite.

According to another classification they are divided into *substantive* and *adjective* pronouns:

The substantive pronouns are: я I, ты thou, онъ he, она́ she, оно́ it, себя́ one's self, кто who, никто́ nobody, нѣкто somebody, ничто́ nothing, нѣчто somewhat, ко́е-кто, кто-то, кто-нибу́дь, кто-ли́бо somebody, ко́е-кто, что-то, что-нибу́дь, что-ли́бо something.

The adjective pronouns are: мой my or mine, твой thy or thine, на́шъ our or ours, вашъ your or yours, свой his, кото́рый who or which, чей whose, э́тотъ, сей this, тотъ that, о́ный that or the said, како́й what, тако́й such, самъ self, са́мый same, most, нѣкоторый a certain, some, ка́ждый each, вся́кій every, весь all.

DECLENSION OF SUBSTANTIVE PRONOUNS.

Singular.

	of all genders.		masc.	fem.	neut.
N.	я, I.	ты.	онъ.	она́.	оно́.
G.	меня́, of me.	тебя́.	его́.	ея́.	его́.
D.	мнѣ, to me.	тебѣ.	ему́.	ей.	ему́.
A.	меня́, me.	тебя́.	его́.	её.	его́.
I.	мно́ю, by or with me.	тобо́ю.	имъ.	е́ю.	имъ.
P.	о́бо мнѣ, of me.	о тебѣ.	о немъ.	о ней.	о немъ.

Plural.

	of all genders.		masc.	fem.	neut.
N.	мы, we.	вы.	они́.	онѣ́.	они́.
G.	насъ, of us.	васъ.	ихъ.	ихъ.	ихъ.
D.	намъ, to us.	вамъ.	имъ.	имъ.	имъ.
A.	насъ, us.	васъ.	ихъ.	ихъ.	ихъ.
I.	на́ми, by or with us.	ва́ми.	и́ми.	и́ми.	и́ми.
P.	о насъ, of us.	о васъ.	о нихъ.	о нихъ,	о нихъ.

N.	—	кто.	что.
G.	себя́.	кого́.	чего́.
D.	себѣ́.	кому́.	чему́.
A.	себя́.	кого́.	что.
I.	собо́ю.	кѣмъ.	чѣмъ.
P.	о себѣ́.	о комъ.	о чемъ.

Like кто are declined: ко́е-кто, кто-то, кто-нибу́дь, кто-ли́бо, никто́. Like что are declined: что-то, что-нибу́дь, что-ли́бо, ко́е-что, ничто́.

DECLENSION OF ADJECTIVE PRONOUNS.

	Singular.			Plural.
	masc.	fem.	neut.	of all genders.
N.	мой.	моя́.	мое́.	мои́.
G.	моего́.	мое́й.	моего́.	мои́хъ.
D.	моему́.	мое́й.	моему́.	мои́мъ.
A.	N. G.	мою́.	мое́.	N. G.
I.	мои́мъ.	мое́ю.	мои́мъ.	мои́ми.
P.	о мое́мъ.	о мое́й.	о мое́мъ.	о мои́хъ.

According to this example are declined: твой, твоя́, твое́, and свой, своя́, свое́.

	Singular.			Plural.
	masc.	fem.	neut.	of all genders.
N.	нашъ.	на́ша.	на́ше.	на́ши.
G.	на́шего.	на́шей.	на́шего.	на́шихъ.
D.	на́шему.	на́шей.	на́шему.	на́шимъ.
A.	N. G.	на́шу.	на́ше.	N. G.
I.	на́шимъ.	на́шею.	на́шимъ.	на́шими.
P.	о на́шемъ.	о на́шей.	о на́шемъ.	о на́шихъ.

In the same manner are declined: вашъ, ва́ша, ва́ше.

	Singular.			Plural.
	masc.	fem.	neut.	of all genders.
N.	сей.	сiя́.	сiе́.	сiи́.
G.	сего́.	сей.	сего́.	сихъ.
D.	сему́.	сей.	сему́.	симъ.
A.	N. G.	сiю́.	сiе́.	N. G.
I.	симъ.	се́ю.	симъ.	сiми.
P.	о семъ.	о сей.	о семъ.	о сихъ.

	Singular.			Plural.
	masc.	fem.	neut.	of all genders.
N.	э́тотъ.	э́та.	э́то.	э́ти.
G.	э́того.	э́той.	э́того.	э́тихъ.
D.	э́тому.	э́той.	э́тому.	э́тимъ.
A.	N. G.	э́ту.	э́то.	N. G.
I.	э́тимъ.	э́тою.	э́тимъ.	э́тими.
P.	объ э́томъ.	объ э́той.	объ э́томъ.	объ э́тихъ.

	Singular.			Plural.
	masc.	fem.	neut.	of all genders.
N.	чей.	чья.	чье.	чьи.
G.	чьего́.	чьей.	чьего́.	чьихъ.
D.	чьему́.	чьей.	чьему́.	чьимъ.
A.	N. G.	чью.	чье.	N. G.
I.	чьимъ.	чье́ю.	чьимъ.	чьи́ми.
P.	о чьемъ.	о чьей.	о чьемъ.	о чьихъ.

	Singular.			Plural.
	masc.	fem.	neut.	of all genders.
N.	самъ.	сама́.	само́.	сами́.
G.	самого́.	само́й.	самого́.	самі́хъ.
D.	самому́.	само́й.	самому́.	самі́мъ.
A.	N. G.	саму́ (самое́).	само́.	N. G.
I.	сами́мъ.	само́ю.	самі́мъ.	самі́ми.
P.	о само́мъ.	о само́й.	о само́мъ.	о самі́хъ.

	Singular.			Plural.
	masc.	fem.	neut.	of all genders.
N.	тотъ.	та.	то.	тѣ.
G.	того́.	той.	того́.	тѣхъ.
D.	тому́.	той.	тому́.	тѣмъ.
A.	N. G.	ту.	то.	N. G.
I.	тѣ́мъ.	то́ю.	тѣмъ.	тѣми.
P.	о томъ.	о той.	о томъ.	о тѣхъ.

	Singular.			Plural.
	masc.	fem.	neut.	of all genders.
N.	весь.	вся.	все.	всѣ.
G.	всего́.	всей.	всего́.	всѣхъ.
D.	всему́.	всей.	всему́.	всѣмъ.
A.	N. G.	всю.	все.	N. G.
I.	всѣмъ.	всёю.	всѣмъ.	всѣми.
P.	о всемъ.	о всей.	о всемъ.	о всѣхъ.

All the remaining adjective pronouns are declined regularly like adjectives, excepting that како́й and тако́й take the termination ого (instead of аго) in the genitive singular of the masculine and neuter genders.

In the use of the pronouns attention must be paid to the following peculiarities of the Russian language:

1. The substantive pronoun *себя́* and the adjective pronoun *свой* always replace the subject or nominative of the phrase, of whatever person, gender or case it may be. Consequently *себя́* must be rendered in English not only by *one's self*, but by *myself, thyself, himself, herself, itself, ourselves, yourselves, themselves;* and *свой* not merely by *his*, but just as often by *my, thy, her, its, our, your, their (own):* f. ex. я недово́ленъ самі́мъ собо́ю, I am not satisfied with *myself;* ты самъ *себя́* обма́ныва́ешь, thou deceivest *thyself;* вы должны́ купи́ть *себѣ́* но́выя тетра́ди, you must buy *yourself* new copy-books; нашла́ ли она́ *свою́* шля́пку, has she found *her* bonnet; мы лю́бимъ *свои́хъ* учи́телей, we like *our* teachers; они́ *свои́мъ* прилежа́ніемъ заслужи́ли похвалу́, by *their* diligence they have deserved praise.

2. The English possessive pronouns, his, her, hers, its, their, theirs, when not relating to the subject of the phrase, must be rendered in Russian by the genitive case of the personal pronouns онъ, она́, оно́, они́; as сестра́ потеряла *его́* кни́гу, his sister has lost his books:

я читáлъ ужé *ея́* кни́ги, I have already read her books; мы ви́дѣли *ихъ* лошадéй, we saw their horses. These pronouns are indeclinable, and subject to no variations of gender.

3. The Russian pronoun *чей*, whose, being an adjective pronoun, agrees with its substantive in gender, number, and case; as, чь*и* э́ти кни́ги? whose books are these? чь*ю* кни́гу потеря́лъ ты? whose book have you lost?

4. To the pronouns, *онъ, онá, онó*, when preceded by a preposition, an *н* must be prefixed in all cases, as *къ немý* (not къ емý), to him, *отъ нея́*, from her, etc.

5. If the compound pronouns *никтó, ничтó*, are preceded in their declension by a preposition, it must be placed between *ни* and *кто* or *что*; f. ex. ни въ чемъ, in nothing (not въ ничéмъ), ни о комъ, of nobody, ни у когó, with nobody, etc.

VERBS.

Russian verbs may be divided into *active, passive, neuter, reflective, reciprocal,* and *common.* *

They are varied by *mood, tense, branch, person, number, gender, participle,* and *gerund.*

There are three *moods* in the Russian verb: the *indicative, imperative,* and *infinitive.* As to the *subjunctive* or *conditional* mood, employed in other languages, it is rendered in Russian by adding the conjunction *бы* to the past tense, as, онъ хотѣ́лъ *бы* ви́дѣть васъ, he would like to see you.

There are three *tenses:* the *present,* the *past,* and the *future.*

* These last have the signification of either active or neuter verbs. Common verbs, as well as reciprocal and reflective, terminate in *ся* (an abreviation of себя́).

The variations in form of the same action are expressed by what is called in Russian *branches* (виды) of a verb. There are four branches: the *indefinite*, the *perfect*, the *semelfactive*, and the *iterative*. The *present* tense has no branches; the *past* tense has all the four branches; the *future* tense has three branches: the *indefinite*, the *perfect*, and the *semelfactive*.

The variations of meaning expressed by the four branches are the following:

1. The *indefinite* expresses the action indeterminately with regard to its completion, as, я писа́лъ I have written, онъ бу́детъ чита́ть he will read.

2. The *perfect* shows that the action has either been quite finished, or will be so, as, я написа́лъ I have written (finished writing), вы прочита́ете, you will read over.

3. The *semelfactive* marks the sudden and single occurrence of an action, as, сту́кнуть to knock (once), онъ мигну́лъ he winked (once).

4. The *iterative* expresses the frequent repetition of the action, as, я чи́тывалъ I frequently read, онъ ха́живалъ he often went.

Rem. From the nature of the Russian verb a fifth branch might be added: the *inchoative*, marking the beginning of an action, as, я *запѣ́лъ* I began to sing, онъ *запое́тъ* he is going to sing, вѣтеръ *поду́лъ* the wind began to blow.

The indicative mood has all the tenses with their branches.

The imperative has three branches: 1. the *indefinite*, as, пиши́ write, стучи́ knock; 2. the *semelfactive*, as, сту́кни knock (once); 3. the *perfect*, as, напиши́ write down.

The infinitive has no tenses, but all the four branches: the *indefinite* — чита́ть, to read; the *perfect* — прочита́ть, to read over; the *semelfactive* — сту́кнуть, to knock (once); the *iterative* — чи́тывать, to read repeatedly.

There are three *persons* usually expressed by the personal pronouns: the 1st person — *я* пишу́ I write, *мы* пи́шемъ we write; the 2d person — *ты* пи́шешь thou writest, *вы* пи́шете you write; the

3d person — *онъ* писа́лъ he wrote, *она́* писала́ she wrote, *оно́* писа́ло it wrote, *оні́, онѣ̀* писа́ли they wrote.

There are two *numbers*: the *singular* and the *plural*.

The *gender* of verbs regards only the past tenses, as, сынъ чита́лъ the son read, дочь чита́*ла* the daughter read, дитя́ чата́*ло* the child read.

The *participle* is an adjective derived from a verb, and replaces two words: the pronoun *кото́рый* and a *verb* in the indicative mood. Thus, юноша *обогаща́ющій* свой умъ нау́ками, and юноша́, *кото́рый обогаща́етъ* умъ свой нау́ками, may both be rendered by: a youth who enriches his mind with knowledge. Participles partaking of the nature of both the verb and the adjective have voices, tenses, branches, gender, number, and case.

The *gerund* is a form of the verb, which, to express a meaning, must be supplied by another verb, as, *чу́вствуя* приближе́ніе сме́рти, оте́цъ позва́лъ четве́рыхъ сынове́й свои́хъ, the father feeling the approach of death called his four sons; *возврати́вшись* изъ вавило́нскаго плѣ́на, Изра́ильтяне не впада́ли уже́ въ идолопокло́нство, the Israelites having returned from the Babylonian captivity fell into idolatry no more. Gerunds, like verbs, have all voices, tenses, and branches.

There are two conjugations: the *first* has *ешь* in the 2d person singular number present tense of the indicative mood, as, ты чита́*ешь* thou readest, ты гуля́*ешь* thou walkest; and the *second* — *ишь*, as, верт*и́шь* thou turnest, ко́рм*ишься* thou supportest thyself.

CONJUGATION OF THE AUXILIARY VERB БЫТЬ, TO BE.

Infinitive Mood.

Indefinite branch — быть, to be; iterative branch — быва́ть, to be.

Indicative Mood.

Present Tense.

	I.	II.
Sing.	я есмь,	бываю, I am.
	ты есѝ, *	бываешь, thou art.
	онъ, она́, оно́ есть,	бываетъ, he, she, it is.
Plur.	мы есмѝ, *	бываемъ, we are.
	вы есте́, *	бываете, you are.
	онѝ, онѣ́ суть,	бываютъ, they are.

Past Tense.

	Indefinite Branch.	Iterative Branch.
Sing.	я былъ,	бывалъ, I was.
	ты былъ,	бывалъ, thou wast.
	онъ, она́, оно́ былъ, а, о,	бывалъ, а, о, he, she, it was.
Plur.	мы бы́ли,	бывали, we were.
	вы бы́ли,	бывали, you were.
	онѝ, онѣ́ бы́ли,	бывали, they were.

Future Tense.

Singular.*	я бу́ду, I shall be.
	ты бу́дешь, thou wilt be.
	онъ бу́детъ, he will be.
Plural.	мы бу́демъ, we shall be.
	вы бу́дете, you will be.
	онѝ, онѣ́ бу́дутъ, they will be.

* not used.

Imperative Mood.

Singular. будь ты, be thou.
пусть онъ, она́, оно́ бу́детъ, let him, her, it be.
Plural. бу́дьте вы, be you.
пусть они́, онѣ́ бу́дутъ, let them be.

Participle.

Present. сущій, быва́ющій, being, who or which is.
Past. Indefinite Branch. бы́вшій, who or which was.
— Iterative Branch. быва́вшій, who or which has been.
Future. бу́дущій, who or which is to be.

Gerund.

Present. бу́дучи, being.
Past. Indefinite Branch. бывъ, бы́вши, having been.
— Iterative Branch. быва́въ, быва́вши, having been.

The auxiliary *стать* has only two tenses — the future: я ста́ну, I shall, and the past: я сталъ, I began; f. ex. я ста́ну писа́ть, I shall write, я сталъ писа́ть, I began to write.

Verbs are conjugated according to the following table:

TABLE FOR THE CONJUGATION OF REGULAR VERBS.

<table>
<tr><th>TENSES.</th><th>BRANCHES.</th><th colspan="2">INFINITIVE MOOD.</th></tr>
<tr><td rowspan="4">Wanting.</td><td>Indefinite.</td><td colspan="2">ть, чь, ти, f. ex. рѣша́ть to decide, печь to bake, нести́ to carry.</td></tr>
<tr><td>Perfect.</td><td colspan="2">ть, чь, ти, f. ex. рѣши́ть, испе́чь, понести́.</td></tr>
<tr><td>Semelfactive.</td><td colspan="2">нуть, f. ex. ду́нуть to blow (once), сту́кнуть to knock (once).</td></tr>
<tr><td>Iterative.</td><td colspan="2">ивать, ывать, f. ex. нашива́ть to sew on (repeatedly), дѣлывать to do (often).</td></tr>
<tr><td rowspan="3">Present.</td><td rowspan="3">Wanting.</td><td colspan="2">INDICATIVE MOOD.</td></tr>
<tr><td>Singular.</td><td>Plural.</td></tr>
<tr><td>ю, ешь, етъ; у, ишь, итъ</td><td>емъ, ете, ютъ, утъ; имъ, ите, атъ, ятъ</td></tr>
<tr><td rowspan="3">Past.</td><td>Indef. and Perf.</td><td>-лъ, -ла, -ло</td><td>-ли</td></tr>
<tr><td>Semelfactive.</td><td>-нулъ, -нула, -нуло</td><td>-нули</td></tr>
<tr><td>Iterative.</td><td>ивалъ, ывалъ, ла, ло</td><td>ивали, ывали</td></tr>
</table>

<table>
<tr><th>TENSES.</th><th>BRANCHES.</th><th colspan="2">INDICATIVE MOOD.</th></tr>
<tr><td rowspan="3">Future.</td><td>Indefinite.</td><td>бу́ду
бу́дешь
бу́детъ } ть, чь, ти</td><td>бу́демъ
бу́дете
бу́дутъ } ть, чь, ти</td></tr>
<tr><td>Perfect</td><td>terminates like</td><td>the Present Tense.</td></tr>
<tr><td>Semelfactive</td><td>-ну, -нешь, -нетъ</td><td>-немъ, -нете, -нутъ</td></tr>
<tr><td rowspan="3">Wanting.</td><td rowspan="3">Alike for all branches.</td><td colspan="2">IMPERATIVE MOOD.</td></tr>
<tr><td>Singular.</td><td>Plural.</td></tr>
<tr><td>(ты) и, ь, й
(пусть онъ) етъ, итъ</td><td>(вы) ите, ете, йте
(пусть они́) ютъ, утъ, ятъ, атъ.</td></tr>
</table>

Verbs terminating in *ся* are also conjugated according to this table, adding *сь* or *ся* to each person, as, я занима́юсь I occupy myself, ты прогу́ливаешь*ся* thou walkest, вы смѣ́етесь you are laughing.

Verbs with regard to their forms of conjugation are: *regular*, *irregular*, *copious* (having two different terminations in their present tense, but which convey the same meaning, as движу and двига́ю, I move), *defective*, *impersonal*, and *frequentative* (denoting a certain duration of time in the action, as поха́живать, to walk a little).

With regard to their composition verbs may also be divided into *simple* and *compound* verbs.

CONJUGATION OF REGULAR VERBS.

1. CONJUGATION OF ACTIVE AND NEUTER VERBS.

Branches.	*Infinitive Mood.*			
Indefin.	дѣлать, to do.	стучáть, to knock.	жить, to live.	вíдѣть, to see.
Perfect.	сдѣлать	постучáть	пожíть	увíдѣть
Semelf.	wanting	стýкнуть	wanting	wanting
Iterat.	дѣлывать	not used	живáть	вíдывать

Indicative Mood.

Present.

я дѣлаю, I do.	стучý, knock.	живý, live.	вíжу, see.
ты дѣлаешь	стучíшь	живёшь	вíдишь
онъ дѣлаетъ	стучíтъ	живётъ	вíдитъ
мы дѣлаемъ	стучíмъ	живёмъ	вíдимъ
вы дѣлаете	стучíте	живёте	вíдите
онí дѣлаютъ	стучáтъ	живýтъ	вíдятъ

Past.

Indefin.	я дѣлалъ, I did.	стучáлъ, knocked.	жилъ, lived.	вíдѣлъ, saw.
Perfect.	я сдѣлалъ	постучáлъ	пóжилъ	увíдѣлъ
Semelf.	wanting	стýкнулъ	wanting	wanting
Iterat.	я дѣлывалъ	not used	живáлъ	вíдывалъ

Future.

Indefin. я бу́ду, I shall / ты бу́дешь / онъ бу́детъ, etc. } дѣ́лать do, стуча́ть knock, жить live, ви́дѣть see.

Perfect.	я сдѣ́лаю	постучу́	поживу́	уви́жу
	ты сдѣ́лаешь	постучи́шь	поживе́шь	уви́дишь
	онъ сдѣ́лаетъ	постучи́тъ	поживе́тъ	уви́дитъ
	мы сдѣ́лаемъ	постучи́мъ	поживе́мъ	уви́димъ
	вы сдѣ́лаете	постучи́те	поживе́те	уви́дите
	они́ сдѣ́лаютъ	постуча́тъ	поживу́тъ	уви́дятъ
Semelf.	wanting	сту́кну	wanting	wanting

Imperative Mood.

Indefin.	дѣ́лай, do (thou).	стучи́, knock.	живи́, live.	wanting
	пусть онъ дѣ́лаетъ, let him do.	стучи́тъ	живе́тъ	ви́дитъ
	дѣ́лайте, do (you).	стучи́те	живи́те	ви́дите
	пусть они́ дѣ́лаютъ, let them do.	стуча́тъ	живу́тъ	ви́дятъ
Perfect.	сдѣ́лай	постучи́	поживи́	wanting
Semelf.	wanting	сту́кни	wanting	wanting

Participles.

Present.

дѣ́лающій, who or which does,	стуча́щій	живу́щій	ви́дящій

Past.

Indefin.	дѣлавшій, who or which did.	стýчавшій	жúвшій	вúдѣвшій
Perfect.	сдѣлавшій	постучáвшій	пожúвшій	увúдѣвшій
Semelf.	wanting	стýкнувшій	wanting	wanting
Iterat.	дѣлывавшій	not used	живáвшій	видáвшій

Gerunds.

Present.

дѣлая, doing.	стучá, knocking.	живя́, living.	вúдя, seeing.

Past.

Indefin.	дѣлавъ (ши), having done.	стучáвъ (ши)	жúвши	вúдѣвъ (ши)
Perfect.	сдѣлавъ (ши)	постучáвъ(ши)	пожúвши	увúдѣвъ (ши)
Semelf.	wanting	стýкнувъ (ши)	wanting	wanting

2. CONJUGATION OF REFLECTIVE, RECIPROCAL, AND NEUTER VERBS.

Infinitive Mood.

Indefin.	хвалúться, to praise one's self.	сражáться, to fight.	улыбáться, to smile.
Perfect.	похвалúться	сразúться	wanting
Semelf.	wanting	wanting	улыбнýться

Indicative Mood.

Present.

я хвалю́сь,	сража́юсь,	улыба́юсь,
I praise myself.	fight.	smile.
ты хва́лишься	сража́ешься	улыба́ешься
онъ хва́лится	сража́ется	улыба́ется
мы хва́лимся	сража́емся	улыба́емся
вы хва́литесь	сража́етесь	улыба́етесь
они́ хва́лятся	сража́ются	улыба́ются

Past.

Indefin.	я хвали́лся,	сража́лся,	улыба́лся,
	I praised myself.	fought.	smiled.
Perfect.	я похвали́лся	срази́лся	wanting
Semelf.	wanting	wanting	я улыбну́лся

Future.

Indefin.	я бу́ду хвали́ться,	сража́ться	улыба́ться
	I shall praise myself.		
Perfect.	я похвалю́сь	сражу́сь	wanting
	ты похва́лишься	срази́шься	—
	онъ похва́лится	срази́тся, etc.	—
Semelf.	wanting	wanting	я улыбну́сь

Imperative Mood.

Indefin.	хвали́сь,	сража́йся,	улыба́йся,
	praise thyself.	fight.	smile.
	пусть онъ хва́лится,	сража́ется	улыба́ется
	let him praise himself.		
	хвали́тесь,	сража́йтесь	улыба́йтесь
	praise yourselves.		
	пусть они́ хва́лятся,	сража́ются	улыба́ются
	let them praise themselves.		
Perfect.	похвали́сь	срази́сь	wanting
Semelf.	wanting	wanting	улыбни́сь

Participles.

Present.

хваля́щійся,	сража́ющійся	улыба́ющійся
who praises himself.		

Past.

Indefin.	хвали́вшійся,	сража́вшійся	улыба́вшійся
	who praised himself.		
Perfect.	похвали́вшійся	срази́вшійся	wanting
Semelf.	wanting	wanting	улыбну́вшійся

Gerunds.

Present.

хваля́сь,	сража́ясь,	улыба́ясь,
praising one's self.	fighting.	smiling.

Past.

Indefin.	хвали́вшись, having praised one's self.	сража́вшись	улыба́вшись
Perfect.	похвали́вшись / похваля́сь	срази́вшись / сразя́сь	wanting / —
Semelf.	wanting	wanting	улыбну́вшись

3. CONJUGATION OF PASSIVE VERBS.

Infinitive Mood.

Indefin.	быть хвали́му, to be praised.	награжда́ему, rewarded.	посыла́ему, sent.
Perfect.	быть похва́лену	награ́ждену	по́слану
Iterat.	быва́ть хвали́му	награжда́ему	посыла́ему

Indicative Mood.

Present.

The old form of the conjugation of the present tense: я есмь or я быва́ю хвали́мъ, награжда́емъ, посыла́емъ (I am praised, rewarded, sent) etc. — is now superseded by the following: меня́, его́, насъ, васъ, ихъ хва́лятъ, награжда́ютъ, посыла́ютъ, they praise reward, send me, thee, him, us, you, them.

Past.

Indefin.	я былъ хвали́мъ, I was praised.	награжда́емъ	посыла́емъ
or:	меня́ хвали́ли, they praised me.	награжда́ли	посыла́ли
Perfect.	я былъ похвалёнъ	награждёнъ	по́сланъ
or:	меня́ похвали́ли	награди́ли	посла́ли
Iterat.	я быва́лъ хвали́мъ	награжда́емъ	посыла́емъ
or:	меня́ быва́ло хвали́ли	награжда́ли	посыла́ли

Future.

Indefin. Instead of the obsolete: я бу́ду хвали́мъ, награжда́емъ, посыла́емъ (I shall be praised, rewarded, honoured) the following forms are used:

	меня́ бу́дутъ хвали́ть, they will praise me.	награжда́ть	посыла́ть
Perfect.	я бу́ду похва́ленъ	награждёнъ	по́сланъ
or:	меня́ похва́лятъ	наградя́тъ	пошлю́тъ

Imperative Mood.

Indefin.	пусть тебя́ хва́лятъ, let them praise thee.	награжда́ютъ	посыла́ютъ
Perfect.	пусть тебя́ похва́лятъ	наградя́тъ	пошлю́тъ

Participles.

Present.

	хвали́мый,	награжда́емый	посыла́емый
	who or which is praised.		

Past.

Indefin.	хвале́нный,	wanting	wanting
	who or which was praised.		
Perfect.	похвале́нный	награжде́нный	по́сланный

Gerunds.

Present.

бу́дучи хвали́мъ,	награжда́емъ	посыла́емъ
being praised.		

Past.

бывъ похвале́нъ,	награжде́нъ	по́сланъ
having been praised.		

CONJUGATION OF

Infinitive Mood.		*Indi-*
Indefinite Branch.	Perf. Br.	Present.
берéчь, to preserve	сберéчь	берегý, бережéшь
брать, to take	взять	берý, берéшь
везтú, to carry	повезтú	везý, везéшь
вестú, to lead	повестú	ведý, ведéшь
влечь, to draw	повлéчь	влекý, влечéшь
грызть, to gnaw	изгры́зть	грызý, грызéшь
давáть, to give	дать	даю́, даéшь
идтú, to go	пойтú	иду́, идéшь
класть, to put	положúть	кладý, кладéшь
лѣзть, to climb	полѣзть	лѣ́зу, лѣ́зешь
ложúться, to lie down	лечь	ложýсь, ложúшься
мочь, to be able	смочь	могý, мóжешь
нестú, to bear	понестú	несý, несéшь
облекáть, to invest	облéчь	облекáю, облекáешь
обрекáть, to devote	обрéчь	обрекáю, обрекáешь
пастú, to pasture		пасý, пасéшь
печь, to bake	испéчь	пекý, печéшь
растú, to grow	вы́рости	растý, растéшь
садúться, to sit down	сѣсть	сажýсь, садúшься
стерéчь, to guard	постерéчь	стерегý, стережéшь
спасáть, to save	спастú	спасáю, спасáешь
стричь, to shear	острúчь	стригý, стрижéшь
сѣчь, to flog	вы́сѣчь	сѣкý, сѣчéшь
отвергáть, to reject	отвéргнуть	отвергáю, отвергáешь
отверзáть, to open	отвéрзть	отверзáю, отверзáешь
терéть, to rub	потерéть	тру, трешь
трястú, to shake	потрястú	трясý, трясéшь
умирáть, to die	умерéть	умирáю, умирáешь
ѣсть, to eat	съѣсть	ѣмъ, ѣшь, ѣстъ, ѣдúмъ, ѣдúте, ѣдя́тъ
ѣхать, to drive	поѣхать	ѣ́ду, ѣ́дешь, ѣ́детъ, ѣ́демъ, ѣ́дете, ѣ́дутъ

IRREGULAR VERBS.

…cative Mood.			*Imperative Mood.*	
Past Indef.	Past Perf.	Fut. Perf.	Indef. Br.	Perf. Br.
берéгъ	сберéгъ	сберегу́	береги́	сбереги́
бралъ	взялъ	возьму́	бери́	возьми́
везъ	повéзъ	повезу́	вези́	повези́
велъ	повéлъ	поведу́	веди́	поведи́
влекъ	повлéкъ	повлеку́	влеки́	повлеки́
грызъ	изгры́зъ	изгрызу́	грызи́	изгрызи́
дава́лъ	далъ	дамъ	дава́й	дай
шелъ	пошéлъ	пойду́	иди́	поди́
клалъ	положи́лъ	положу́	клади́	положи́
лѣзъ	полѣзъ	полѣзу	лѣзь	полѣзь
ложи́лся	легъ	ля́гу	ложи́сь	лягъ
могъ	смогъ	смогу́		
несъ	понéсъ	понесу́	неси́	понеси́
облека́лъ	облéкъ	облеку́	облека́й	облеки́
обрека́лъ	обрéкъ	обреку́	обрека́й	обреки́
пасъ			паси́	
пекъ	испéкъ	испеку́	пеки́	испеки́
росъ	вы́росъ	вы́росту	расти́	вы́рости
сади́лся	сѣлъ	ся́ду	сади́сь	сядь
стерéгъ	постерéгъ	постерегу́	стереги́	постереги́
спаса́лъ	спасъ	спасу́	спаса́й	спаси́
стригъ	остри́гъ	остригу́	стриги́	остриги́
сѣкъ	вы́сѣкъ	вы́сѣку	сѣки́	вы́сѣки
отверга́лъ	отвéргъ	отвéргну	отверга́й	отвéргни
отверза́лъ	отвéрзъ	отверзу́	отверза́й	отверзи́
теръ	потéръ	потру́	три	потри́
трясъ	потря́съ	потрясу́	тряси́	потряси́
умира́лъ	у́меръ	умру́	умира́й	умри́
ѣлъ	съѣлъ	съѣмъ	ѣшь	съѣшь
ѣхалъ	поѣхалъ	поѣду		поѣзжа́й

Rem. Of the above irregular verbs there are only two which are used in the *semelfactive* branch: трястí — тряхнýть and стричь — стригнýть; and in the *iterative:* везтú, вестú — вáживать, нестú — нáшивать, сѣчь — сѣкáть, ѣсть — ѣдáть, and ѣхать — ѣзжáть. The verb мочь cannot be used in the future tense of the indefinite branch: it would be incorrect to say: я бýду мочь.

OBSERVATIONS.

The conjugations of verbs are subject to a great many rules with still more exceptions: here will be pointed out only such rules as are more fixed and less liable to exceptions.

I. *On the Infinitive Mood.*

1. Verbs in the infinitive mood of the *indefinite branch* generally end in *ть* preceded by the vowels: *а, е, и, о, у, ы, ѣ, я,* as чит*áть* to read, тер*éть* to rub, хвал*úть* to praise, кол*óть* to sting, тон*ýть* to sink, р*ыть* to dig, им*ѣть* to have, забавл*ять* to amuse; and by only two consonants: *з* and *с,* as, лѣ*зть* to climb, гры*зть* to gnaw, пле*сть* to twist, цвѣ*сть* to bloom; only very few verbs terminate in *чь* and *ти,* as, вле*чь* and ид*тú.*

2. The *perfect branch,* in its infinitive mood, has the same termination as the indefinite branch, but with various modifications. Some verbs have a perfect branch of their own, as, отличáть, to distinguish — *отличúть,* принимáть, to receive — *принять,* одѣвáть, to clothe — *одѣть,* брать — *взять;* others form their perfect branch by prefixing prepositions, as, любúть, to love, to like — *полюбúть,* писáть, to write — *написáть;* or borrow their perfect branches of compound verbs, as, берéчь — *сберéчь,* from the verb сберегáть, готóвить, to prepare — *приготóвить,* from the verb приготовлять, смотрѣть, to look — *посмотрѣть,* from посмáтривать.

3. The *semelfactive branch* terminates in *нуть*, as, мигну́ть to wink (once), свистну́ть to give a wistle, дёрнуть to give a pluck.

4. The *iterative* — in *ивать* and *ывать*, as ха́живать to go (often), чи́тывать to read (often). Only few verbs have the iterative branch which, in writing as well as in conversation, ought to be used with great discrimination. Verbs ending in *ивать* and *ывать* have no iterative branch, as, разсма́тривать to examine, обя́зывать to oblige.

II. *On the Indicative Mood.*

1. The 1st person singular of the present tense has two terminations: *ю* and *у*, the latter of which is always preceded by a consonant, as, сижу́ I sit, иду́ I go; the 2d — *ешь* and *ишь;* the 3d — *еть, ить;* the 1st person plural — *емъ, имъ;* the 2d — *ете, ите;* the 3d in verbs of the *first* conjugation — *ютъ* and *утъ:* чита́ешь — чита́ютъ, ведёшь — веду́тъ; of the *second* — *атъ* and *ятъ*: молчи́шь — молча́тъ, смо́тришь — смо́трятъ. To this rule only two verbs are an exception: бѣжи́шь, (thou) runnest — бѣгу́тъ, not бѣжа́тъ; хо́чешь, (thou) wilt — хотя́тъ, not хо́чутъ.

2. Verbs terminating in the present tense in *гу*, change *г* in the 2d and 3d persons singular, and the 1st and 2d persons plural into *ж*, as берегу́, бережёшь, бережётъ, бережёмъ, бережёте; but in the 3d person plural they retain *г*: берегу́тъ, стерегу́тъ.

3. Verbs ending in the present tense in *ку*, change *к* in the 2d and 3d persons singular and the 1st and 2d persons plural into *ч*, as, влеку́, влечёшь, влечётъ, влечёмъ, влечёте, but in the 3d person plural retain *к*: влеку́тъ, пеку́тъ.

4. Monosyllabic verbs in *ить* form their present tense by changing *ить* into *ью*, as, пить to drink, шить to sew, бить to beat — *пью, шью, бью*, except брить, to shave — *бре́ю*.

5. The present tense sometimes expresses a future action, f. ex. за́втра я *ѣ́ду* въ дере́вню, I am going into the country to-morrow;

на дняхъ онъ *отправляется* за границу, he is going abroad one of these days.

6. The *past* tense of the *indefinite* and *perfect* branch terminates in *лъ*, and is generally formed from the infinitive mood of the indefinite and perfect branch, by changing *ть* into *лъ*, f. ex. чита́*ть* — чита́*лъ*, хотѣ́*ть* — хотѣ́*лъ*, мя*ть*, to crumple — мя*лъ*; *сти* into *съ*, as, не*сти́* — не*съ*; *зти* into *зъ*, as, ве*зти́* — ве*зъ*; but цвѣ*сти́*, to blossom, has *цвѣлъ*, ве*сти́* — *велъ*. The *semelfactive* branch ends in *нулъ:* миг*ну́лъ*. The *iterative* branch in *ивалъ, ывалъ:* the two last branches are formed from their infinitives by changing *ть* into *лъ*, ха́жива*ть* — ха́жива*лъ*. Verbs which want the iterative branch replace it by adding the word *бывáло* (it used to be) to their past indefinite, f. ex. быва́ло встрѣча́лъ, used to meet.

7. The *future* of the *indefinite* branch is composed of the future of the auxiliary *быть*, and the infinitive of the principal verb, as, я бу́ду хвали́ть I shall praise, я бу́ду спра́шивать I shall ask. The *future* of the *perfect* branch has the terminations of the present tense; but the rules for the formation of this tense and branch, from their great variety, will be better learned by by practice. The *future semelfactive* ends in *ну*, and is formed from the infinitive of the same branch by eliding *ть*, дви́ну*ть*, to stir — дви́ну, ки́ну*ть*, to fling — ки́ну.

III. *On the Imperative Mood.*

1. In the imperative generally only two persons are used: the 2d and 3d, f. ex. чита́й, пусть онъ чита́етъ, чита́йте, пусть они́ чита́ютъ; but there are cases in which also a first person can be used, f. ex. *будь я* бога́тъ, я бы помо́гъ ему́, were I rich, I should help him; *учи́сь я* приле́жнѣе, я бы тепе́рь не раска́явался, did I learn more diligently, I should not repent now; likewise in the plural by employing the 1st person plural of the present and future perfect: идёмъ, пойдёмъ let us go, ѣдемъ, поѣдемъ let us drive, остано́вимся let us stop, ся́демъ let us sit down. In such cases the syllable

те is often added to the 1st person plural, as, сядем*те*, остано́вим*тесь*.

2. Sometimes the infinitive is used instead of the imperative, as, молча́*ть*, silence! не шумѣ́*ть*, no noise!

3. In elevated style, to the 3d person of the imperative the particle *да* is added, as, *да* здра́вствуетъ Императоръ, long live the Emperor! (instead of: пусть здра́вствуетъ).

IV. *On the Participle.*

In active and neuter verbs the *present* participle terminates in *щій*, and is formed from the 3d person plural of the present indicative by changing *тъ* into *щій*, as, смо́трятъ, (they) look — смо́тря*щій*, встрѣча́ю*тъ*, (they) meet — встрѣча́ю*щій*, живу́*тъ*, (they) live — живу́*щій*. — The *past* participle ends in *вшій*, and is formed from the singular of the past tenses of the indicative, by changing *лъ* into *вшій*, as, смотрѣ́*лъ*, смотрѣ́*вшій*, жи*лъ*, (he) lived — жи́*вшій*; and in verbs having no *л*, by changing *ъ* into *шій*, as, росъ — ро́с*шій*, берёгъ — берёг*шій*, везъ — вёз*шій*; but from the verb вести́, велъ — *ве́дшій*, идти́, шелъ — *ше́дшій*, цвѣсти́, цвѣлъ — цвѣ́*тшій*.

In reflective, reciprocal, and common verbs the syllable *ся* is added to the above-mentioned terminations, as, смо́тря*щійся* who sees himself, встрѣча́*вшійся* who met.

The participles of passive verbs are formed only from active verbs. Their *present* tense ends in *мый*, and is formed from the 1st person plural present indicative by changing the last letter *ъ* into *ый*, as, хва́лимъ — хвали́*мый*, обижа́емъ, we offend — обижа́е*мый*. Exceptions: иска́ть, to seek, has *иско́мый*, пасти́ — *пасо́мый*, вести́ — *ведо́мый*, везти́ — *везо́мый*, нести — *несо́мый*. — The *past* terminates in *нный* and *тый*, and is formed from the past tenses plural by changing the termination *ли* into *нный* and *тый*, as, дѣ́ла*ли* — дѣ́ла*нный*, ви́дѣ*ли*, saw — ви́дѣ*нный*, избра́*ли*, elected — и́збра*нный*; мы́*ли*, washed — мы́*тый*, ши́*ли*, sewed — ши́*тый*; except: хвали́ть — хвале́*нный*, носи́ть, to carry — но́-

шенный, прощáть, to pardon — прощéнный, забывáть, to forget — забы́тый and забвéнный.

Participles have no future tense, except *бýдущій* (future or that is to be) from the auxiliary *быть*.

Participles are declined like adjectives.

The participles of passive verbs have *apocopated* terminations; thus, from the full termination уважáемый (who is esteemed) — уважáемъ, уважáем*а*, уважáем*о*; чи́танный — чи́танъ, чи́тан*а*, чи́тан*о*; взя́тый — взятъ, взя́т*а*, взя́т*о*.

Participles, in general, are used only in writing; in conversation are employed only those of *passive* verbs with *apocopated* terminations, as, э́тотъ домъ хорошó *пострóенъ* that house has been well built, э́та кни́га прочи́тана this book has been read over, приказáніе испóлнено the order has been executed; and such participles as have the signification of adjectives: онъ *сýщій* ребéнокъ he is quite a child, *бывáлый* человѣ́къ an expert man, *бýдущая* жизнь a future life, непроходи́мый лѣсъ an impassable forest.

V. *On the Gerund.*

Gerunds of active and neuter verbs terminate in the *present* tense in *а*, *я*, *учи*, *ючи*, as, стуч*á*, си́д*я*, читá*я*, читá*ючи*, жив*ýчи*; and in the *past* tense in *въ* and *ши*, as, сидѣ́*въ*, сидѣ́в*ши*, читá*въ*, читáв*ши*. The terminations *а*, *я*, *въ*, are *aprocopated* ones, and *учи*, *ючи*, *ши* — *full* ones; the former are employed in writing and speaking, and the latter in the vulgar tongue.

The *present* gerund is formed, like the present participle, from the 3d person plural of the present tense, by changing the terminations: *атъ* into *а*; *ятъ*, *утъ* and *ютъ* into *я*, as, молч*áтъ*, they are silent — мóлч*а*; хóд*ятъ* — хóд*я*; вед*ýтъ* — вед*я́*; жел*áютъ*, they wish — жел*áя*. The *past* gerund is formed from the past participle by changing *ій* into *и*, as, молчáвш*ій* — молчáвш*и*; or *шій* into *ъ*: молчáв*шій* — молчáвъ.

The gerunds of reflective, reciprocal, and common verbs add *сь (ся)*, in the *present* tense to the apocopated termination, and in the *past* to the full one, as, пря́ча, hiding — пря́чась, спря́тавшись; возвраща́я, returning — возвраща́ясь, возврати́вшись.

The gerunds of passive verbs, in order to form the *present* tense, add *бу́дучи* to the apocopated termination, as, *бу́дучи* хвали́мъ; and *бывъ*, to form the *past*, as, *бывъ* хвале́нъ or похвале́нъ.

ADVERBS. *

Adverbs are invariable. Those however, which are derived from qualificative adjectives, have the degrees of comparison. Their comparative degree is like the apocopated comparative of the adjectives from which they are derived, as, ску́чно tediously, скучнѣ́е more tediously; хорошо́ well, *лу́чше* better; ра́но early, *ра́ньше* earlier; бли́зко near, *бли́же* nearer or more nearly. The superlative is formed: 1. by prefixing the adverbs *о́чень, весьма́* very, or the syllable *пре*, 2. by the word *всего́* joined to the comparative, as, *о́чень* ску́чно, *весьма́* ску́чно, *прескучно́* very tediously, *всего́* скучнѣ́е most tediously.

Russian adverbs of quantity can be used as substantives, and govern the genitive case of actual nouns. Such are: *нѣсколько* some, *сколько* how much or how many, *столько* so much or many, *мно́го* much or many, *ма́ло* little, as, *мно́го наро́да* (наро́ду) стоя́ло внѣ́ це́ркви, many persons stood outside the church; чрезъ *нѣсколько вре́мени*, after some time; *ско́лько уроковъ* у васъ до обѣ́да? how many lessons have you before dinner?

PREPOSITIONS. *

Prepositions may be *separable* and *inseparable*.

Separable prepositions govern the following cases: 1. the *genitive*

* See a list of adverbs p. 69.

* For a list of prepositions with their significations see p. 75.

— безъ, для, ради, до, изъ, отъ, у, and the compound prepositions изъ-за, изъ подъ; 2. the *dative* — ко (къ); 3. the *accusative* — про, чрезъ, сквозь; 4. the *instrumental* — надъ; 5. the *prepositional* — при; 6. the *genitive* and *instrumental* — между; 7. the *accusative* and *instrumental* — за, подъ, предъ; 8. the *accusative* and *prepositional* — въ, во, на, о (объ); 9) the *genitive, accusative*, and *instrumental* — съ (со); 10. the *dative, accusative*, and *prepositional* — по.

Several adverbs denoting place, and governing the genitive case, may also be considered as *separable* prepositions, as, близъ, во́злѣ, по́длѣ, о́коло, про́тивъ, ми́мо, среди́, впереди́, позади́, etc.

The *inseparable* prepositions govern no case, but merely modify the signification of the words of which they form a component part, as, веде́ніе leading — *воз*веде́ніе raising, го́дный fit — *вы́*годный profitable, до́брый kind — *пре*до́брый very kind, etc.

CONJUNCTIONS
and
INTERJECTIONS.

Classifications of conjunctions and interjections, as well as of prepositions and adverbs, being of no particular practical value to the student have, for want of room, been omitted. But for a list of conjunctions and interjections, see p. 76—78.

APPENDIX I.

COMPARATIVE TABLE OF RUSSIAN AND ENGLISH COINS, WEIGHTS AND MEASURES.

COINS.	ESTIMATION			
	IN RUSSIAN COINS.		IN ENGLISH COINS.	
IN GOLD.	Roubles.	Copeeks.	Shillings.	Pence.
The imperial (имперiáлъ). . . .	10	30	33	6
The half-imperial (полуимперiáлъ	5	15	16	9
The ducat (червóнецъ)	3	—	9	9
IN SILVER.				
The rouble (рубль).	—	100	3	4
The half-rouble (полтíнникъ) . .	—	50	1	8
The quarter of a rouble (четвертáкъ).	—	25	—	10
A twenty kopeek piece (двугрíвенникъ)	—	20	—	8
A fifteen kopeek piece (пятналтывникъ)	—	15	—	6
A ten copeek piece (грíвенникъ)	—	10	—	4
A five copeek piece (пятáкъ in copper, пятачéкъ in silver). . . .	—	5	—	2
IN COPPER.			Pence	Farthings.
A three copeek piece (три копéйки)	—	3	1	1
A two copeek piece (двѣ копéйки)	—	2	—	$3^{1}/_{8}$
A copeek piece (копéйка)	—	1	—	$1^{3}/_{8}$
A half-copeek piece (дéнежка) . .	—	$^{1}/_{2}$	—	$^{4}/_{8}$
A quarter-copeek piece (полýшка)	—	$^{1}/_{4}$	—	$^{2}/_{8}$

WEIGHTS.	ESTIMATION IN RUSSIAN WEIGHTS		ESTIMATION IN ENGLISH WEIGHTS. Avoir du poids	
	Pounds.	Zolotneeks.	Pounds.	Ounces.
The berkovets (берковецъ) . . .	400	—	361	3
The pood (пудъ)	40	—	36	2
The pound (фунтъ)	—	96	—	14½
The lot (лотъ)	—	3	—	0,45
The zolotnik (золотникъ)	—	1	—	0,15
The zolotnik has 96 dolee (доли).	—	—	—	—

MEASURES.	ESTIMATION IN RUSSIAN MEASURES.		ESTIMATION IN ENGLISH MEASURES.	
LONG MEASURE.	Feet.	Inches.	Yards.	Feet.
The verst (верстá) has 500 sazhanes	3500	—	1164	—
The sazhane (сажéнь) has 3 arsheens	7	—	2	1
			Feet	Inches.
The arsheen (арши́нъ) has 16 vershoks.	2	4	2	4
The vershok (вершóкъ).	—	$1^3/_4$	—	$1^3/_4$
The foot (футъ)	—	12	1	—
The inch (дюймъ) has 12 lines. .	—	1	—	1
SQUARE MEASURE.	Square sazhanes.		Acres.	Roods.
The dessyateena (десяти́на) . . .	2400		2	3

	ESTIMATION			
	IN RUSSIAN MEASURES.		IN ENGLISH MEASURES.	
SOLID MEASURE.	Cubic feat.		Cords.	
The cubic săzhane (кубúческая сажéнь	343		$2\frac{7}{10}$	
LIQUID MEASURE.	Vedros.	Krooshki.	Gallons.	Quarts.
The tun (бóчка)	40	—	108	1
The vedro (ведрó) has 8 shtofs (штóфы)	—	10	2	$2\frac{3}{4}$
The ksooshka (крýжкá) has 10 tsharki (чáрки)	—	1	—	1
DRY MEASURE.	Tshetver.	Garnets.	Gallons.	Quarts.
The tshetvert (чéтверть)	8	—	46	—
The tshetvereek (четверúкъ) . .	—	8	5	3
The half-tshetvereek (получетверúкъ).	—	4	2	$3\frac{1}{2}$
The garnets (гáрнецъ)	—	1	1	$2\frac{7}{8}$

APPENDIX II.

A LIST OF THE PRINCIPAL TECHNICAL TERMS

FOR THE USE OF

CIVIL ENGINEERS, MECHANICS, ETC.

A.

actual power, s. **power**.
to **adjust** (or to fit), провѣшивать (шпангоуты).
adjusting an engine, установка паровой машины.
aft, задняя часть корабля; сзади.
ahead, впереди, передъ носомъ корабля.
air pump, s. **pump**.
alternative motion, s. **motion**.
Alum, квасцы.
anchor, якорь.
angle iron, s. **iron**.
anthracite, антрацитъ (уголь).
anvil, наковальня.
apparatus, апаратъ, снарядъ; distilling -, перегоночный ап.; moving -, движущій ап.; self acting feed -, самодѣйствующій спабжающій приборъ.
arc, дуга, погибъ.
arch, **archade**, аркадъ, сводъ.
Archimedian screw, s. **screw**.
areometer, ареометръ.
arm, рукавъ, ручка.
ash, **ashes**, зола, пепелъ.
atmospheric engine, s. **engine**.
axe, топоръ.
axis, ось, внутренникъ.
axle, **axletree**, ось, вертлюгъ, ось балансира.
awash, въ уровень съ водою.

B.

back balance, противовѣсъ.
to **back**, давать задній ходъ, ходить заднимъ ходомъ.
balance valve, s. **valve**.
ballast, баластъ; - basket, угольная корзина.

to bank the fires, s. fire.
bar, брусокъ, поперечина; - surface, поверхность колосниковъ въ топкѣ; bearing - for furnace, перекладина подъ колосниками; boring -, сверлильный стержень.
bare, матка.
barrel, анкерокъ; pump -, корпусъ помпы.
baton, палка, жезлъ.
bead, фризъ.
beam, бимсъ, брусъ; main -, главная нога (береговой машины); working -, балансиръ.
bearer, подпора, подставка.
bearing bar for furnace, s. bar.
to beat, бить, колотить, вбивать.
beater, баба, чекмарь.
bell metal, s. metal.
bellows, раздувальный мѣхъ.
belly stay, s. stay.
bench, скамейка; joiner's -, верстакъ.
to bend, гнуть, нагибать.
bib cock, s. cock.
bilge pump, s. pump.
binding, поясъ, оковка, связь.
black lead, s. lead.
blackening, угольная пыль, черненіе литейной формы.
blacksmith, кузнецъ.
blast-furnace, s. furnace.
blast-pipe, s. pipe.
blaze, пламя, сіяніе, блескъ; to -, пылать.
blister, плена (въ металлахъ), пузырь.
blister steel, s. steel.
block, чурбанъ, блокъ.
to blow off or out, продувать (паровой котелъ).
blow off cock, s. cock.
blower, раздувальщикъ, вентиляторъ.
blowing machine, s. machine.
blunt chisel, s. chisel.
boat, шлюпка, лодка, ботъ; gun -, канонерская лодка; long -, барказъ.
bobin, шпулька, катушка.
boiler, **marine boiler**, паровой котелъ; body of -, корпусъ пароваго котла; tubular -, трубчатый котелъ; waggon -, вагонный пар. котелъ.
bolt, задвижка, болтъ; clench -, заклепной болтъ.
bore, буравъ, сверло; to -, буравить, сверлить; to - out, разсверливать; to - through, просверливать; -r, сверлильщикъ, сверло, буравъ.
boring bar, s. bar.
bow, носъ (корабля); - sprit, бугшпритъ.
box, коробка, камора.
brace, скоба, подпора, подставка.
bracket, подставка, подстилка.
brass, зеленая мѣдь, латунь; yellow -, желтая мѣдь.
break, изломъ, прорывъ, отверстіе.
brick, кирпичъ.
bridge, **flame bridge**, печной мостикъ, порогъ.
brine pump, s. pump.
bronze, бронза.
brush wheel, s. wheel.
bunker, **coal bunker**, угольный ящикъ.
to burn, горѣть, жечь.
bush, трубка.

C.

cable, канатъ, кабельтовъ; канатный.
caliber or **caliper**, кронциркуль, кривой циркуль.
Caloric engine, s. **engine**.
to **cant**, кантовать.
cap (chape plate), крышка, верхняя часть подшипника.
capacity, вмѣстительность, емкость.
capillary tube, s. **tube**.
card, индикаторная діаграмма.
cargo, грузъ.
carling, распорка, подпорка.
carpenter, плотникъ.
to **cast**, отливать.
cast iron, s. **iron**.
cast steel, s. **steel**.
catch, защепка, палецъ, эксцентриковая лодыжка.
to **caulk**, конопатить.
central boss, яблочко по срединѣ поперечника.
centre, центръ, центральная ось; meta -, метацентръ; top and bottom -, мертвая точка.
chain, цѣпь.
chamber of a pump, s. **pump**.
chalk, мѣлъ; to -, мѣлить; to - out, намѣливать.
charcoal s. **coal**.
check, палъ, защепка.
check, доска двойнаго балансира.
chest, ящикъ, камора.
chief engineer, s. **engineer**.
chimney, дымовая труба.
to **chip**, отщепывать, оскабливать, срубать.
chips or **chippings**, щепки.
chisel, **blunt chisel**, рѣзецъ, долото, стамеска.
cinder, пепелъ, зола, угольный мусоръ.
circumgyration, вращеніе вокругъ центра.
cistern, цистерна; oil -, цистерна для масла.
clamp, нажимъ, тиски.
to **clench**, заклепывать.
clench bolt, s. **bolt**.
clinch, заклепка.
coal, уголь, каменный уголь; - bunker, угольный ящикъ; char -, древесный уг.; glance -, сухой каменный уг., шотландскій уг.; pit -, каменный уг.
cock, **bib cock**, кранъ; pet -, кранъ на днѣ цилиндра; blow off -, продувательный кранъ; feed -, снабжающій кр.
cog, деревянный зубъ колеса; - wheel, s. **wheel**; depth of a -, углубленіе зубца.
column, колонна.
comb, гребенка, чесалка, мѣчикъ, рѣзокъ для нарѣзки винтовъ.
combination, соединеніе, смѣшеніе.
combined vapor engine, s. **engine**.
combustible, топливо; сгараемый, горючій.
communication valve, s. **valve**.
compass, компасъ; - es, циркуль.
condensation, сгущеніе, охлажденіе.
conductor, проводникъ.
conduct, проходъ, трубка.
connecting rod, нога, шатунъ.
convolution, шагъ (винта).
copper, мѣдь; - can, мѣдная лейка; red -, красная мѣдь.
cotton, хлопчатая бумага.
counter, счислитель.

crab winch, s. **winch**.
crack, трещина.
crane, лебедка, кранъ.
crank, мотыль.
culm, угольный мусоръ.
cut, слѣдъ нарѣза; to - off, ослаблять, опускать.
cylinder, цилиндръ, валъ.

D.

to **damp the fires**, s. **fire**.
dead point, мертвая точка.
deck, декъ, палуба; quarter -, квартердекь, шканцы, ютъ.
delivery valve, s. **valve**.
density, плотность, густота.
depth of a cog, s. **cog**.
die or dye, басма, матрица въ штампѣ.
dip view, планъ, горизонтальная проэкція.
to **discharge**, выпускать, опоражнивать.
to **disconnect**, разводить, разъединять.
distilling apparatus, s. **apparatus**.
dock, докъ; - yard, адмиралтейство, портъ.
donkey, снабжающая машина, донки.
door, дверцы; fire -, печныя дверцы.
double acting engine, s. **engine**.
drawing, чертежъ,
draught of water, осадка судна на водѣ, углубленіе корабля въ водѣ, обстояніе въ грузу.
to **draw the fires**, s. **fire**.
drilling machine, s. **machine**.
dropping out, течь, скважина.
dust, пыль, порошокъ.
duty, полезная работа.
dynamics, динамика.

E.

ear, ушко, проушина.
to **ease the engine**, уменьшать ходъ машины.
eccentric pulley, эксцентрическій шкивъ.
edge, кромка.
effective power, s. **power**.
elasticity, упругость, эластичество, эластичность.
elevation, вертикальная проэкція.
embers, горячая зола.
embrayage, муфта, обойма.
endless screw, s. **screw**.
engine, машина; atmospheric -, атмосферная машина; caloric -, теплородная или духовая м.; combined vapor -, м. двойнаго пара (воды и эфира); double acting -, м. двойнаго дѣйствія; land -, береговая м.; locomotive -, паровозъ; portable -, переносная м.; single acting -, м. простаго дѣйствія; steam -, паровая м.
engineer, инженеръ, машинистъ; chief -, старшій механикъ; civil -, механикъ; naval -, корабельный инженеръ; second -, второй механикъ.
escape valve, s. **valve**.
to **evaporate**, испарять, испаряться.
evaporation, испареніе.
even, гладкій, ровный; to make -, уравнивать.
to **exhaust**, сгущать, охлаждать.

to **expand**, расширять.
explosion, взрывъ.
eye (or boss), очко, яблоко.

F.

fanner, вентилаторъ.
feed cock, s. **cock**.
file, пила, напилокъ; to -, пилить.
fire, огонь; - fan, заслонка; - iron, кочерга; - man, кочегаръ; - proof, непроницаемый огнемъ; - wood, дрова; to damp, back or put the -s, отодвигать или загребать огни въ глубь топки; to draw the -s, тушить огни; to light the -s, зажигать огни, затопить печи; to urge the -s, усиливать огонь въ печахъ, раздувать огни.
to **fit**, устанавливать, сбирать.
fitter, сборщикъ машины.
flame, пламя,
fleet, флотъ.
flower of sulphur, сѣрный цвѣтъ.
fluid, токъ; текучій.
fly wheel, s. **wheel**.
forge, горнъ, ковальна, молотовая; -r, ковачъ; to -, ковать.
to **form a screw**, нарѣзать винтъ.
to **found**, плавить, лить, выливать.
founder, плавильщикъ, литейщикъ.
frame, шпангоутъ.
frigate, фрегатъ.
fuel, топливо.
full power, s. **power**.
funnel, труба, труба излишняго пара.
furnace, печь; - bar, колосникъ; blast -, доменная печь, домна.
fusion, плавленіе, плавка.

G.

gage, **gauge**, мѣра, мѣрило, масштабъ; glass -, индикаторная или указательная трубка; water -, водомѣрный приборъ.
galvanism, галванизмъ.
gas, газъ.
generator, женераторъ, производитель паровъ.
to **get hot**, нагрѣваться.
to **get up the steam**, поднимать пары.
glance coal, s. **coal**.
glass gauge, s. **gauge**.
glue, клей.
governor, уравнитель, регулаторъ.
gouge, рѣшетчатый золотникъ.
grain, втулка.
grate, **grating**, рѣшетка.
grease, жиръ.
grindstone, точильный камень, точило.
to **gripe**, хватать, сжимать.
gross effect power, s. **power**.
ground plan, планъ, горизонтальная проэкція.
gudgeon, вертлюгъ, ось, шейка.
guide, проводникъ для паралельнаю движенія; rod -, направляющій стержень или прутъ.
gun-boat, s. **boat**.

H.

half power, s. **power**.
hammer, молотъ, молотокъ; lift -, хвостовый молотъ; to -, бить молоткомъ, ковать.
hammered iron, s. **iron**.
hand, рука; ручной; - bellows, ручной мѣхъ; - hole, дира, отверстіе; - hammer, ручной молотокъ; - lantern, ручной фонарь; - vice, ручные тиски.
handle, черепокъ.
hanging valve, s. **valve**.
to **harden iron**, закалывать желѣзо.
hatchet, топорикъ.
head way, впередъ.
heat, жаръ; -ed air, нагрѣтый воздухъ; -ed, super -ed steam, нагрѣтый паръ; latent -, скрытый теплородъ; white -, бѣлокалильный жаръ.
heel, наконечникъ.
helix, винтъ, гребной винтъ.
helm, руль, руммель.
helve, ручка, рукоятка.
high pressure, s. **pressure**.
hold, трюмъ.
horse power, s. **power**.
hot, горячій; горячо; on -, до каленія.
hub, патронъ гребнаго колеса.
hydraulic, гидравлическій.

I.

impetus, моментъ, количество движенія.
incrustation, накипъ.
indicated power, s. **power**.
induction, впусканіе.
injection, инжекція.
introduction, введеніе, впусканіе.
iron, желѣзо; - ship, желѣзное судно; angle -, угловое желѣзо; bar -, полосовое ж.; cast -, чугунъ; hammered -, кованное ж.; sheet -, кровельное желѣзо; Z -, желѣзо Z.

J.

jack, домкратъ.
jaw, тиски, клещи.
jerk, сотрясеніе, толчекъ.
jet, струя; a - of steam, струя пара.
joint, соединеніе шарниромъ; universal -, повсемѣстное соединеніе.
junction plate, соединительная доска.

K.

keel, киль; - son, кильсонъ, лежень подъ машиною.
key, ключъ, чека, ключъ для гаекъ, отвертка; - bit, отвертка.
Kingston's valve, s. **valve**.
knee, колѣно, загибъ.

L.

ladder, крыло станины, по которой ходятъ черпаки землечерпательной машины.
land engine, s. **engine**.
lantern, фонарь.
larboard, лѣвая сторона корабля.
latent heat, s. **heat**.
lathe, токарной станокъ.
lead, свинецъ; black -, графитъ, черный карандашъ.
lead, веди впередъ!
leak, течь, капельная течь.

leather belt or strap, кожаный поясъ или ремень.
length of the stroke, ходъ поршня эксцентрика.
level, уровень.
lever, рычагъ.
lift hammer, s. **hammer**.
lifter, скоба съ нарѣзными концами.
lifting gear, подъемная рама гребнаго винта.
lifting valve, s. **valve**.
to **light the fires**, s. **fire**.
liner, подкладка подъ подшипники.
to **link**, соединить бугелемъ.
liquid, жидкость; жидкій.
lobe plate, фундаментная доска.
lock, замо́къ; - smith, слесарь; pick -, отмычка.
locomotive, паровозъ, локомотивъ.
loose, вольно, свободно, съ зазоромъ.
lowering, отдача (снасти), спускъ (машины).
lying shaft, s. **shaft**.

M.

machine, машина; blowing -, продувательная м.; drilling -, сверлильный станокъ, пробойная м.; punching -, прессъ для пробиванія диръ; -ry, механизмъ.
machinist, машинистъ.
main beam, s. **beam**.
male, винтъ или наружная нарѣзка.
mallet, мушкель.
man-hole, man-way, горловина (въ паровомъ котлѣ).
man-of-war, военное судно.
management, управленіе (машиною).
manometer, манометръ.
marine boiler, s. **boiler**.
mass, масса.
mast, мачта; fore -, фокъ-мачта; main -, гротъ-мачта; mizen -, бизань-мачта; top -, стеньга; top-gallant -, брамъ-стеньга.
materials, матеріалы.
mechanic, ремесленникъ, мастеровой; -ian, механикъ.
to **melt**, плавить (металлъ), сплавливаться.
merchantman, купеческое судно.
metacentre, s. **centre**.
metal, металлъ; bell -, колокольный металлъ; soft -, мягкій м.
middle shaft, s. **shaft**.
model, модель.
motion, движеніе; alternative -, движеніе то взадъ то впередъ попеременно; reciprocating -, попеременное движеніе.
mouth, отверстіе, проходъ.
moving apparatus, s. **apparatus**.
moving power, s. **power**.
mud hole, грязная горловина (въ паровомъ котлѣ).

N.

nail, гвоздь.
natural steel, s. **steel**.
nippers, клещи, щипцы.
nominal horse power, s. **power**.
number of strokes, число оборотовъ или ходовъ поршня.
nut, гайка.

O.

oar, весло.
oil, масло, олифа; - pipe, трубка для масла; *to -, помазать или натирать масломъ.*
to **open**, *открывать.*
ordinate, ордината.
orifice, отверстіе, окошко.
oscillator, качающійся цилиндръ.
oscillation, качаніе, вращеніе, колебаніе.
outer shaft, s. **shaft.**
to **oxydate**, окислять.
oxyde, окись.

P.

packing, набивка.
paddle, лопасть; - arm, радіусъ гребнаго колеса; - shaft, гребной валъ; - wheel, s. **wheel.**
pan, чашечка или шайка для смолы или масла.
pedestal, подушка подъ валомъ.
piece, штука, кусокъ.
piercer, буравъ, пробойникъ.
pilaster, пилястра.
pin, мотылевой стержень.
pincers, щипцы, клещи.
pipe, труба; blast -, труба отработаннаго пара; steam -, паропроводная труба; waste steam -, (funnel), труба излишняго пара.
piston, поршень; - rod, пистонный стержень; velocity of the -, скорость поршня.
pitch of a screw, шагъ (винта).
pitcoal, s. **coal.**
plane, рубанокъ, стругъ; to -, стругать.
play, зазоръ, игра.
plumbago, plumbagine, карандашъ, графитъ.
poop, корма, кормовой.
***port**, портъ; - hole, пушечный портъ; - way, проходъ, трубка.*
portable engine, s. **engine.**
power, сила; actual -, effective -, полезная или дѣйствительная с.; full -, полное дѣйствіе; gross effect -, динамическій моментъ; half -, средній ходъ, средняя сила; horse -, лошадиная с.; indicated -, индикаторная с.; moving -, движущая с., двигатель; nominal horse -, нарицательная с.
preserve valve, s. **valve.**
pressure, давленіе; high -, высокое д.; middle -, среднее давленіе.
to **prime**, вскипать.
priming, вскипаніе.
proof, проба, испытаніе, опытъ.
prow, носъ (корабля).
pulsation, ходъ поршня.
pulley, блокъ.
pumice, пемза.
pump, помпа; barrel, chamber of a -, корпусъ помпы; air -, воздушный насосъ; bilge -, трюмная п.; brine -, разсольная п.
punching machine, s. **machine.**
to **put back the fires**, s. **fire.**
pyrometer, пирометръ, огнемѣръ.

Q.

quicksilver, ртуть.

R.

radius, радіусъ.
rail, рельсъ, шина, перила; - road, - way, желѣзная дорога.
ram, баба.
rasp, терпугъ.
rat's tail, рѣдька (оплетенный конецъ снасти).
reaction, обратное дѣйствіе.
reactive, обратно дѣйствующій.
reciprocating motion, s. **motion**.
red copper, s. **copper**.
register-tonnage, вмѣстимость судна за вычетомъ вѣса машины.
to **regulate**, уравнять.
regulator, уравнитель.
rent, трещина.
reservoir, резервуаръ, бассейнъ.
to **reset**, выпрямлять, выправлять.
revolution, оборотъ.
rhimer, развертка.
rigging, оснастка, такелажъ.
ring, кольцо, рымъ.
rivet, заклепка; to -, заклепывать.
roof, вершина или сводъ печи.
rope, снасть, веревка.
rosin, **resin**, гарпіусъ.
rotation, вращеніе.
rudder, руль; рулевой.
rut, пересѣченіе, захватываніе.

S.

safety valve, s. **valve**.
sail, парусъ, судно; to -, ходить подъ парусами, плыть; to make -, поднимать паруса; to set -, вступать подъ паруса; fore -, фокъ; main -, гротъ; mizen -, бизань.
to **saturate**, насыщать.
saw, пила.
scissors, ножницы.
screw, винтъ, гайка; - bolt, болтъ съ винтовымъ нарѣзомъ; - driver, отвертка; - jack, домкратъ; - nail, гвоздъ съ винтовымъ нарѣзомъ; - nut, винтовая гайка; - plate, винтовальная доска; - shaft, s. **shaft**; - thread or worm, винтовой нарѣзъ; Archimedian -, Архимедовъ винтъ; endless -, worm -, безконечный в.; turn -, отвертка; to un-, отвинчивать, развинчивать; to unship the -, поднимать гребной винтъ.
scraper, скрябка.
seat, гнѣздо.
second engineer, s. **engineer**.
sediment, осадокъ.
self acting feed apparatus, s. **apparatus**.
shackle, скоба, обойма.
shaft, валъ, воротъ; lying -, лежачій валъ; middle -, средній в.; outer -, гребной в., валъ гребнаго колеса; screw -, винтовой в.
to **sharpen**, точить, завастривать.
shaving, стружка, щепка.
shears, большія ножницы.
sheet, листъ; - iron, s. **iron**.
shell, коробка крана.
ship, корабль, судно; корабельный; - builder, кораблестроитель; - building, кораблестроеніе; - of the line, линейный корабль; - wright, корабельный мастеръ.
shock, ударъ, столкновеніе.
shovel, лопата.

shrouds, ванты; main -, гротъ ванты.
shut off valve, s. **valve**.
single acting engine, s. **engine**.
to **slacken**, ослаблять.
sleeper, поперечина.
slide valve, s. **valve**.
slip, отступаніе, скольженіе.
slit, расчепъ, выемка, фальцъ.
smith shop, **smithy**, кузница.
smoke, дымъ; - pipe, дымовой ходъ.
soft metal, s. **metal**.
to **solder**, паять, сваривать.
sole plate, фундаментная доска.
spanner, раздвижной ключъ.
speed, скорость.
spelter, цинкъ.
spindle, шарниръ, стержень клапана.
spring, пружина.
stack, дымовая труба.
standard, подпора, подставка.
standing vice, s. **vice**.
starboard, правая сторона корабля.
stay, распорка, подпорка, штагъ; belly -, ванты у трубы.
steam, паръ; - boat, -er, пароходъ; - boiler, паровикъ, паровой котелъ; - chest, паропріемное пространство; - engine, s. **engine**; - gauge, манометръ, паромѣръ; - pipe, s. **pipe**; - ship, - vessel, паровой корабль, паровое судно; - tight, непропищаемый паромъ; - tug, буксирный пароходъ; heated -, superheated -, s. **heat**; wet -, мокрый паръ.
steel, сталь; blister -, пузырчатая ст.; cast -, литая ст.; natural -, естественная ст.
stem, стемъ, форштевень.
stern. корма; кормовой.
stoker, истопникъ, кочегаръ.
stop, **stop piece**, ладышка или задержка на валѣ, усы.
strain, напряженіе, усиліе, натуга.
strap, ремень.
strength of man, человѣческая сила.
striker, молотобоецъ.
strip, выступъ, приливъ, мѣтка, шкало, мѣдная линейка для установки механизма.
stroke, ходъ или длина хода поршня паровaго цилиндра.
suction, всасываніе (насоса).
support, подпорка, подставка.
surface, поверхность.
swage, штампъ, форма или басма въ штампѣ, бородокъ, осадка или гладилка кузнечная.

T.

tallow, сало.
tank, ушатъ, чанъ, водоемъ.
tap-wrench, метчикъ для нарѣзыванія внутреннихъ винтовъ.
teethed wheel, s. **wheel**.
tell-tale-valve, s. **valve**.
tenacity, вязкость, упорство.
tender, тендеръ.
throat of a chimney, дымовой выходъ.
tie-rod, распорка (между стѣнами паровaго котла).
to **tighten**, натягивать, укрѣплять.
timber, строевой лѣсъ; the filling -, наборный шпангоутъ; the cant -, поворотный шпангоутъ.

tire, шина (у колеса).
tongs, клещи, щипцы.
tool, инструментъ, орудіе.
tooth, желѣзный зубецъ.
top and bottom centre, s. centre.
to **tow**, буксировать.
travel of the valve, s. valve.
trunnion, цапфа.
tube, труба, трубка; - brush, банникъ.
tubular boiler, s. boiler.
turf, торфъ, дернъ.
turnplate, вертящаяся платформа.
turnscrew, s. screw.
twiers, фурма, форма (въ доменныхъ печахъ, кричныхъ горнахъ).
tyre, патронъ гребнаго колоса.

U.

unit of labour, единица работы.
universal joint, s. joint.
to **unscrew**, s. screw.
to **unshackle**, расклепывать.
to **unship the screw**, s. screw.
upper valve, s. valve.
upright, стойка стандерсъ.
to **upset**, опрокидывать.
to **urge the fires**, s. fire.
useful effect, полезное дѣйствіе, полезная сила.

V.

vacuum, безвоздушная пустота.
valve, клапанъ; balance -, равновѣсный кл.; communication -, - shut off -, стопарный или разобщительный кл.; delivery -, выпускной кл.; escape -, preserve -, safety -, предохранительный кл.; hanging висячій кл.; Kingston's Кингстонный кл.; lifting подъемный кл.; slide -, задвижной золотникъ; tell - tale -, клапанъ со свисткомъ; travel of the -, ходъ золотника; upper -, верхній паровой кл.
vapor, паръ.
velocity of the piston, s. piston.
vent, отверстіе, выходъ.
vertical plan, поперечный чертежъ.
vibrating, качаніе, колебаніе.
vibration, вибрація, качаніе.
vice, тиски; standing-, стуловые тиски.
vitriol, купоросъ.

W.

waggon boiler, s. boiler.
water, вода; - gauge, s. gage.
wear, порча.
wedge, клинъ.
wet steam, s. steam.
wheel, колесо; - barrow, тачка; - blade, лопасть гребнаго колеса; brush -, трущееся колесо; cog -, teethed -, зубчатое к.; fly -, маховое к.; paddle -, гребное к.
white heat, s. heat.
wimble, коловоротъ.
wire, проволока; copper -, мѣдная пр.; iron -, желѣзная пр.
winch, брашпиль; crab -, воротъ.
wood, дерево, дрова.
to **work**, дѣйствовать, ходить.
working beam, s. beam.
worm screw, s. screw.

Y.

yard, рей; main -, грота-рей; top -, марса-рей; main-top -, гротъ-марса-рей.
yarn, пряжа.
yellow brass, s. brass.

Z.

Z iron, s. iron.
zinc, цинкъ, шпіаутеръ.

ERRATA.

Page.	Line.	Printed.	Ought to be.
2	13	å	ŏ, å
6	5	вѣчéрия	вечéрия
»	9	катихизйсъ	катихйзисъ
12	3	pȧ-rȧ-vŏ-tshtshīk	pȧ-rȧ-vŏ-shtshīk
»	7	землеѣдлецъ	земледѣлецъ
»	22	sŭīn	sŭīn
16	3	nyĕrr-vŭī	nyĕrr-vŭī
18	15	сáмолюбіе	самолю́біе
21	1	самóвáръ	самовáръ
22	9	пирóжиное	пирóжное
23	22	grŏ-shȧ	grŏ-shȧ
26	5	catin	satin
»	26	рчýка	рýчка
27	2	lobly	lobby
»	4	stŏ-pȧ-nĕ	stŏ-pȧ-nĕ
28	30	пéчька	пéчка
32	18	nȧ-bĕ-rĕsh-nȧ-yȧ	nȧ-bĕ-rĕzh-nȧ-yȧ
33	1	bui ding	building
36	4	mĕrr	mĕrr
38	19	īss-pȧ-rȧ-nĕ-yĕ	īss-pȧ-rȧ-nĕ-yĕ
49	11	nyȧ-stshȧt-lyĕ-vŭī	nyȧ-stshȧst-lyĕ-vŭī
56	33	[illegible]-tshĕ-vŏ	nyĕ-tshĕ-vŏ
72	19	[illegible]kh-dȧ	nyĕ-kŏgh-dȧ
84	29	reso[illegible]	reasonably
90	13	перед[illegible]	передáть

94	24	нрибавляются	прибавляются
96	18	желѣзное	стальнóе
100	16	меня́	меня́
102	13	бáльше	бóльше
115	20	пять въ или	пять и́ли
116	6	in second	in a second
122	6	хорошó	хорошá
124	11	enough. *	enough.
»	12	For pity's sake	For pity's sake
»	30	Ни́чéго	Ничегó
125	26	Подви́нтесь	Подви́ньтесь
126	10	прогу́лку	прогу́лки
»	17	ру́ки	ру́ку
139	1—2	the the	the
141	2	учи́лели	учи́тели
»	19	кáмень	кáмень
142	7	помѣстье	помѣстье
»	15	щипц*óвъ*	щипц*óвъ*
143	18	plvral	plural
144	20	срéдлтво	срéдство
147	12	пусты́е	пусты́е
158	12	áвше	вáше
160	25	bonnot	bonnet
162	28	hranches	branches
163	1	писáлъ	писáлъ
166	15	еме	его
179	2	wistle	whistle
184	11	позади́	позади́
187	12	ksooshka	krooshka
190	11	уголъ	уголь
»	41	мѣдъ	мѣдь
192	14	put the -s	put back the -s
	37	длъ	для

CPSIA information can be obtained
at www.ICGtesting.com
Printed in the USA
LVHW040425110522
718423LV00002B/461

9 783375 007447